*The*
# Little Grey Men

# The
# Little Grey Men

*A Story for the Young in Heart*
*by BB*

*With illustrations by*
DENYS WATKINS-PITCHFORD

THE JULIE ANDREWS COLLECTION
HARPERCOLLINS*PUBLISHERS*

The Little Grey Men
Copyright © 2004 by James William Donnelan Drake-Lee and
James Edward Lamb, Trustees of the late Denys Watkins-Pitchford
First published in 1942 by Eyre & Spottiswoode

Library of Congress Cataloging-in-Publication Data
BB.
    The little grey men : a story for the young in heart / by 'BB' ;
illustrated by Denys Watkins-Pitchford.—1st ed.
        p.      cm.
    "Julie Andrews Collection."
    Summary: In Warwickshire, England, three gnomes set out on
a dangerous journey to find their long-lost brother, who left years
ago seeking the source of the Folly brook, on whose shores they
make their home.
    ISBN 0-06-055448-7 — ISBN 0-06-055449-5 (lib. bdg.)
    [1. Adventure and adventurers—Fiction.   2. Gnomes—
Fiction.   3. Brothers—Fiction.   4. Nature—Fiction.
5. Animals—Fiction.   6. Warwickshire (England)—Fiction.
7. England—Fiction.]   I. Title.
PZ7.W324Li   2004                                    2003024142
[Fic]—dc22

Typography by Larissa Lawrynenko
1 2 3 4 5 6 7 8 9 10

# CONTENTS

*A Note from*
## JULIE ANDREWS EDWARDS

I have been in love with this book since my early childhood.

My father and I were spending some precious moments together and had gone into our local bookstore—a W.H. Smith & Son, as I recall. He was a great lover of literature, poetry, and nature—and he must have been searching for exactly the right book to ignite the spark of those passions in me. Suddenly, he handed me a narrow, linen-bound book and said, "Here, darling. This is for you. I think you'll love it." His timing could not have been more perfect.

As I paged through *The Little Grey Men*, my attention was immediately drawn to the intricate detail of the charming woodcut illustrations inside, and as soon as I got home I sat down to enjoy it further. I vividly remember struggling through the exposition of the first two or three pages, but the moment Baldmoney emerged from the base of the oak tree I was completely engaged. As I continued to read, there was not a moment that didn't connect for me; it spoke to everything I loved and held dear. Growing up as I did on the banks of the River Thames in England, I identified with every detail of the little Folly brook. I could smell the water, see the reeds, visualize the countryside, recognize the wildlife—I entered the world of the gnomes and never wanted to leave. The imagery was so rich, and combined with such a marvelous adventure, that the book enhanced my awareness of the natural world from that point forward and cemented forever my love of reading.

Over the years I went back to *The Little Grey Men* again and again. I read it to my own children, and they are now reading it to my grandchildren. The magic in these pages has stood the test of time. Having carried it in my heart all these years, it is especially meaningful for me to make *The Little Grey Men* available to a new generation of readers. I hope that young people everywhere will enjoy this exquisite classic as much as I still do.

—*Julie Andrews Edwards*

# INTRODUCTION

This is a story about the last gnomes in Britain. They are honest-to-goodness gnomes, none of your baby, fairy-book tinsel stuff, and they live by hunting and fishing, like the animals and birds, which is only proper and right.

This story concerns their exploration of the Folly brook, on whose banks they dwell, and of their search for Cloudberry, their long-lost brother, who years ago went up the Folly and never returned. You may not believe in the Little People, but that is because most fairy books portray miniature men and women with ridiculous tinsel wings, doing all sorts of impossible things with flowers and cobwebs. That sort of make-believe is all right for some people, but it won't do for you and me.

If you don't believe in the Little People, I would ask you to make yourself as small as possible (which is horribly difficult) and keep very quiet (which is more difficult still) and watch and wait by the streams and in the woods, as I have done. And suddenly you will understand that the birds and wild animals *are* the Little People! Such a simple fact, and yet we never realized it!

There are water-sprites, such as wagtails and kingfishers, reed warblers, buntings, water-voles, and water-shrews. And there are goblins! Watch the wood-mice among the leaves, the hedgehog hunting at twilight, the squirrels swinging among the trees. There are goblins with wings, goblins of the night, such as nightjars and owls, which are rather frightening. And in the larger, wilder woods are trolls, the lumbering cautious badgers, who walk by night and are seen by few mortals.

And, alas! There are giants. But you must read this book to find out to what order giants belong.

My gnomes are but a very short step (for the normal imagination) from the wild woodland people. They live with birds and beasts, and can never be far from water. That is the reason why children instinctively love water, and why Ireland is the last stronghold of the Little People; it is wild and wet, and there is no locality a gnome likes so much as a place which is "wild and wet."

In telling this story I must ask the reader's indulgence for one flight of fancy. I have found it necessary to allow my gnomes and animals the power of speech. As this is a book for young people no doubt they will forgive me, for it makes the story easier to follow. In other respects it does not often go beyond the realms of possibility. Warwickshire is one of the last English counties where one might meet with a fairy; surely William Shakespeare knew this when he wrote *A Midsummer Night's Dream.*

The Author

1942

# Sneezewort, Baldmoney, Dodder, & Co.

IT WAS ONE OF THOSE DAYS at the tail end of the winter when spring, in some subtle way, announced its presence. The hedges were still purple and bristly, the fields bleached and bitten, full of quarreling starling flocks; but there was no doubt about it, the winter was virtually over and done with for another seven months. The great tide was on the turn, to creep so slowly at first and then to rise ever higher to culminate in the glorious flood, the top of the tide, at midsummer.

Think of it! All that power, all those millions of leaves, those extra inches to be added to bushes, trees, and flowers. It was all there under the earth, though you would never have guessed it.

After a soft grey morning, the sun had slowly broken through the clouds, and every blackbird and thrush in Lucking's Meadow began to warble and tune up; the first opening bars of a great symphony in praise of Life.

The willow bush by the Folly brook showed silver buttons up every slender wand, and on the rough grey bark of the leaning oak tree on the other side of the pool three sleepy flies were sidling about, enjoying the warm rays.

At this spot, for some reason known only to itself, the Folly brook turned at a right angle.

Beneath the oak the water had washed away the sandy bank, and many winter floods had laid bare some of the massive hawser roots which projected in a twisted tangle from the soil of the bank. The sun, shining full on the steep bluff, threw shadows from the overhanging roots, so that underneath all was darkness.

Close to the margin of the glittering water, there was a miniature beach of colored shingle and white sand; and from the glare on the stream, wavering bars of reflected light played to and fro on the bulging trunk of the oak. These light bars moved up and down in ripples, fading away when the sun was dimmed for an instant by a passing cloud.

It had been a dry winter and the Folly brook was running fresh and clear, higher than in summer, of course, but quite undimmed by flood-cloud. It was so clear that near the beach every stone and pebble on the bottom could be seen, though where the water was deeper, all was tawny obscurity, the color of ripe old ale.

Near the bank, the tangled reeds were as white as bleached bone, though if you had looked more closely, sharp green sword points could have been seen just beginning to pierce the dead vegetation. Later these reeds formed a deep green thicket, the strong juicy blades growing so close together that only a water-vole could slip between. The bank on the side opposite to the oak shelved gradually to the water's edge, and here Farmer Lucking's cattle came to drink. They had poached and punched the soil at the "marge" until it was in an awful mess and the grass for some way up the bank was quite worn away. But in the stream itself there was little mud, for the bottom was hard sand and shingle. Most of the mud which the heavy stolid beasts had collected to their knees was soon washed off by the current if they stood long enough in the stream.

Something moved in the shadow under the root. At first you might have thought it was a water-rat or a mouse; then, if you had waited long enough, keeping very still (for the Little People usually know when any mortal is about), you might have been lucky enough to see Baldmoney. He came out from under the root very slowly, peeping first one way and then another, listening.

\* \* \*

Up among the silver willow studs swung a tit, a beautiful little sprite splashed with a blue as azure as the patch of spring sky above.

"Tit tee, tit tee, tit tee!"

It was the "all clear" for Baldmoney. The little man ran,

like a mouse, out onto the colored shingle.

You must remember that Baldmoney and his brothers were (as far as I know) the last gnomes left in England. Rather surprisingly, he was extraordinarily like the pictures of gnomes in fairy books, even to the pointed skin hat and long beard. He wore a short coat and waistcoat of mouse-skin with a strip of snakeskin round his middle; moleskin breeches tied in below the knee, but no shoes or stockings. He had no need of these, for gnomes are hairy little folk; in summertime they sometimes dispense with clothes alto-gether. Their bodies are not naked like ours, but clothed in long hair, and as to their feet, if you had not worn boots or shoes since you were born, you would have no need of them either. He carried a hunting knife in his belt, made of ham-mered iron, part of an old hinge which he had found in the stream.

Bluebutton, the Bluetit, flipped down, leaflike, to the lowest wand of the willow which projected a little way over the pool and watched the gnome with his beady eye.

"Well, Bluebutton, it's good to see you again; what sort of winter have you had?"

"Not too bad, Baldmoney," replied the tit, hopping about among the soft willow buds.

Before I proceed I must tell you that of course the wild things did not talk to the gnomes in our language. They had one of their own which the gnomes understood. Naturally

in this book I have made them talk in our language, otherwise you would not make head or tail of what they were
saying.

"And your wife, Bluebutton, how is she?"

Here the bluetit looked very sorrowful. He sat still and
said nothing.

"Oh, I'm sorry, Bluetit, so sorry," said Baldmoney sym-
pathetically. "I know, it has been a terrible winter, one of the
worst since we've been on the stream . . . poor, poor
Bluebutton. Never mind," he added lightly, "spring is here
again, think what that means, plenty of food, no more frost,
and . . . and . . . you must find another wife. After all, you've
still got your children."

But Bluebutton would not be comforted and indeed was
so overcome with grief that he could stay no longer, but flew
away up the Folly brook.

Baldmoney sat down in the sun. It was warm on the
shingle, and he found his mouseskin waistcoat irksome, so
he took it off and hung it on an old withered stalk of beaked
hedge-parsley that grew out of the bank nearby.

His little red face, the color of an old hip berry, was
puckered and creased like the palm of a monkey's hand. His
whiskers were whitish grey, the beard hanging down almost
to his middle. The tiny hands with their grubby nails were
like moles' hands, though smaller. Gnomes have large hands
for their size, larger in comparison than those of a mortal.

His ears were long, sharply pointed, and covered with silky hair. After sitting a minute or two on the smooth stones he half turned round, looking towards the root. "Come on, you two, it's lovely out here in the sun . . . wake up, spring is here again."

Two more gnomes immediately emerged; one, Sneezewort, rubbing his eyes, the other, Dodder, blinking in the strong sun. Sneezewort, the youngest, was a little shorter than Baldmoney and was also clad in a mouseskin coat and moleskin breeches, though, strange to say, he was without whiskers, which is unusual in a gnome. For some reason nobody could ever understand (by "nobody" I do not mean people like you and me, but the animals, birds, and the Stream People generally) Sneezewort had never grown whiskers. It was not because he shaved, for no gnome would think of doing such a thing. Beards keep you warm in the winter. As I say, nobody knew why he had never grown whiskers, not even Sneezewort himself. But his round little face was just as red and puckered as Baldmoney's, and in some ways he looked older for he had lost most of his teeth and gnomes don't know how to make false teeth.

Dodder, the eldest and wisest of the three, was the shortest in stature, but that was because he had a wooden leg. It was a very cleverly designed leg made out of an acorn cup into which the leg stump fitted neatly, with a stout thorn twig morticed firmly into the outside end. The trouble was that this leg was always wearing out and in the summertime poor Dodder had to make a new one every month. His beard was a beauty, it hung below his belt, almost to his knees, and would have been snow white if he had not dyed it with walnut juice, for white beards would be too conspicuous, and that would never do. Secrecy was of utmost importance, especially in these modern days when discovery would mean the end of everything. Why these little creatures had survived for so long is puzzling, because, though they lived in this rural countryside, it was by no means "wild" in the sense that some parts of Devon and Cornwall are wild, and there are, to my knowledge, no gnomes left now in either of these last two localities, though I understand they are still to be found in some parts of Ireland.

Perhaps the reason is that nobody in their senses (and only a few out of them) would dream of looking for a gnome in Warwickshire, a county intersected in all directions by roads and railways, with modern villas and towns everywhere.

Unlike the others, Dodder wore a coat and breeches of batskin, with the ears left on. He drew this almost over his head in cold weather, so that he looked like a very curious elongated bat without wings. He always maintained that batskins were more supple than those of mice, and allowed greater freedom of movement.

As soon as he joined Sneezewort and Baldmoney he sat

down and took off his wooden leg, laying it on the shingle beside him.

"I shall have to make another leg, Baldmoney," he said in a sorrowful voice. "This peg is wearing out and I shall want another one now the spring is coming. I do wish I could find something that would wear better."

Baldmoney took up the leg and examined the end, rubbing his beard and puckering his already wrinkled forehead until his eyes seemed to disappear.

"I believe we could find something better. I'll ask the King of Fishers."

Just at that moment, as if in answer to a prayer, a streak of flashing blue darted round the bend of the stream and a kingfisher came to rest just above their heads on a branch of the oak tree, close to five little round oak-apples.

The gorgeous bird glanced below him with side-cocked head, and every now and then bobbed up and down, gulping something.

"Our respects, your Majesty," said Baldmoney humbly (he always seemed to be the spokesman of the party); "you're just the one we wanted to see. Brother Dodder here requires a new leg of more durable stuff than thorn. What can you suggest, humbly begging your pardon?"

But for a moment or two the Kingfisher could not reply for the very good reason he had just swallowed six sticklebacks and his gullet was crammed.

The gnome waited politely for him to digest his meal, and at last he spoke. "Wood is no good, it's bone you want. What I don't know about bone isn't worth knowing, seeing that we build our nests of them."

The gnomes remained silent for they knew Kingfishers' nests of old; did not they have to hold their noses every time they passed them? Kingfishers are filthy birds in their nesting habits, and it was always a source of utmost amazement that such gorgeous and kingly beings could be so dirty. Why kingfishers possess such lovely plumage, the most lovely of any British bird, is another story.

"That's an idea," said Dodder. "I never thought of bone."

"Fishbone isn't tough enough," said the Kingfisher. "I'll keep a look out and bring you something stronger."

Lulled by the music of the babbling stream, all sat silent for a space. Just above the bend it ran over the shillets, creased and full of broken sky reflections. It was so shallow there that the gnomes could wade across, but it soon deepened and ran smooth and polished into the sherry-brown deeps under the oak root.

"Well, your Majesty, and how goes the fishing?" asked one of the gnomes.

"Rotten, never had worse, though it's better up above Moss Mill. But the miller's brats catch a lot—they're at it all day long. One of them tried to hit me with a stone from his catapult yesterday. You'll be starting fishing soon, I suppose?

Excuse me . . ." (and here the Kingfisher made rather a rude noise in his throat, for his meal was not yet quite digested). "Yes," said Dodder, politely pretending not to notice, "I shall be starting soon, but we've fished the stream out about here, and that's the truth. The minnows and sticklebacks don't seem to run up as far as they used to. I don't know what we shall do now that the tar is coming in off the new road. Beastly stuff, it kills the fish. It was bad enough when they used to dip the sheep up above Moss Mill. The poison killed off several gnomes when they began it, that was many Cuckoo summers ago, before your Majesty was born. Do you remember that, Sneezewort?" But the little gnome did not reply, he was gazing wistfully upstream. "He's thinking of poor Cloudberry, our lost brother, you know," said Baldmoney in an undertone to the Kingfisher. "Cloudberry went up the stream to find the Folly Source and never came back. That's months ago now." Baldmoney sighed, and they all sighed. For a space there was nothing but the undertone of the brook, and the wind in the trees.

"Did you ever go to look for him, Baldmoney?" the Kingfisher asked, glancing down at the three sorrowful little gnomes sitting below him on the shingle. "Yes," whispered Baldmoney, "we went upstream below Moss Mill and Joppa but we could find no trace. The water-voles said they saw him up above the mill, but nobody saw him after that. Your Majesty's father saw him too, walking through the Dock forest by Lucking's water meadows, but nobody else could help us. Your Majesty's father went all the way to the wood of Giant Grum, but could not find him." "Perhaps Giant Grum saw him, though," said the Kingfisher darkly. "There's been a Giant Grum in Crow Wood for years. He tried to shoot me once, but missed, and I give the place a wide berth now, though the fishing's the best in the stream." "Have you ever been right up, beyond the wood?" asked Baldmoney in an awed voice.

"No, not right up. Beyond Crow Wood is the Big Sea and an Island, and then the Folly gets very narrow, and the fishing's poor; it goes on for miles and miles. Perhaps I will go one day, though."

Baldmoney sighed again. "I wish I had wings like your Majesty, then I could go right up to the Birth of the Folly. Our people have always wanted to go, but it's such a long weary way, and our legs are so small."

The sun had gone in and the wind began to rise, ruffling the water. Baldmoney reached for his waistcoat and put it on and Dodder strapped on his wooden leg again.

"Well," said the Kingfisher, shaking himself, "I must be off; my wife is downstream somewhere. I won't forget your leg, Dodder," and with a flick he left the branch and arrowed away like a blue bolt across the angle of the meadow.

The three gnomes, left alone, began to collect some dead twigs from under the bank. It would be cold when the sun went down. Baldmoney went up the shingle to search for flints, and the others crept back into the shadow of the root carrying their fuel with them.

Lucking's cows came trooping across the meadow in a long line on their way to the ford. They waded in, the water dribbling from their mouths, their pale-lashed eyes gazing stupidly at the current as they sucked in long draughts.

Baldmoney came back along the shingle carrying a dead branch. The cows saw him but paid no heed. They went on sucking in long draughts of cold water and the mudsmoke rolled away from their huge hairy legs, dimming the clear stream. They had seen the gnomes many times and took no more notice of them than if they had been water-voles. Why should they ? For all wild creatures were the same to them. After all, the little wild people *are* fairies and gnomes; birds and beasts alike.

As each one finished drinking, it stood for a moment or two with dribbling mouth and then wheeled round, hoisting itself up the bank and wandering off into the pasture, where it began noisily to crop the grass.

\* \* \*

When Baldmoney entered the hollow under the oak root he pulled the branch in after him. Though it was only sixteen inches long it was all he could manage.

There was quite a large space of trampled sand under the root (in the high floods of winter the water sometimes

*Baldmoney carries firewood into Oak Tree House*

came right up to the door of their house). This door was not more than eight inches high but excessively thick. It was part of an old Sunlight soap box that had been washed down the stream years before and it had taken the gnomes many weeks to cut through with the blade of a pocket knife which belonged to Cloudberry. He had found the knife in the Willow Meadow below Moss Mill, and when he went away he had taken it with him. The hinges of the door were made of wire, filched from a fencing post. Holes had been bored in the door and the wire passed through and the whole contraption was hinged to the living root of the oak.

Baldmoney broke up the stick as well as he could and, shouldering the bundle, opened the door and passed inside, shutting it behind him. Before him the earth sloped upwards between two cheeks of oak root through which he had to squeeze, and beyond he found himself in the actual living space. This was cozy enough and gave them ample room, for under the root there was a great chamber, fully three feet across. The floor was lined with dried rush, gathered from the stream, and the smoke from the gnomes' fire went right up inside the tree, coming out through a knothole in the top.

When their fire was burning there was only a filmy thread of smoke, but they took the wise precaution of never lighting it save on a windy night when the smoke would not be noticed, or during bad weather when people would be indoors. On calm nights when there was no breeze, even the tiniest wisp might have been observed by any mortal outside.

As it was a windy evening the gnomes had a good blaze burning and the ruddy light of the flames lit up the interior of the tree, throwing dark shadows everywhere. Looking upwards, a tiny point of dim light was seen where the tree was open to the sky.

Sneezewort was seated cross-legged, making fish-hooks out of a mouse's bone; Dodder was slitting the stomach of a fat minnow. He had seven other little fish in a pile beside him. When all were cleaned he hung them in a row in the smoke from the fire to kipper them. Baldmoney flung down the fagots and stacked them neatly at the side of the cave.

They all worked without speaking, each at his own job. Dodder, owing to his wooden leg, was the chief fisherman of the three, and he was also the cook, and no mean cook either, as he often said. Certainly his kippered minnow and beechnut girdle cakes were *very* good indeed.

After a meal, taken in silence round the fire, the gnomes lay down, each snuggling into his moleskin sleeping-bag. They lay gazing at the embers which now smoldered redly. The wind was rising outside and they heard Ben the owl leave the tree and go a-hunting. It was Ben who provided them with skins, as many as they wanted, for gnomes do not kill warm-blooded things save in self-defense; all birds and animals with the exception of stoats and foxes (wood dogs, as the gnomes called the latter) were their friends.

For a while nobody said a word; they lay stretched out under their moleskins, their tiny eyes glowing like moths' eyes in the red glow of the dying fire. At last Baldmoney spoke.

"I've been thinking over what the King of Fishers was saying about going up the stream and looking for Cloudberry. Well, why shouldn't we? We've got the whole summer for the trip and can get back here before the fall of the leaf. I don't see why we shouldn't try it." Nobody replied. Indeed the other two were so silent that Baldmoney thought they must be asleep. But on looking at his companions he saw their eyes as brilliant points in the dusky interior of the cave.

Diamonds flashed from Sneezewort's eyes for he was weeping silently. Of the three gnomes he was the most easily moved, and Cloudberry had been his favorite brother. At last Dodder burst out, rather irritably.

"You know, Baldmoney, you're as bad as Cloudberry, always restless, always wanting to leave the Folly and find a better place, always talking, like poor Cloudberry, of the Folly Source. We should never find him or meet any other gnomes up the stream who could help us. The fishing is poor here, I know, but we still get enough to eat and the oak has been a good friend to us. Besides, what about my leg? I can't go with you. Still," he added in an injured tone, "leave me behind, I don't care. I shall be all right, but if you never came back, like poor Cloudberry, I should be all alone, but . . . I suppose I could manage very well by myself," and he sniffed in an aggrieved way.

"Oh, we shouldn't leave you, Dodder, you'd have to come with us, wouldn't he, Sneezewort?"

"I'll go, Baldmoney, if Dodder comes. I've always wanted to go up the stream to find Cloudberry, always. . . ."

There was a short silence again; the wind piped in the shadowy cavern above and sang a song in the twisted branches of the old tree.

Dodder growled, "Absurd, it's sheer stupidity, and we will never come home again. How can we go all that way? Why, it takes us hours to reach Moss Mill!"

"Ah, but I've been thinking," said Baldmoney, "thinking a lot just lately. Why shouldn't we build a boat, not a fishing boat" (they used coracles made of frogs' skins stretched over a withy frame, Indian-wise), "but a proper boat with paddles. I've got it all planned out in my mind."

Dodder snorted angrily.

"And do you suppose, my dear Baldmoney, that we could ever paddle against the current of the Folly? Why, it's all we can do now to manage our fishing boats!"

"Well, I think we could in *my* boat," observed Baldmoney. "I've got it all planned out. At any rate we could manage in the smooth reaches and we might carry it over the rapids, like the Dartmoor gnomes used to do in the old days, in the country of Running Waters."

"I've got a better idea than that," broke in Sneezewort. "Let's get Water-vole to tow us up the rough water, or if he won't, Otter would."

"What a splendid notion, Otter and Water-vole! They'll help us; why, they might take us right up to the Folly Source if we wanted to go. Why ever didn't we think of that before?" Sneezewort and Baldmoney were warming to their subject.

Dodder snorted again. "Well, you can go, the pair of you, and I'll stay behind and live a few years more. What about Giant Grum and Crow Wood? You're fools, the pair of ye, and I'll have nothing to do with the madcap scheme. You can go, *I* won't come with you. It's all very well for you, with two good legs, but I've only one, and that won't help me run away from any Giants, or swim if I fall in the Folly."

But the other two gnomes argued on until the last spark of the fire winked out and they were left in the intense darkness with the wind "bluntering" round outside. Soon even Baldmoney was tired out and a silence fell in the dark cave under the old oak.

Out in the cold meadow the cows had lain down one by one, and from beyond Hallfields spinney a wood dog (fox) was barking. Half veiled by the scudding clouds, the stars glimmered through ragged gaps, and under the root, which smelt of oak smoke and kippered minnow, three tiny snores rose up like elfin horns. The sun was on the other side of the big round world, the soft tide of darkness cloaked every living thing. Only the night hunters, like the red wood dogs, and Bub'ms (as the gnomes called the rabbits) were out, and as for Ben, why, he was away beyond Collinson Church, hunting the new plow!

# CHAPTER 2

# The Launching of the Boat

NEXT MORNING BALDMONEY and Sneezewort found that Dodder was still adamant in his decision not to go on any foolhardy trip up the Folly. Up to now the three gnomes had been inseparable and had always lived in harmony; this was the first time they had seriously disagreed. Dodder was sulky, refusing even to talk, and consequently an unnatural gloom descended on the trio.

By passive resistance to the projected plan Dodder hoped to change their minds. It was not the first time the trip had been suggested, and perhaps, as before, Baldmoney and Sneezewort would forget all about it.

What with the feel of spring in the air and the continued sunny weather, the gnomes had much to do. There was the cave to spring-clean, and the little men carried out all their portable furniture into the sun and burnt the old rush matting. Dodder went through the store cupboards and reviewed their stocks. First he sorted out the piles of kippered minnow, which had been harvested in the autumn. He found they still had one hundred and sixty bundles of dried fish, making four hundred and eighty fish in all. The store had carried them through the winter very well, for gnomes do not eat much during hard weather. Like dormice, they hibernate during the colder months of the year. Next he counted out the dried mushrooms; it had been a poor autumn for them, and there was only a bundle of thirty remaining. As for the acorn cake, it was practically all gone. Of wheat cakes there was a goodly store; fortunately for the gnomes, Lucking had been forced to plow up the big meadow below Moss Mill, a thing which had never been known before. This was, of course, very convenient as it was not far to fetch gleanings, and the gnomes had made the most of their opportunity the preceding autumn and had laid in a fine supply. They had worked hard, well into October, going every moonlight night to the stubbles and coming back loaded with grains of wheat which they carried in little sacks made of dock leaves. As to sweetmeats . . . six combs of wild bees' honey remained; the gnomes were pigs for honey. The piles of dried wild berries, hips and haws, beech and hazel nuts, crab-apples and dried sloes, would carry them on until the next fruiting season, and Dodder was well satisfied with his inventory.

Then he went over the wine cellar. The wine was kept in snail shells (the big, brown garden kind) sealed with bungs of wood. Each was neatly labeled with the name and vintage, and they were arranged in racks at the back of the oak root. Elderberry 1905 (a good vintage year), Sloe 1921, Cowslip 1930, Buttercup 1919, and so on; Dodder had a neatly written list. This wine was his especial pride, and it was only brought out on very rare occasions, such as Animal Banquets (when they asked their friends), Hallowe'en, or on Midsummer's Eve. It was drunk direct from the shell, and one was just about as much as a gnome could manage at a sitting.

Next Dodder overhauled the fishing tackle, throwing away all the rotten horsehair which had served as gut, replenishing his stocks with fresh horsehair casts which he had made during the long dark nights of November and December. Baldmoney and Sneezewort had amassed more than a dozen bone fish-hooks, beautifully fashioned complete with barbs. With long practice the gnomes could make these in about an hour or two. They were about a quarter of an inch long, excessively sharp, with a tiny hole drilled through the shank. The end of the twisted horsehair cast was passed through this hole and knotted firmly. The best hook they had was of steel. Dodder had found it inside a minnow's mouth. This minnow had evidently been caught by one of the miller's brats and had broken the gut, and got away. Dodder prized this hook so much he always carried it about with him in an inside pocket of his batskin coat.

Sneezewort beached the boats and went over his gear. He pulled the frogskin coracles up the shingle and scrubbed them out. Though these boats were easily upset, they were very streamworthy and durable, lasting for several seasons.

The moleskin sleeping-bags were turned inside out and laid in the sun to air, and soon the cave was scrubbed and fresh until it was as trim as a newly spring-cleaned house.

The question of the trip up the Folly was not mentioned by any of the gnomes for the next few days, there was so much to do. But Baldmoney, as he went about his work, never ceased to plan and think, for he had set his mind on it and nothing would turn him.

At last came April with its gentle showers and springing buds. Already the oak was thickening in its upper twigs and the rooks called all day from the rookery behind Lucking's farm. They came to the oak for the live twigs, twisting them off with their mighty pickaxe bills from the upper branches.

Ben's wife was sitting on her three rough eggs up in the knothole and soon the wheezing naked owlets would be born. Though the owls were very good friends to the gnomes, supplying them with all the skins they required, they were a bit of a nuisance to the little men. Beetle wings and castings were always tumbling down the interior of the tree and making a mess of the dwelling chamber; poor Sneezewort spent a lot of his time sweeping up. Later, when the owlets were bigger, their wheezing calls for food kept the gnomes awake at night. But the owls were helpful birds, so no complaint was made, and after a while they became accustomed to the persistent squeaking.

It was possible to climb up inside the oak to the owls' nest; Baldmoney and Sneezewort frequently paid a visit to Ben's family to see how they were getting on. The young owlets were at first rather ill-mannered, standing up in the nest and snapping their bills at the gnomes. But after a while they became friendly and were pleased to see them.

There was another inhabitant of the oak tree . . . Zeete, the bat. Zeete seemed to spend the greater part of his life upside down below a knothole, hanging by his needle-like hooks. Only in the evening, when the light dimmed and the midges danced over the water, did he unhook himself and go flittering away like a scrap of burnt paper. He was also useful to the gnomes, for he kept watch for the greatest enemy they had to fear, Man, and warned them of his approach. Through no fault of his own, he was a verminous little person.

One afternoon, when the gnomes were sitting round the mouth of the cave enjoying the warm sun, Kingfisher shot over the meadow and perched on his favorite twig next to the oak-apples. He held in his bill a straight piece of white bone which he dropped on to the shingle at Dodder's feet.

"There you are, Dodder, a nice sound bit of bone for your new leg. I found it outside the wood dog's earth in Hallfields spinney. It's rabbit bone and should serve the purpose." Dodder took it up and examined it.

"Thank you, King of Fishers, it will do well; I'm much obliged to you, I'm sure!"

"When are you going up the Folly?" asked the Kingfisher after a pause. "I thought . . . excuse me . . ." (here he gulped prodigiously) "you would have started by now."

An awkward silence fell. "Well . . . er . . . as a matter of fact, we've been so busy," replied Baldmoney rather shame-facedly. "We've had the house to clean, and I haven't made a start on the boat yet. But I'm going to, this week. I've got all the plans in my mind."

"Well, that's good news, gnomes—I wish you luck; mistake to stay in the same place all your life. I shall see you up the brook; let me know when you are going, and remember I'm always willing to do anything I can to help." And with that he darted from his perch and went away down stream.

After he had gone the gnomes said no word. Dodder began work on his new leg at once. He shaved it down with the edge of a sharp flint (they used flints for lighting their fires), and he whittled and worked, bending low over his task. His beard kept getting in the way until he tucked it inside his batskin coat. He picked out a new acorn cup and fitted the stalk into the hollow end of the bone and after an hour had made a very neat job of it. He braced it up on to his leg, making it secure by strips of mouseskin, and then stumped up and down the shingle, still grim and silent. The other gnomes said no word.

The silence and tension became unbearable and at last Sneezewort ventured to speak, rather timidly.

"When *are* we going to make a start on the boat, Baldmoney? It seems to me if we are to begin we'd better make it soon because the summer will be here and it's going to take a long time getting everything ready."

"Well . . . er . . . what about this afternoon? There's no time like the present. If Dodder won't come he'll have to stay behind, and we must go without him. After all, he can be laying in the winter's supply, and he likes fishing." (Dodder had gone away down the shingle in a huff and the two were left alone.) "You know, it's stupid of Dodder to behave like this," burst out Baldmoney in a low undertone. "He'll be miserable all by himself. Oh dear! Why is he so stubborn? Anyway, even if we don't find Cloudberry the change would do us good; we haven't stirred from this spot for years. Everyone wants a change some time, and I'd like to explore the stream and perhaps find the Folly Source. Come on, let's get some wood to make the boat—it shouldn't take us long to build."

The two gnomes walked up the bank in the opposite direction to Dodder and clambered over the roots of an old thorn-tree which grew on a sandy slope. A few yards away there was a thick spinney in the angle of two hedges where the gnomes collected their fuel. Already the new spring growth was pushing up, soon it would be a veritable jungle of nettles, couch grass, and willow-herb.

Primroses were all over the place in vivid yellow splashes, and up in a thorn tree two chaffinches were building a nest, a wonderfully neat affair of felted lichen. They saw the gnomes but were so busy they couldn't even spare a moment to talk. After a while, however, the cock bird noticed Baldmoney struggling with a stout piece of wood, and stopped his work.

"Hullo, Baldmoney, getting some firewood?"

Baldmoney looked up and mopped his forehead. "No, we're building a boat, Spink." (Spink was the chaffinch's name.) "We're thinking of going up the Folly to find Cloudberry, our lost brother."

"My! My! My! But you will have some fun," exclaimed Spink. "That's the most surprising piece of news I've heard for a long while; I thought you gnomes never went anywhere!"

He was so full of the news he went straight off and told his wife. She, like all females the world over, loved a juicy bit of gossip, and you may be sure it would not be long before all the birds on the stream knew of the coming adventure.

Bub'm (a wild rabbit friend of theirs) was sunning herself at the mouth of the burrow close to the plantation. She heard the gnomes pushing about in the underwood; the tiny snap of twigs and rustle of leaves made her suspicious. She thought at first it must be a stoat. She stood up on her back legs with her paws hanging down against her whitish tummy, her ears went in a V. Then she caught sight of Sneezewort through a gap in the bushes and saw who it was. In a very short time Bub'm also had the news, and as rabbits are also gossiping creatures, it was not long before all the animals knew of the Folly trip.

It took the gnomes some time to collect enough suitable wood, and longer still to portage it down the bank to the oak tree root. But at last the job was done and they began hammering, shaping, and planing for all they were worth. They tapped like woodpeckers and worked so hard that when Dodder returned, still grumpily stumping along with his hands behind his back and eyes on the ground, the boat was taking shape.

When he saw what they were doing he said nothing, but went straight into the cave and did not come out again. The gnomes worked on until it was too dark to see. All the next day and the next they toiled, stopping only for a bite of food. By the end of the month the boat was nearly finished and looked something like this:

For paddles they used strips of wood, cleverly wedged into wooden hubs, and the two handles were made out of bent wire, filched from a fence. The bending of the wire was the most difficult job of all, for it took their united strength to hammer it to the right shape; the little corner of the brook rang like a blacksmith's shop.

All the animals and birds up and down the stream had got wind of what was happening, for the tidings had been passed from beak to beak and from mouth to mouth. Everybody came to look at the new boat, for it was the finest boat ever built by gnomes.

As it neared completion it was tied up under a log which lay among the stinging nettles of the bank so that all could admire it. Baldmoney and Sneezewort were very proud of their handiwork for, as you can see, it was a splendid boat and very ingeniously made. Even Dodder was secretly impressed. He used to go and peep at it when he thought the others were not looking. But still he refused to talk and went about with his eyes on the ground. Poor little gnome; secretly he wished that he was going too, for in all his life he had never been alone and the idea of the long summer months without his companions would not bear dwelling on. But he was of a very proud nature, and once gnomes make up their minds about a thing it takes a lot to change them.

By the first week in May the boat was finished. It was varnished with gum from a nearby sycamore and looked very smart and streamworthy. The launching was a great moment. Gnomes never waste time over anything. The boat was finished on the Second of May, at five o'clock in the evening, and at seven o'clock they decided to launch her in the pool. They put wooden rollers under her and tied a twisted grass rope to the prow. They pulled for all they were worth to get her down the bank, but they could not stir her. Baldmoney's feet kept slipping on the loose shingle. This held up matters for a bit, for of course Dodder was nowhere to be seen; he was sulking in the house. I doubt if they ever would have got her down the bank had not a passing toad lent a hand. They tied the grass halter round his neck and all three pulled and pulled. "It's moving," said Baldmoney excitedly; "pull, you fellows, pull." And sure enough the heavy little boat began to jerk forwards towards the stream, nearer and nearer to the water's edge until at last, with one final heave, it slid in with a faint splash. The trouble they had in getting the grass halter off the toad you wouldn't believe, for he kept trying to swim away. After a tremendous amount of splashing and noise they at last pulled the boat back to land and tied it up to a hawthorn bough. Then, thanking the toad, they went off to plead with Dodder.

They found him inside the house, right up in the corner by the cellar, and Baldmoney noticed that he had been crying. His eyes were very red, but he pretended it was the smoke from the fire.

"Come on, Dodder, we're going to try the boat. Toad helped us to launch her and she floats beautifully. We're going to paddle her up the Folly as far as the Stickle. *Do* come, Dodder!"

They coaxed and wheedled but the little man said no word and shook them off roughly. So they left him alone and went out to try the boat.

It was late now, and Zeete was out, flickering round over the water. The two gnomes were wildly excited as they climbed aboard. Sneezewort pushed off with a willow stick and the little boat swung gently into the current of the deep pool.

Looking upstream they saw the smooth water winding away towards the rapids, the reflections of the bushes and willows, dark and mysterious, at the bend in the brook.

A song thrush, singing among the white blackthorn blossom, stopped his song when he saw the boat put out from the bank and sat watching the gnomes with interested eye.

Two male blackbirds who were running round each other in a love duel (their tails fanned and crests depressed) also saw the boat push off, and even they forgot their jealous anger and flew up to the oak tree to see how the gnomes fared.

Baldmoney took one of the paddle handles and Sneezewort the other and they began to turn them round. At first the gentle current still pushed the boat backwards but, as the paddles got to work, the backward movement ceased, the boat became stationary, and then oh, joy! It began to slowly forge upstream!

As the gnomes got into their stride, each working his handle in rhythm, the boat gathered speed until it was steadily pushing a furl of water before it and heading up the center of the pool.

Neither of the gnomes spoke. As they were bent over the handles they did not see the dim face of Dodder peering round one corner of the oak root. The poor little man could not resist coming to see how the boat worked. When Baldmoney stopped paddling for a moment to wipe away a bead of sweat from his brow Dodder immediately bobbed back into the shadow, for he didn't want to be seen.

Out of the corner of his eye Sneezewort saw the sturdy green rushes and young nettles growing on the opposite bank slowly sliding past. He worked with all his might, delighted with the success of the boat and with the ease with which it slid through the water. It was infinitely better than paddling one of the coracles.

But the test was yet to come. As they neared the Stickle the sound of the water furling against the prow of the boat loudened into a chuckle and a thin film swept over the bottom boards, wetting the gnomes' feet. But they worked with a will and inch by inch they crept upstream until the smooth water round the bend was reached.

They headed into the bank and tied up to an iris flag. "Phew," gasped Sneezewort, "that was hard work. We can do it, but we shall have to get Water-vole to help us at the rapids; unless we meet any bigger ones below Crow Wood we ought to get up without a lot of trouble."

Baldmoney was sitting in the prow, mopping his forehead. "Don't tell me I can't design boats; Sneezewort; we can go anywhere in this!"

He got out and surveyed the craft proudly. Under the opposite bank there was a sudden plop and a second later they saw Water-vole swimming across with a rush in his mouth.

"Hi, Water-vole, we want to speak to you!" called Baldmoney. The rat altered course and came over across the current, his body twisted sideways, swimming with a consummate ease which the gnomes envied. He climbed out on to a pad of rotten reeds and cleaned his whiskers.

"That's a fine ship you've got there, gnomes!"

"Yes, it's our new boat, we've just made it," said Sneezewort with pride, "and we want to ask a favor of you, Water-vole. We're going up the Folly to find Cloudberry and we want you to help us. Is there any rough water below Moss Mill?"

"Rough water! I should think there is," replied Water-vole. "You'll never get your boat up to Moss Mill; it takes *me* all my time working up the bank."

"That's just what we want to see you about," broke in Baldmoney and Sneezewort together. "We want you to give us a tow in the rapids; we can manage all right in the smooth water but with your help we can get up."

"Of *course*, I'll help you, gnomes," said the good-natured animal, "and so will all the other voles below the mill. I'll let them know about it, unless, of course, they know already—about the trip, I mean. I knew two days ago, Bub'm told me; the whole stream probably knows it. But take my advice and wait a day or two; the Folly will be lower then and it will be easier to get up the rapids. You should start when the first wild iris bud splits, not before."

The Water-vole took up a piece of green root and, holding it between his forepaws, began chewing busily. The grateful gnomes nearly danced for joy.

"When will that be?" asked Sneezewort eagerly. "When do you think we can start, Water-vole?"

"Well," he replied between mouthfuls, "I should say in

about two days' time. We're going to have a dry summer by the look of the stream, and all you've got to worry about is thunder showers and, of course, Giant Grum. I shall feel happier when you are through Crow Wood. Of course, I don't know what the Folly's like above Moss Mill, because I've never been, but the higher you get the less water there is. I should make a map as you go along, it'll be useful to you afterwards, and you can mark in all the good fishing grounds. The minnows in the mill-stream are whoppers."

"Have you ever seen Giant Grum?" asked Sneezewort rather timidly.

"No, I've never seen him, but he has a dreadful reputation. He'll kill you if he catches you there. Crow Wood is a terrible place. I'll see you safely up to Moss Mill, but after that I shall have to come back. I'm a family man and my wife would worry. As it is, I daren't tell her I'm going with you, because she made me promise not to go even as far as Moss Mill. You see, her mother went up to Crow Wood and she, like your poor Cloudberry, never came back. I expect Giant Grum got your brother as well."

"Well, thanks a lot, Water-vole; we'll make a start when the first iris breaks its bud. Good-bye, Water-vole, and don't forget your promise!"

The gnomes climbed aboard again and pushed off into the current. They had no need for paddles. They drifted gently along on the surface of the stream. It was good to sit down in luxuriant ease and watch the scenery go by; the reed spears already forming a forest, the grass so long and lush, hanging over the edge of the bank, with here and there bunches of cuckoo pint, and the wild cherry glorious in bloom.

When they reached the rapids it was nearly dark. The boat gathered speed and the gnomes crouched, half fearful, half exultant, hanging on for grim death. They swept down the rough water, rocking a little but always stream-worthy until they glided into the quiet reaches of the Oak Pool.

They tied up the boat under a wild rose bush and walked back across the shingle, tired but happy, to the tree house. Dodder was curled up in his moleskin bag pretending to be fast asleep, though in reality he was wide awake, listening with all his ears.

"Dodder's asleep," whispered Sneezewort. "Don't wake him." After a hurried supper they crawled into their skin bags round the dead fire. Sneezewort was soon fast asleep, but Baldmoney lay awake. The thought of the coming great adventure heated his blood, and his imagination got busy with all manner of things. There was so much to think of; supplies, for instance. They would have to raid Dodder's store cupboard and there was bound to be a scene. Why *was* the little man so troublesome? They would have to take fishing gear and a change of clothes in case they got wet. Gnomes hate damp, especially when they reach a great age.

For you must remember that they had lived by the stream since it first began to run, way back in the dim, dim past, almost before Man walked the earth.

Oh dear! There was so much to think of, and he had to do it all. It had always been the same, it was he who had to think for the others, while Dodder gave the orders.

At last, worn out, he began to snore, and Dodder, who had cried himself to sleep (the moleskin bag was quite wet with tears), began to snore in unison.

# CHAPTER 3

# The Start of the Journey

THE NEXT DAY WAS spent in feverish preparation and frequent visits to the wild iris clump to see if the rather ungainly branching buds showed any sign of splitting.

Dodder refused to let them touch his store cupboard. He sat on a three-legged stool in front of it, looking very white and determined, gripping his stick. They pleaded and wheedled until at last he gave in, but he stood silently by whilst they packed their provisions. Baldmoney selected ten bundles of kippered fish, a pot of wild bees' honey, three loaves of wheaten bread, two cups of acorn paste, and a packet of big mushrooms. Dodder refused to let them have any more. They carried away the provisions and stacked them by the inner door of the house.

Then began a rather painful period of waiting. Dodder knew that their departure was a matter of hours, and he went about with a heart like lead. He just dare not think of the awful moment when, for the first time in his life, he would be left alone.

That evening Sneezewort was winding some new horsehair fishing line onto a piece of stick, a present from Spink, when he suddenly jumped to his feet.

"What's the matter, Sneezewort?" exclaimed Baldmoney in surprise.

"Why, I've just thought of something, something very important—we haven't named the new boat! It's awfully unlucky to go on a voyage in a new boat which has no name. What shall we do?"

"Why, name it, of course," said Baldmoney with a superior air. "We must do the thing properly, though, and fetch some spring water from over the meadow." So they got a frogskin bucket and went across.

There was a soft rain falling from a luminous sky, sturdy half-grown lambs frolicked in the small green meadow by the distant lane and bird song echoed on every hand. The spring was close to the spinney where they had gathered the wood for the boat. Green ferns almost hid it from view, pushing up like bishops' croziers from the dead leaves of last November.

Baldmoney leaned among the fronds and dipped the bucket into the very center of the spring, where the water came pushing up in little hillocks from a dusky hole in the sandy bowl.

They carefully carried the brimming bucket back to the

Oak Pool and sat down on the shingle to think of a name. This took them a long time. The little men sat with their knees drawn up under their chins.

"What about Mayfly?" suggested Baldmoney.

"That won't do—mayflies only live a few hours."

"Dragonfly, then."

"That's better; Dragonfly would be flattered too."

They went down to the wild rose bush and Sneezewort pushed the boat off into the pool with Baldmoney aboard her. As the boat began to move he dashed the contents of the bucket over the prow, intoning in a solemn voice, "I name you *Dragonfly*, and may you bring luck to all who sail in you; and may we find Cloudberry," he added as an afterthought, as the boat swung out into the current.

This ceremony over, Baldmoney paddled in again and they spent the rest of the evening carving the name (a picture of a dragonfly) on the prow of the boat. It was dark when they had finished, and so as to save time on the morrow, they packed away the provisions under the seat.

Early next morning Water-vole awakened them by scratching on the door of the cave.

"Wake up, gnomes, the iris bud up the stream has broken; it's time you were off."

Baldmoney and Sneezewort came tumbling out, carrying their moleskin sleeping bags. They were breathless with excitement. "Where's Dodder?" asked Water-vole in a surprised voice. "Sshhh," hissed Baldmoney, "he won't come with us, and I'm afraid he's very upset. He thinks the whole scheme is mad and that we shall never come back. Says he'd rather stay at home and live a few years longer!"

"That's a pity," said Water-vole ruefully; "do you think I can do anything with him?"

"You can try," whispered Sneezewort, "but I don't think anyone can make him change his mind. There's no earthly reason why he shouldn't go, because the King of Fishers has given him a brand new leg and he'd be as right as rain. But see what you can do: tell him we're starting before sun-up." So Water-vole went into the cave.

Dodder was a mere shapeless ball inside his moleskin. He had drawn it right over his head and refused to emerge. Water-vole shook him gently, wheedling and coaxing, but was only answered by stifling sobs.

"It's no good, gnomes," Water-vole told them on his return. "Dodder won't come, he won't say a word and seems very upset. If you take my advice you will get off as soon as you can."

Baldmoney and Sneezewort tiptoed back into the cave. "Well, good-bye, dear Dodder, we'll soon be back, we will really; and we'll bring Cloudberry with us, you see if we don't!" There was no answer from the darkness, so, each shedding a tear, the gnomes tiptoed out and quietly closed the door.

They climbed into the boat and untied the grass rope. As they pushed off into the Oak Pool they were aware of rustlings and flutterings on every hand.

All the animals of the stream were assembled to see them off—Spink and Bub'm, water-voles and wood-pigs, dormice, moles, and squirrels; they never knew they had so many friends! There was quite a flutter of excitement as the gnomes manned the paddles and turned the nose of the *Dragonfly* upstream.

Within the root Dodder heard the commotion on the bank, and hastily slipping out of his sleeping-bag he scrambled for the door. He was in such a hurry he quite forgot to strap on his leg and fell sprawling among the rushes. Sobbing bitterly, the poor little gnome hobbled to the door and peeped out.

A fine rain was falling, making tiny rings on the brown water, and away behind the willows the first flush of a red-eyed dawn was brightening the eastern sky.

He saw the animals gathered on the bank, and the water-side trees and bushes thick with hopping birds and far away, at the other end of the pool, the tiny blur of the boat with Baldmoney and Sneezewort working at the paddles as they headed for the rapids. Smaller and smaller they grew until they reached the bend in the stream and in another moment they were hidden from view.

It was the most bitter, indeed the only bitter moment, in

the little gnome's life. There seemed nothing to live for now, and the future was black with the horror of loneliness.

A cloud of birds, thrushes, finches, reed buntings, and titmice were hovering over the Stickle beyond, circling round and round, all singing; truly a right royal send-off! He watched the birds drifting away over the tops of the bushes, their silver voices becoming fainter and fainter, and then there was nothing but the gentle dribble of rain falling into the smooth water of the Oak Pool.

He crawled back into his sleeping-bag and wished he were dead.

\*    \*    \*

The *Dragonfly* made light of the rapids, for with Water-vole's help, the gnomes soon gained the deep reach above. One by one the circling birds dropped away to get their breakfasts, and the attendant flotilla of moorhens and water-voles fell away and dispersed.

The gnomes worked hard at the paddles and in smoother water made fine progress. Familiar bends in the stream came into view; the osier thicket veiled in new green; the clumps of wild iris, all breaking into bud, and here and there the big flat lily pads, just breaking surface, dotted with raindrops so that they seemed studded with pearls. It was a great pity that the sun was not shining; instead, the rain fell steadily. But it was warm rain and not unpleasant, and the scents and smells of the waterside vegetation were glorious.

In one little bay which opened out from the stream there was a perfect carpet of water-daisy as white as snow, in another, some early water-lily buds, like huge poppy heads from which the petals had fallen, covered a deep backwater.

The gnomes had not much time to notice all these wonders as for the most part their eyes were fixed on the floor of the boat.

They passed the old red-roofed cattle shed which stands in the corner of Lucking's meadow and saw the sable-backed swallows gathered along the roof ridge. The Folly turned this way and that, always wonderfully interesting and never monotonous.

Before long they had passed under Pingle Bridge which carries the farm track to Lucking's place, and glimpsed the rose-red chimneys and the black-and-white half-timbering peeping through the apple orchard.

The cocks were crowing in the straw-yard and from a wild crab-tree a cuckoo was shouting "cuckoo, cuckoo!"

Water-vole swam easily alongside, sometimes going far ahead to see if the coast was clear.

The gnomes found that after a while their backs began to ache with the unaccustomed effort of paddling, and towards midday they were glad to tie up under a willow thicket and have a "breather." Water-vole had disappeared; no doubt he was higher up the brook, but as he was a reliable person the gnomes did not worry. After all, they would soon have to get used to relying on themselves, for as they got higher up the Folly, the water-voles living along the banks would become few and far between.

The rain stopped and soon the sun burst forth, gilding every bush and twig, from which hung rows of glittering drops which flashed back a multitude of exquisite colors. All the lush new vegetation was steaming, and a white mist was smoking over the surface of the stream.

"Where are we now?" queried Sneezewort, standing up in the boat and peeping through the thicket of willow.

"Must be somewhere near the Dingles, below Moss Mill, I should think," replied Baldmoney, rather breathlessly, for he was still feeling the effects of the constant bending. "I'll tell you one thing, Sneezewort, we're going to have terrible lumbago tomorrow." He pressed his hand gingerly behind his back. "It'll take us a bit of time to get used to this paddling, you know."

After a pause Sneezewort wiped a tear from his left eye. "I do wish Dodder had come with us. I wonder what he's doing now; in the cave, I expect, crying his heart out!"

"Oh, don't let's think about it," said Baldmoney with some irritation. "If he likes to be so stupid and stubborn it isn't our fault. He'll soon get used to being alone, and probably quite like it after a bit."

Neither spoke. They lay full length on the bottom of the boat and watched a green caterpillar swinging to and fro by a long thread from a willow leaf.

A marsh tit with a black head came flitting through the thicket. He never saw the gnomes down amongst the tangle below. But he saw the caterpillar, and there was a tiny snap as his bill closed over it. He then flew away higher up the thicket.

The water, chuckling among the willow roots, made such a sleepy sound that Baldmoney found himself nodding. "Here, this won't do," he exclaimed, jumping up, "we will never get up the Folly at this rate; come on, Sneezewort, back to work. We've got to make Moss Mill before the bats are out."

"I wonder where Water-vole's got to," murmured Sneezewort sleepily, not moving from his comfortable position. "I hope he won't just go off and leave us."

"Oh, don't you worry about him; he's probably swum on to the next lot of rapids; you can't expect him to keep with us all the time."

After attending to a hurried toilet the gnomes reembarked and pushed on.

The sun was now very hot, so much so that they had to keep under the bushes which grew along the bank. Luckily the water was quite deep (about five inches) and as they were out of the force of the main current they made better progress. Even so it was warm work and soon the gnomes were fairly dripping. But they stuck to it and by the middle of the afternoon they saw the two tall black poplars which marked the site of Moss Mill, on the other side of the Dingle meadows.

Moss Mill was an attractive place and the mill was in working order. It was surrounded by willows, loud with the sound of many waters and rank with the rather exciting "river smell" which always seems to pervade such places.

There was a large square mill pond, bright green in color, like a lawn (it looked as though you could walk on it), and here the miller's white ducks played about, pushing their way amongst the green weed and leaving an inky black path behind them which, however, quickly closed again after they had passed.

In high summer Moss Mill was embowered with trees, willows, elms, oaks, and thickets of alder. Being a damp sort of place, weeds of all kinds flourished: all those plants which love water crowded round; giant dock, appearing not unlike the riverside plants of a tropical stream, with huge hairy columns for stalks as thick round as trees, with curious beetles and flies crawling about on the undersides of their green umbrella-like leaves, fool's parsley, bog myrtle, water-betony, marsh marigold, and huge buttercups.

All through the summer you could hear the murmur of the weir hidden under some alders twenty yards above the mill, a sort of sleepy sound which was not unlike the whisper of the wind in the tall black poplars at the head of the mill pond. The place fairly smelt of pike, trout, and all sorts of cool silvery-scaled water creatures.

The Folly divided above the mill, one arm going down the mill leat which fed the giant, chunking wheel, and the other, the main branch of the stream, winding away through willow groves to join up with the leat about thirty yards below.

Mighty trout were to be found under the wheelhouse, where the force of the water had scoured out a deep hole. It was rather an awesome place, for the darkness there was loud with the wheel's thunder and full of a roaring and a rushing. Sinister green hart's tongue ferns grew out of the stonework; the spined perch (their backs banded like zebras and with sealing-wax red fins) mouthed and backed in the shadowed depths. A pleasant place in which to be on a hot day in May or June.

\* \* \*

The gnomes paddled onwards until they were too weary to go farther, and finding a dense bed of graceful reeds they pushed their way in as far as they could and tied up to a stem. Already they were feeling the pangs of hunger, for they had had nothing to eat since breakfast.

Baldmoney got out the kippered minnows and gave Sneezewort one of them, eating two himself when Sneezewort had his back turned. Washed down with Folly water the little fish tasted delicious.

There was a reed warbler's nest slung in the tall reeds close by, a cunning little basket as deep as a purse. The hen was sitting and her little sulphur and brown head could just be seen peeping over the edge at them. The nest was deep because when the wind smote the tall slender wands there was a danger of the eggs or young falling out.

The gnomes did not know the reed warblers well because no tall reeds grew downstream. These birds will only build in a certain species of reed and never nest in the low broad-bladed sedges.

"We'd better have a sleep," said Baldmoney; "it's no good passing Moss Mill in daylight. We must wait until dusk or we might be seen. Besides, the village lovers are fond of sitting by the mill bridge; really we should not start until it's dark."

"Lovers won't notice us," replied Sneezewort scornfully; "they're always far too occupied with each other. Lucking's carter was in love two years ago and he and his wench used to walk along the Folly by Pingle Bridge. I was often fishing there, but they never saw me. I saw *them*, though," he added darkly.

Baldmoney ignored this last remark. "We'd better get our nap now. Besides, if we chatter too much we shall disturb Mrs. Reed-warbler." And having said this Baldmoney pulled up his skin bag to make himself a pillow and soon both gnomes were fast asleep, lying on their backs with their thumbs together, lulled by the sweet breeze, rushing, rushing, through the stately reeds, and by the murmur of the stream.

When they awakened it was late evening. The gnats were a-dance over the water in fairy fountains, and now and again there was a loud plop as a trout jumped for a fly.

After the heat of the day it was wonderful on the stream. You must remember that the time the gnomes had picked for their journey was the best of the whole year; May and June in the heart of England, given the right weather, are our finest months. And you must not for a moment imagine that the gnomes were blind to these beauties—indeed, being halfway between the animals and our unhappy selves, they appreciated the beauties of the world far more than a great many mortals. To them the whole year was lovely (as indeed it is to all right-thinking folk), and not an hour passed by but they found something to admire and relish.

A faint sound of chewing came from the reeds close at hand and they saw Water-vole, sucking a juicy bit of reed stalk.

"Hullo, Water-vole, we thought you'd left us," exclaimed Baldmoney, half in fun.

"Oh no, I've been close to you all the time. I want to see you past Moss Mill."

He hunched himself with a curious little shuffle into a

*In the quiet of evening the gnomes paddle along happily:*
*There is a smell of water weeds and fish*

more comfortable position on his reed pad and went on chewing busily.

"Well, what about it, Sneezewort?" Baldmoney stretched and yawned.

"Yes, I'm ready, Baldmoney—all aboard!"

They untied the boat and pushed her off into the stream. "You'd better look out, gnomes," called the Water-vole after them; "the old Colonel from Joppa Manor is fishing just below the mill, but I don't think he'll spot you, because when I last saw him his line was hung up in a hawthorn, and he was using the most awful language!"

They kept the *Dragonfly* well into the reeds, and when at last they turned the corner they saw that the Colonel was indeed in difficulties. His rod was on the ground and he was sitting on the fence wrestling with a tangled cast, a white handkerchief under his cap to keep off the midges.

"He won't see us," whispered Baldmoney. "Keep her well into the side."

Here and there a tangle of gnats were weaving about in clouds just above the surface of the water and white-tailed moorhens jerked among the lily pads. As the gnomes approached the mill they moved with the utmost wariness.

When they were about a hundred yards from the engrossed fisherman they stopped paddling and begged a tow from Water-vole, for the splash of the paddles might have attracted attention.

They had hardly got going again when, without warning, Water-vole dived. Quick as lightning (for gnomes can move so fast you can hardly follow them) they slipped the tow-rope and let the *Dragonfly* drift in among the water-betony which grew by the edge of the stream.

For the Colonel, having retied his cast, was now flogging the water and, to the gnomes' horror, he began to move slowly towards them!

"I wish we'd waited until it got dark," breathed Sneezewort, feverishly working the boat in among the water plants by pulling at the tough stems. "Wouldn't it be perfectly *awful* if he saw us! What *should* we do?"

Just at that moment, as bad luck would have it, the Colonel was into a big trout. They heard the scream of the reel and in another second something like a torpedo shot downstream, sending a furl of water slapping among the weeds. The bank vibrated with heavy footfalls and in a moment they could hear violent breathing close at hand.

The trout, which was a big one, fought about with much splashing just opposite the gnomes. Then to their horror it came diving in, right among the water plants at their feet. They heard the gut twanging as it tightened, and muttered curses from the perspiring and excited Colonel.

"It's all right," whispered Sneezewort. "He's so intent on his fish he won't see us. And he's playing it well, too; just see the way he keeps the line tight!" Sneezewort and

Baldmoney, being great fishermen, could appreciate every move in the game.

The trout refused to leave his lair and in a moment or two the stifled grunts from the bank were redoubled.

"What's he doing?" whispered Baldmoney, trying to peep between two water-betony stems.

"He's taking off his boots," gasped Sneezewort in a horror-stricken whisper. "He's going to wade in!"

The Colonel, having rolled up his pants to above his knees, began gingerly to enter the water, growling and cursing all the while.

"How cross he is," said Baldmoney.

"What hairy legs!" whispered Sneezewort. "We'd better cut the line or he'll be right on top of us."

The silvery silky gut was close to them, taut as a bowstring, going down into the center of the weeds. Sneezewort drew his knife from his belt and, leaning out of the boat, gently scraped the tight gut. It parted instantly and there was a violent outburst from the Colonel.

The gnomes lay low, hugging themselves. Then a quiver in the reed bed told them the big fish had bolted upstream.

Winding in his line, the Colonel got out on to the bank and, after putting on his stockings and boots, walked away, still muttering to himself.

When all was quiet the gnomes emerged. They found Water-vole chuckling among the reeds.

"That was as neat a bit of work, gnomes, as ever I saw; I was quite anxious at one time, especially when I saw him taking off his boots. It's all quiet now, the old fellow's gone home."

Away over the water meadows the sun had long dipped down and bats were out, hawking over the willow swamps. Sedge-warblers chattered unceasingly and there was a lovely smell of wet water-weed and fish.

"Hark!" Baldmoney suddenly stopped paddling.

Far away they heard the faint "chunk, chunk" of the millwheel. "Miller's working late," said Sneezewort in a puzzled tone; "he usually stops before now. I wonder why it is."

"It doesn't matter," said Baldmoney; "he'll be so busy with his corn-grinding he won't see you, and there are no lovers on the bridge."

"Don't you be too sure," broke in Water-vole. "They may be lying on the other side of the green palings, where the village boys bathe. I'd better go on and see."

He pushed off, cleaving the water in a V which glimmered and lapped among the red willow roots on the opposite bank. He soon returned with the news that the coast was clear so the boat got under way again.

As they neared Moss Mill the Folly widened; here and there masses of arrow-head weed grew near the bank and the yellow knobs of the water-lilies showed between their round flat leaves.

They saw before them the rose-red tiles on the mill roof splashed with grey and gold lichen seals, and behind, the rounded masses of horse-chestnut trees, now a patterned curtain of white candles from top to bottom which glimmered in the fragrant dusk. The rooks in the upper branches were quite hidden by the foliage, only a sleepy "caw, caw" told of a wakeful rookling.

Farther away still, the course of the brook was marked at intervals by more poplars, and beyond that again lay the unknown country which the gnomes had never seen, as mysterious and alluring as the darkest African interior.

Though it was now barely three hours to midnight there was a great deal of light in the sky, and from the mill the chunking of the wheel sounded louder and louder as the *Dragonfly* approached.

Numerous bats were hawking about, dipping and flitting over the reeds, and from all sides came the splash of rising fish.

A new sound filled the air, a distant thunder which, like the mill-wheel's beat, grew louder with every stroke of the *Dragonfly*'s paddles. This was the water going down the leat. Where the two streams joined below the mill the Folly swirled and bored.

The gnomes did not like the look of this maelstrom; the rapids above the Oak Pool were insignificant by comparison. But by keeping to the bank and with Water-vole's help they got past without much bother, and in a short time won through to the smooth water above the mill. Now they were on the threshold of the unknown and the first of the obstacles seemed behind them.

Baldmoney, working at the paddles with unvarying rhythm, felt elated at their success. Water-vole, having slipped the tow-rope, came through the duskiness, a gleaming ripple at his nose, for he was coming downstream to them.

"Well, gnomes, you're past Moss Mill. I'll leave you now—good luck!"

"Good luck, Water-vole, and thank you for your help; we won't forget you, and we shall be with you again before long. Tell Dodder to cheer up and say we'll soon be back!" And, with a final word, Water-vole glided away towards the mill which was bulking behind them against the afterglow of the sunset.

And then—a dreadful thing happened.

The two gnomes were working at the paddles, all was going swimmingly in every sense of the word, when, without warning, Sneezewort's paddle broke! They had struck a half-submerged snag which was almost invisible in the dark reflection of the chestnut trees. In another moment the *Dragonfly* was spinning slowly and aimlessly in midcurrent, back, back, towards the mill.

For a moment or two neither of the gnomes realized

what had happened. Sneezewort only knew that the paddle handle spun round in a foolish sort of way and would not "bite" the water. Baldmoney tried to head the *Dragonfly* for the bank, but with only one paddle they simply described a circle which took them farther from the shore and more into the pull of the current. I do not think that either gnome knew of the real danger of the situation. They thought that, at worst, they would be carried below Moss Mill and bring up in the calm reach by the lily pads.

But their peril was soon abundantly clear. Instead of following the by-pass stream, the current, ever quickening, bore them straight for the mill house.

With a sudden horror the two gnomes saw the huge cliff of brick drawing nearer with an ever-increasing impetus, and the ghastly rumble of the water was soon drowned in the rumbling thresh of the massive wheel.

"We must swim for it!" shouted Baldmoney, seizing a bundle of his most cherished possessions, for the turmoil was now so loud as to almost drown speech.

"Quick, over you go, take your bundle with you, make for the brickwork!"

Gnomes are splendid swimmers in calm water, but this sucking Niagara was something very different. It whirled them like dead twigs, or drowning beetles, helpless.

They saw the ill-fated *Dragonfly* spinning round and round. The hideous yawning gulf of the archway, through which the mill-stream fed the great wheel, rushed on them. Nearer, nearer . . . Baldmoney was gasping; fighting for air, Sneezewort had vanished. The tunnel advanced like a mammoth mouth and engulfed them; Baldmoney, Sneezewort, and boat were as minnows to a giant whale. A thunder which drowned all, flying spray, and streams of shimmering bubbles.

Baldmoney had a nightmarish glimpse of black iron bars rising and falling, was dimly aware of a clanging and a crashing, and the stifling inrush of water to his lungs; tons and tons of water pressing him down, down into the very depths; down! down! down!

# CHAPTER 4

## Dodder

For some hours after the departure of the *Dragonfly* and her intrepid crew Dodder lay in the cave, sobbing violently.

Nobody came near him, no one showed him sympathy. And because of this he was brought to his senses. Self-pity never helped anybody, least of all a gnome. He dried his tears at last, and putting on his leg, came out from under the root to find a new world of sunshine and glistening raindrops.

From the overhanging boughs of the oak tree, spots of moisture kept plopping into the pool, sending miniature ringlets which quivered away, to be lost in the smooth breast of the sliding stream.

He took his fishing-rod and hobbled up to the Folly Stickle.

After the shower the minnows were hungry, and it was not long before he was playing a fat one which took him all over the place until it was brought to bank. He soon became so engrossed with his fishing that he forgot all his troubles, and the glorious morning put new life into him.

A faint breeze brought him the scent of cowslips and ladies' smocks in the meadow, and the fragrance of the hawthorn. A cuckoo was calling continuously from the coppice in the corner.

Sable swallows swept the Oak Pool from end to end, dipping lightly with fairy touch into the crinkling surface of the stream. A tattered tortoise-shell butterfly (which had been hibernating in a crevice of the old oak tree) settled on the withered head of a reed mace close by, spreading its wings luxuriantly in the warm sun.

Dodder fished on until he had caught seven fat minnows and a stickleback. The latter was a cock fish, very smart in a rose-red gorget and with a beautiful blue back, shot with all the colors in the spectrum. Then he wound in his line and watched the little fishes swimming past in the shallow water, questing about among the stones on the Folly bed, and bringing up against the current.

As the minutes passed he was aware of a growing desire for company. All the animals and birds were too busy to stop and talk, for nearly everybody had families to look after, nests to build, and food to collect for clamoring babies and sitting wives.

Putting his catch in the rush creel slung across his back,

Dodder walked up the bank. As he went along he began to think very hard. One thing was soon apparent, he could not stand this loneliness, which was becoming more menacing every moment. Some way or another he must go after Baldmoney and Sneezewort and find them; the perils of the journey would be nothing to this intense feeling of desolation.

But the question was, how? He was lame, he could only progress at half the pace of his brothers even when walking. To attempt to overtake the *Dragonfly* was a hopeless task.

There was a fallen willow above the Stickle, a very old tree which had been riven by lightning. The searing bolt had split the tree in half and it had fallen athwart the stream, bridging it from bank to bank. Along the top of the trunk there was a hollow, like a trough, and into this the rains had washed mud and dead leaves. Bright green grass grew there and strange leathery-lipped fungus. Dodder climbed up and sat down in the hollow, his one sound leg dangling over the stream and his game leg straight out in front of him.

From here he could look down into the brook. There was quite a deep pool beneath, but the water was gin clear and he could see every pebble on the sandy floor. It looked so inviting he almost wished he was a fish.

As his eyes became accustomed to the shadows and play of sunlight on the stream-bed things began to take shape.

If the sun is shining on a clear stream it is not easy for

the unpracticed eye to see fish; even for Dodder it was difficult. By shifting his position he at last could make out the form of a very large perch which was lying on the bed of the pool, its head upstream and with faintly quivering fins. It was a handsome fish. The bars on its back were like branch shadows, and only the occasional whitish gleam of its blowing gills showed that it was a fish at all. The spines along its back were almost invisible, for a perch will not raise them unless excited or frightened.

Dodder was very astonished. Such monsters rarely came up the Folly as far as this, and if he could catch it, he would be assured of some days' supply. He put a wriggling brandling on his hook (brandlings are most appetizing worms of a clear red color) and with great skill threw it in just above the perch in such a way that it looked as if it had fallen off the willow.

Immediately it touched the water. Dodder saw it wriggling this way and that, borne by the current, but sinking lower and lower until it came to rest an inch or two above the sluggish fish.

Perch are unlike the dace or roach—they do not cruise about in lightsome shoals, but rest on the mud and sand waiting, like Mr. Micawber, for what may turn up.

As soon as the worm touched the sandy floor it began to crawl about and the perch showed signs of movement. Its fins trembled slightly and the spines rose on its back. Then there was a little swirl of sand particles and the line tightened.

Luckily Dodder was such a thorough fisherman he had plenty of line, wound on a reel made of the leg bone of a weasel. Immediately the perch felt the hook it made a great rush upstream and ran out nearly two yards of tackle. It was luck Dodder had a reel or he might have been pulled in, for you must remember that the perch was a big fish and weighed almost as much as himself. But he was a good angler and he played it with the skill of a practiced salmon fisher.

In about an hour it began to tire and show its white tummy. Dodder scrambled down off the log and pulled it to the side. It took all his strength to get it up the bank. It was a magnificent fish, the best he had caught for a long time. He drew his hunting knife and began to skin it, making an incision down the stomach and pulling hard at the thick leathery skin, folding it back as he worked his knife along. The flesh was veined with blue threads, juicy and firm. He skillfully cut himself fillets about two inches in length and soon there was nothing left but the bones.

He twisted a sedge into four thongs, tying the fillets up neatly into a bundle, and with this on his back made his way to the oak root. He went into the cave and collected his moleskin sleeping-bag, and took a bundle of wheat cakes from the store cupboard.

For Dodder had finally made up his mind: somehow or

other he was going up the Folly to join the others. The thought of a night alone in the cave was unbearable, he must be up and doing.

* * *

There was no excited company of animals to wish *him* God Speed, and nobody saw the little halting figure, with a bundle on its back, making its way up the Folly brook.

By nightfall he had made good progress and was in sight of the reed bed where the other gnomes had rested in the heat of the day. His sharp eyes soon found traces in the soft mud where Baldmoney and Sneezewort had pulled the boat among the sedges, and from the reed-warbler he learnt how they had rested awhile before going on up to the mill.

The little gnome was very tired and his leg was aching, so he decided to look for a place to sleep. It was still a long way to Moss Mill and he would have no chance of reaching it before the following night.

He found a hollow under the roots of an ash tree growing on the bank of the Folly and dumped all his gear in a dry cavity. He undid the bundle of perch steaks and, making a little fire, grilled two of them in several thicknesses of water-dock leaf. They tasted delicious and he felt much stronger. Truth to say, Dodder was even beginning to enjoy himself. He lit a pipe of nettle tobacco and sat on a log, puffing away contentedly, and watched the light die off the stream.

As darkness fell, the sound of the water was intensified, for the banks and bushes seemed to send back an echo. Water-voles swam across under the hawthorns, whose blossom-laden boughs hung low over the water, almost dipping into it. Dead sticks and dried grass still hung in swinging curtains from these lower branches, relics of the last floods of March.

Dodder finished his pipe and turned in, snuggling down inside his sleeping-bag. He slept soundly, only waking once when some animal, he did not know what, came down to drink just before dawn. Had he known it was a wood dog he would have been terribly scared.

He awakened just as the east was greying and the first lark singing somewhere up on the high arables above the farm. Though it was May a cold wind was astir, and the water meadows were cloaked in a milky mist.

Dodder lay curled up under his root listening to the birds. For some time only the lark held the stage, its thin pure notes faint and far, dropping down from an immense height. No doubt it could view the sun, peeping over the rim of the world. Then a wren sang very loudly just outside the ash root. Dodder could see it, perched on a mossy stone. It was amazing that such a tiny creature could make so much noise.

Dodder called out to it. "Hullo there, wren, you're early astir!"

The little bird sat for a moment looking rather alarmed, for it could not see Dodder under the root, and its quick little head turned this way and that. It seemed so scared that Dodder laughed, and then the wren saw him, sitting up in his moleskin bag with his hands clasped round his one good knee.

"Why, gnome, whatever are you doing up here? I never knew the Little People came up as far as this!"

"Well, we don't usually; we live by the Oak Pool. But I'm going up the Folly to find my brothers. They made a boat, and a very fine one too, and said they were going up above the mill to find Cloudberry."

And Dodder told the wren the whole story.

*   *   *

By now the birds were getting into their stride and the dawn chorus was quite deafening. Few of us hear this wonderful hymn of praise, for we lie snoring in our beds like pigs in a sty, thereby missing one of the most lovely things in the whole of Nature.

Blackbirds and thrushes warbled and piped, the sedge-warblers chattered their songs full of water music copied from the Folly, and two cuckoos competed with each other from their respective hawthorn trees. They made so much noise that Dodder at last had to block his ears. The cuckoo's song is maddening if repeated incessantly. And all the while, as it grew lighter and lighter, and the hawthorn bushes more distinct, the bird chorus increased in volume.

At this time of year, when all the birds are so busy with their domestic affairs, the dawn and late evening are the only times that they can spare for singing: their only chance to show their love for this wonderful earth and the gift of life.

Dodder must have been sung to sleep, for when he next opened his eyes it was quite light and the sun was beginning to pierce the river mists. Only the tops of the poplars by the farm were visible, looking like monks' peaked cowls above the white vapor. There was all the promise of a glorious day, and Dodder began at once to get his breakfast which he made of beechnuts, another steak of perch (eaten raw), and two wheat cakes. He finished off with a starling's egg which he had found on his way up the stream. This was a great delicacy. It was not often they had the chance of a fresh egg, for the birds were their friends and the gnome did not like robbing their nests, though I'm afraid they sometimes did so when the birds were absent.

This egg he had found among some ladies' smocks; dropped by a starling on its way to its nest. They are slovenly birds and frequently do this. Like the perch steak, Dodder ate it raw, and then finished up with a draught of searing cold Folly water, which is the best drink anyone could wish for.

The sun was well up when he at length started again on his journey. It was difficult, slow work, for at times thick bushes came right down to the water's edge and barred his way so that he had to make long detours to get back to the stream. He knew its course fairly well for he had been up almost to Moss Mill years ago on a fishing expedition.

By midday he was quite exhausted, and to make matters worse, his poor leg was sore from unaccustomed violent exercise. He was still far from the mill and he began to wish he had not undertaken the journey after all. At this rate he would never catch the others, by now they would be many miles away. From a water-vole, however, he gathered some information. It had seen the two gnomes below Moss Mill and the boat was going well. And a moorhen also gave encouragement. Dodder found her sitting a clutch of fine spotted eggs under an overhanging branch. The nest was built on a sunken log and was quite a massive affair, made of dead water weeds and reeds.

"Well, little gnome, this is a surprise to be sure!" said she. "I saw two of your brothers yesterday; they passed me in a very fine boat. Where are you going? Not leaving the Oak Pool, surely?"

"Oh no," replied Dodder hastily, "we are going to find Cloudberry, who went up the stream and never came back."

"Well, I wish you luck, little gnome. If I wasn't chained to my nest I'd come with you, but my babies will be hatching tomorrow. Are they not lovely eggs?" And she stood up fluffing out her feathers. Dodder saw a clutch of six big

*Dodder begins his lonely journey up the Folly brook*

eggs, blotched and streaked with handsome chestnut markings. He could not help thinking what a delicious meal one of them would have made him, new laid. He duly admired the eggs and asked how far it was to Moss Mill.

"Well, it takes *me* six minutes to fly to the mill pool. But that's across the meadow," replied the moorhen.

Dodder's heart sank. He would never reach the mill by nightfall, and he sat down among the willow-herb utterly spent.

He must have fallen alseep, for when next he awakened it was early evening. The first thing he saw was a very tall, aristocratic-looking bird, standing in the shallows of the next bend. It had long greenish legs, a grey body, and a neck like a snake. Its bill was sharp, broad at the base, and a handsome crest drooped backwards from the crown of his head.

It was Herne the heron, a friend of the gnomes, for he often came to the Oak Pool for minnows. Dodder immediately gathered his belongings and went up the bank to have a word with him. To his dismay he found his leg was so stiff and sore that he could hardly stump along.

"Good day to you, Sir Herne; I hope you have had good fishing?" said Dodder, setting his bundle down on the bank among the water forget-me-not, and mopping his forehead wearily.

The graceful bird twisted his head sideways and looked down at him. Dodder did not come up to his knee-joint; the huge bird towered over him.

"Well, well, if it isn't Dodder," said heron kindly. "You look very tired, little gnome. What takes you so far from the Oak Pool? I have not seen you up here for many a long day!"

Dodder told him and then asked the heron how much farther it was to Moss Mill.

"A long way for you, little gnome; you should have stayed at home. I have seen no sign of your brothers, or their boat, and I have come downstream this morning, fishing all the likely pools. They may have reached Crow Wood, and I hope they won't meet any harm there, it's a bad place—a bad place," he repeated meaningly. "I've got a nest in the heronry on Poplar Island, above the wood, so I know. You must not think of going there alone. But I tell you what I will do, Dodder," he added. "If you like to get on my back I will take you up to the mill. You may find Water-vole or somebody who can give news of the others."

"Supposing I fell off?" said Dodder rather nervously.

"Oh, you need not worry about that, little gnome, if you hold on tightly!"

So saying, the bird sat down on the grass and after some difficulty Dodder scrambled up onto the broad back. He held on to his bundle with one hand and gripped a handful of grey feathers with the other and lay trembling violently.

"I hope I shall be all right, Sir Herne; it seems very dangerous."

"Oh, don't you worry, hold on tight—you'll be safe enough," replied the heron, getting up again.

Dodder was horrified, it seemed such a very long way to the ground. The big bird walked in a stately way up the bank, took one look round and then made a short run forward, putting down his head and spreading his great wings.

In a moment Dodder felt a rush of air which flowed over him; it was as though he was in a great gale of wind. Horror-struck, he saw the fields dropping away below, and the course of the Folly all the way back to the Oak Pool, and beyond. He saw the tops of the white hawthorn bushes in the hedges and the roofs of the mill and far, far up the valley, a dark fir wood . . . Crow Wood.

The heron seemed to take only a dozen beats with his wide vanes and then began a long glide. This was rather a delightful sensation, and Dodder began to quite enjoy the novel experience. There was no uneasy "up and down" motion, the sweet air flowed past him like a cool stream. Soon he could see the individual grass blades, the cowslips and buttercups, getting nearer and nearer.

"Hold tight, Dodder," said the heron over his shoulder, "I'm going to land." And as he said this his huge wings lifted up and he "stalled" in the air. Dodder, taken unawares, let go his hold and fell head over heels into the cowslips, quite unhurt, though a little shaken. His fishing-rod fell one way and the bundle another, and he lay on his back gasping.

"All right, Dodder?" asked Sir Herne, rather anxiously, when he saw the little gnome lying in the grass.

Dodder scrambled to his feet, gasping for breath. "Yes . . . I'm all right, Sir Herne. I wasn't quite prepared for that!" He picked up his bundle and fishing-rod and looked about him.

About a hundred yards away he saw the mill and the willow swamp and heard the steady thump of the mill-wheel.

"I must go now, Dodder. I don't like going too near the mill, for I don't trust that miller; he'd shoot me if he could." Then, spreading his wings, and not waiting for Dodder's gasping thanks, he sailed away.

Dodder walked to the water's edge and hid in the sedges. His best plan would be to wait until the sun was setting and visibility was not so great. He lit a pipe and watched the azure dragonflies flitting over the water with their fairy wings tipped with deep blue.

On the opposite side of the stream a fence came down into the water with strands of rusty barbed wire, coiled from post to post. Something was caught in the lowest strand, and at first Dodder thought it was some wreckage of the stream. Then his heart gave a mighty bump. It was the boat! One end was held by a rusty barb, pressed there by the current, and the bow was tilted slightly in the air. Inside it he could see two sleeping-bags and all the gear, which had miraculously survived the descent over the mill-wheel.

Dodder felt quite sick. This, then, was the end of the whole adventure! He would never see Sneezewort and Baldmoney again! Their boat had been wrecked by some-body, or something, and his brothers had no doubt been drowned. Overcome with grief and horror, the poor little gnome buried his head in his hands and the tears ran down his beard, wetting his knees.

Oh dear! What would become of him now? He must return to the Oak Pool and live alone for the rest of his life! He could not bear the thought of it.

Soon a yellow wagtail, with a breast of bright sulphur, came tripping along the margin of the stream. It ran so fast its legs almost seemed to disappear. But it never saw Dodder, weeping among the sedges, and calling "Chissick! Chissick!" It flew away with dipping flight, a bundle of insects in its bill, destined for Mrs. Wagtail, who had a nest out in the middle of the water meadows.

As the evening advanced, little fat persons emerged from the meadow grass and began laboriously crawling towards the stream. They were toads.

With their round staring eyes and rotund stomachs they always tickled Dodder immensely. When they reached the Folly they just fell in, head-over-heels. As Dodder lay watching them from amongst the sedges one of them came up close to him, and he could see a pulse beating in its throat. Its front legs were bowed like a bulldog's, and when it crawled along it looked uncommonly like a fat gentleman in his underpants.

Dodder couldn't help laughing at this sudden apparition and it quite cheered him up. When it caught sight of him its eyes bulged more than ever. Then a green fly which was crawling up a stem suddenly vanished, licked in by a lightning flick of the toad's tongue. Dodder wished it "good evening," and the toad was so surprised it fell backwards into the water and Dodder was alone again. Poor Dodder, nobody would stay and talk, not even the toads! All he could do now was to retrieve the sad relics in the boat and return to the Oak Pool.

✿

# CHAPTER 5

# Baldmoney and Sneezewort

BALDMONEY AND SNEEZEWORT were carried over the wheel and hurled into the mill pool, the concentrated weight and force of the Folly behind them.

They went under again and came up farther down, still hanging on to their bundles, but with scarcely enough strength left to pull themselves up the shingle.

For some time they lay gasping for breath, coughing and choking, and shivering with cold. They took off their wet skin jackets and hung them up on a bush to dry. Luckily there was long grass close by, dead and withered, and they dried themselves as best they could with this. The *Dragonfly* had gone, and with her most of their dry things, all their supplies, and fishing-tackle. It was a serious situation. Luckily for the gnomes, it was a warm night or they might have taken harm.

But gnomes are adaptable and ingenious little creatures. Not very far away there was a haystack in the corner of a field and they ran thither, completely naked, carrying their bundles and clothes with them.

They burrowed inside the stack and soon were beautifully warm, and there they slept until dawn.

As soon as the sun rose they took their clothes and laid them out in the sun to dry, and when this was done went back to the river to see if they could see any sign of the hapless *Dragonfly*. But it was nowhere to be found and they sat down on the shingle and held a council of war.

Should they return to the Oak Pool and fit out again? Should they abandon the expedition altogether, or should they push on? The latter course appealed to them most, but they were sorely handicapped by having no fishing-tackle and no means of getting food. It was a weighty problem.

"If we go back, Dodder will only be superior and say I told you so," said Baldmoney miserably.

"I know, that's just the trouble, and we shall be the laughing-stock of the whole stream. We *must* push on, Baldmoney. We can soon make some fishing-tackle and we can find food as we go along. It will take us a very long time without the boat, but it can be done."

And after further argument and a weighing of the pros and cons they at length decided to continue their journey, come what might.

From a rubbing-post in a field they got a new supply of horsehair, and Sneezewort made some temporary hooks out of thorn-wood. By this time they were feeling very hungry so they dug some worms out of the bank and began to fish. The minnows were uneducated, unlike the Oak Pool fish, and in a very short time they had caught a good number; the wooden hooks seemed to work quite well, though after a while they became soft and useless in the water. But they caught enough to make a meal, and thus fortified they continued on their way. They were glad when Moss Mill was far behind them and the sound of its wheel faint in the distance.

Now a new country opened up before them, fraught with hidden dangers. The Folly became unfamiliar and the meadows alien. Somewhere ahead was the dreaded Crow Wood where Giant Grum was reputed to prowl. The stream ran slow and sluggish between banks of reed, with here and there a deep pool studded with yellow water blobs, or water-lilies. They saw plenty of fish, and at midday they decided to stop for a rest and lay in a supply. Baldmoney found a willow warbler's domed grass nest, cleverly hidden among the dense waterside vegetation, and as the hen bird was absent he took four of the eggs, with Sneezewort to keep *cave* for him.

After a lot of searching they also found some flints and so were able to get a little fire going, though it was rather a risky thing to do. They boiled the eggs in one half of a mussel shell and then had a nap.

High up in the blue sky little fluffy clouds sailed over, the cattle browsed knee-deep in golden meadows, and cuckoos called all the afternoon. Even the buttercups were above them. Standing under this golden forest would have been a wonderful experience for us mortals. The buttercup heads were like miniature golden bowls suspended over their heads and, as far as they could see, this exquisite ceiling stretched away, with the blue sky showing in the open spaces between each flower—an azure sky studded with golden nails.

It was late evening when the gnomes awakened from their nap and, much refreshed, they began to make preparations for continuing their journey.

"I've just had a good idea," exclaimed Baldmoney, as he strapped on his belt and hunting knife. "Do you remember Water-vole saying we must make a map as we go along? All explorers make maps of uncharted country, and anyway it would be most useful to us if ever we get back to the Oak Pool."

"Yes, you're right, Baldmoney, we must make a map surely. What a good thing you remembered; but how are we going to do it—what can we draw our map upon?"

"That's just the question," replied Baldmoney, fingering his beard thoughtfully. "What *can* we use?"

"What about birch bark?"

Baldmoney shook his head. "No, birch bark won't do; we

can't carry it about with us. . . . I have it, my waistcoat!"

"Your waistcoat—how so?"

"Skin, don't you see, the best parchment we could possibly have!"

"Yes, but what are you going to write with? We haven't any walnut juice, and even if we had, we could not carry it about with us—we've got enough as it is."

"Burn it on."

"Burn it?"

"Yes, burn it. We shall always have a fire at night, I hope, and with a piece of wire, heated in the embers, I can draw what I want!" (Baldmoney intended to draw the map pokerwork fashion.) "And what's more, it won't rub off and we shan't have anything extra to carry!"

Sneezewort sighed. "I wish I had your brain, Baldmoney. I should never have thought of that. Let's try it."

Baldmoney took off his waistcoat and turned it inside out, laying it flat on the grass by the embers of the fire. It did not take them long to find a piece of wire from a nearby fence, and Baldmoney made a wooden handle for it, like a penholder. Very soon the wire became red hot and he began to draw upon the skin. He found he could make quite a keen black line. Of course he did not hold the wire in the same place too long, or he would have burnt a hole right through the skin.

In about an hour he had mapped out their route all the

way from the Oak Pool. He even drew in Moss Mill and the mill-wheel and two little dots which were meant to represent their heads being carried under the wheel.

"Why, that's wonderfully drawn!" exclaimed Sneezewort delightedly. "It will be a splendid map, and you can draw little pictures of all our various adventures as we go along. Won't it be interesting to look at it when we get home again, and won't Dodder be pleased!"

Baldmoney put on his waistcoat again and stuck his wire pen in his belt. Westwards the sun was sinking low over the water meadows and a faint mist was rising, spreading like a white veil over the flat fields. A plover called and a distant snipe drummed.

Three rabbits came out into the grass on the bank of the stream and began to feed. The gnomes could just see the tips of their pink ears quivering among the cowslips. These cowslips were not the long-stalked variety, which you find in hedge banks and sheltered places. They were squat and thick-stemmed, and of a very pale lemon yellow tint. In one field alone there must have been acres and acres of them, and their faint fragrance perfumed the evening air.

"It's time we were moving," said Baldmoney at last. "The rabbits are coming out to feed." He got up and buttoned his mouseskin coat. They tightened their belts and cut themselves two stout willow sticks, then set off up the stream keeping as close as possible to the bank.

What a wondrous evening it was, so peaceful, and perfumed with all the smells of growing things: grass, reeds, the
overhanging bushes, the fragrant hawthorn blossom, wild
iris, and cowslips. Oh! It was good to smell the green earth,
to be on their way again! As they went along, Baldmoney
made a mental note of every turn in the stream, every pool
and rapid, so as to be able to draw their journey on the map
later. The Folly began to wind about, so much so that in
some places it almost retraced its course, in figure-of-eights
and S bends, so that after about two hours' walking the
gnomes had not traveled more than a couple of fields. But
it was exciting, nevertheless, and they whistled a tune as
they went along. Perhaps it was a good thing that they did
not realize what a short distance they had covered or they
might have given up in despair. But you must know that
gnomes are persistent little creatures (you may already have
guessed it) and nothing would have made them change
their minds.

You may wonder that they now chose the dusk and
evening to do most of their traveling, but, like rabbits and
hedgehogs, gnomes prefer this time of day to all others,
and they were in strange country. One reason was that they
were less likely to be seen, and another that their eyes were
like those of cats and owls—they could see better then than
at any other time. Perhaps this accounts for the fact that our
great-grandparents so seldom caught sight of the Little

People, and even on those very rare occasions when they did, they put it down to some trick of the imagination; it is so easy to imagine things in the shadows under the bushes. And remember that it is not everyone who *can* see the Little People; even if they were as common now as in medieval times, few would know of their existence. Grown-up people, it is safe to say, hardly ever see them. Why? you will ask, quite naturally. And I should answer, it is because they have grown up. Their heads are higher, like the tops of trees, whereas when we are small we are close to the ground and can see things more easily. But not all children can (or could) see them. As a child I only once saw one and then when I was least expecting to. And another reason is that grown-up people are less like animals than are children. Adults are always so busy with the dull and the dusty affairs of life which have nothing to do with grass, trees, and running streams. I doubt if even you or I were standing by the Folly that May evening, and *knew* that the gnomes were coming up the stream, we should have as much as caught a glimpse of Baldmoney and Sneezewort.

\* \* \*

As it grew darker the stream rattled more loudly, the splash of a fish was magnified, the faint breeze, rustling in the thick foliage on the banks, sounded very sinister.

Baldmoney as usual led the way, stumping along with his stout willow stick and his bundle on his back. After a while the bushes became more scattered until the Folly was winding its way through flat meadows, with here and there a pollarded willow growing by the margin of the brook. These trees seemed like distorted old men in the half light, with their twisted heads and bushy whiskers.

Gleaming rings widened from under one of them and they saw a round black knob pushing through the water towards their side of the stream. Both gnomes dropped in their tracks, for there was no knowing what the creature might be. But in a moment, a beautifully mellow whistle sounded down the winding course of the Folly, and they knew it was an otter. He climbed out on to a sunken log just below them and shook the water out of his rudder. He had such a quaint face which looked as though it had been sat upon, very broad-browed and with two merry little eyes set deep in his head. The otter heard the faint rustling as Baldmoney raised himself to see who it was and for an instant was watchful, strung like a bow, ready to slip back into the water. But in another second he saw the gnomes and came up the bank with astonishing ease.

"Well, gnomes" (all the Stream People seemed to greet them in the same friendly way), "this *is* a surprise. You gave me quite a turn at first—I wondered who it was. What brings you so far from the Oak Pool, little men?"

Once again the gnomes told the story of their journey to find Cloudberry.

Otter listened attentively before he spoke. "Well, I think I can help you, gnomes; but I can't think why you've taken so long to come up from the Oak Pool—it's only a few flicks of a rudder to Moss Mill!" "Indeed it is not!" exclaimed Sneezewort (rather rudely). "We've been tramping for hours; it must be miles away!"

Otter was a tactful beast, so he changed the subject. "It was a pity you lost the boat, especially after you spent all that time in making it. I don't mind telling you gnomes that at the rate you are going, it's going to take you a very long time to reach Crow Wood, and you may not see Cloudberry there. I shouldn't be surprised if he has gone up the Folly Source, and that's a long long way, even for me!"

"I don't care," said Baldmoney doggedly, "we're going, however long it takes us, even if we have to winter up the stream."

"Well, I admire your spirit, gnomes; I wish you all the luck in the world, I'm sure. Even I have not been up to the Folly Source, for there's no fish so high up, not even a minnow. But you will find fish right through the wood and as far as the bridge, beyond there I haven't been. But you must look out for trouble in Crow Wood."

When he had gone Baldmoney whispered, "I *do* wish the Stream People would stop talking about Crow Wood. I'm not afraid of any beastly giant or any dark wood. I love woods anyway, and why should we be afraid?"

A second after both gnomes froze in their tracks. For, from high up the course of the Folly, from somewhere in the direction of where Crow Wood might conceivably be, came a high thin wailing sound which died away to a profound silence. Even the willows seemed to shiver and both gnomes felt very afraid. It was the howl of a wood dog, a sound they were to hear many times before the journey was over.

A tiny chattering noise followed. Sneezewort jumped round and clutched Baldmoney's arm. "What's that?"

"Don't be silly," stuttered Baldmoney, "it's only my t-t-teeth; yours would b-b-be ch-ch-chattering t-t-too if you had any t-t-to ch-ch-chatter with!"

"Oh, I'm afraid," whimpered Sneezewort. "I'm afraid, Baldmoney; let's go back to the Oak Pool and Dodder."

"Pooh!" said Baldmoney, trying to control his teeth, "who's afraid of wood dogs? They never harmed us by the Oak Pool; you can go home if you like, but I'm going on."

Truth to say, Baldmoney was secretly thinking just then how nice it would be to be inside the old oak tree, watching the embers dying in the fire. But he kept this to himself.

They stood quite still in the damp grass looking upstream. Before and over them towered an old willow tree, its ivy-clad crown rustling, its slender, graceful leaves drooped downwards with here and there a shy star peeping.

The cry came again, fainter now, which seemed to make it all the more lonely and dreadful; never had explorers in the pine-clad barrens of the North felt greater fear when, from out of the wilderness, came the far howling of a wolf.

"Pooh," said Baldmoney again, "wood dogs don't eat gnomes in summertime, only in winter when they're hard put to for food. Everybody has enough to eat just now; he'd much rather have a nice young rabbit than a tough old gnome without any teeth."

"Or a long, scraggy beard," put in Sneezewort spitefully.

An owl flew noiselessly across, his great head turning, his eyes like lamps. His face was like a skull peering down at them. For an instant he checked his flight with fanning wings and some instinct made the gnomes crouch. It was a stranger owl, not Ben; when he saw they were gnomes he shrugged his shoulders and vanished.

"Look here," said Baldmoney, "we must pull ourselves together; you'll get me rattled soon. There's nothing to be afraid of—all the Stream People are our friends. As to stoats and wood dogs, we can give a good account of ourselves. Anyway, wood dogs don't like us; we smell too much like humans. Let's get going; the dawn will be coming and we haven't walked a mile yet. Come on!" And picking up his stick again, and settling his pack on his back once more, he led the way up the stream.

The white hawthorn petals (like confetti in the half darkness) were scattered over the grass and bushes; they had fallen everywhere, even in the stream, where the current

*Baldmoney and Sneezlewort continue the journey on foot:*
*The hawthorn is in blossom and white petals fall on the dark water*

carried them away. Some, caught in miniature whirlpools and eddies, span round and round, circular rafts of them revolving like fairy wheels.

The crab-trees, too, were shedding their pink blossoms, white and shell-pink mingled, and the Folly hurried them all along on its crinkling tawny breast.

The gnomes made good progress for the next two hours and nothing untoward happened. The Folly was getting smaller, there was no doubt of that, and there were next to no bushes growing on the banks. Their way led through hayfields not yet cut, full of all manner of wild flowers, delicate cuckoo-pint predominating. In contrast with noonday it was a silent land through which they journeyed, for no birds were singing and they were now beyond the haunts of reed and sedge warblers which sing during the hours of darkness.

I wish I could describe that lovely summer night, the sweet softness of it, the peace. Only the Folly sang to them, a different tune at every bend. They came to a broad ford, where the water scrambled over shingle with a loud clatter.

"We will call this the Meadow of Talking Water," said Baldmoney (he always found an apt name for places), and so he wrote it on his waistcoat, at their next camping place.

Moths buzzed about among the grass stems, big cock-chafers blundered by. One struck Sneezewort in the chest and he cried "Ouch!," which made Baldmoney jump.

They heard some cows grazing over the stream, the "scrush, scrush" as they tore the grass and the smell of newly plucked blades drifted to them. So quiet was it that they could hear the tummies of the great beasts rumbling, the same sound that guides the elephant hunter in the long grass. Many were lying down, very still and silent as though hewn of rock—perhaps they were asleep.

Sneezewort tugged Baldmoney's arm. "Let's have some milk," he whispered. They stole across the shallows, altering the song of the Folly, and crept through the grass to where the cloudy shadows of the drowsy beasts lay.

The smell of these recumbent monsters was strong, a beautiful buttercup and grass smell, mixed with the rough mud-caked hairs on their motionless flanks. It was not the first time that the gnomes had milked cows. It was an old trick they had learnt, ages back, before the steel railroad was made up the valley.

Baldmoney held a mussel shell half under one of the teats and Sneezewort squeezed with skill. Working away under the huge dome of the udder the gnomes looked up to the sky. The side of the recumbent cow was like a black mountain against the stars. The beast's eye opened wider as Sneezewort squeezed, the heavy lashes parted and it whisked its tail uneasily. In another moment it might have stood up, but the shell was full and overflowing with rich, steaming milk, which looked so white in the half darkness.

Carrying their precious burden back to the stream, they drank their fill and felt refreshed. "There's nothing like fresh warm milk for putting new life into you," remarked Baldmoney.

"Ah," sighed Sneezewort, wiping his toothless little mouth, "that's better, a lot better. I was ready for that; I feel I can face anything now . . . hark!"

From away over the mowing grass a lark began to sing. Dawn was breaking, stealing like a silver ghost over the eastern sky.

"The morning sun," whispered Baldmoney. "The sun is coming, soon it will be day!"

Sneezewort yawned a toothless yawn. "Oh, I'm so tired . . . so tired, Baldmoney."

"We must not rest until the flowers wake up," said Baldmoney. "We must push on."

So, as minute by minute the silver in the east paled, and all the meadows grew more distinct, Baldmoney and Sneezewort, stifling their yawns, stumped onwards, following every bend, noticing every pool, until the sky was full of singing birds and the glory of morning.

# CHAPTER 6

# Trespassers Will Be Prosecuted!

WHEN THE GNOMES AWAKENED on the following evening they found a change in the weather. They had slept during the day in a willow root close to a deep brown pool, bored out by the floods of many winters. Hunger demanded immediate appeasement, and they began at once to put their fishing lines together.

Gone was the golden weather which had so far favored their trip; instead the sky was overcast and gloomy, and a strong wind was whipping the trees and bushes, turning the pale undersides of the leaves uppermost. Curious swirls and V-shaped eddy-marks creased the pool by the willow; the reeds bent and bent again before the rude breath of the stormy wind, their sharp tips cutting the water.

On all sides stretched the lush meadows; the gnomes could see the waves of wind passing over the mowing grass so that the surface was undulating exactly like the surface of the sea, the rollers following one behind another, a sea of grass instead of water. Though the evening was not cold, the gnomes were glad of their skin coats.

In a very short time they had caught some thumping perch, and they fished until they had broken all their hooks. They were not used to these heavy game fish. Seven fat fellows lay on the root of the willow when they at last wound in their lines, and you may depend upon it, it was not long before those fish were neatly cut up and grilled over a fire. They ate themselves cross-eyed and for some time were quite incapable of movement.

"It's almost like an autumn night," remarked Baldmoney at length, as he lit his pipe with an ember from the fire. "We're going to have rain before dawn, that's why the fish are biting."

Sneezewort was homesick and also very full of perch, so he did not answer. He watched the wind ripples passing over the mowing grass and the spots of yellow foam spinning slowly round the pool; a little higher upstream there was a big clot of it caught against a submerged reed.

He was thinking how cozy the oak root would be on a night like this, and how the glow of the fire used to light up the rugged interior of the tree. How was the owl family getting on, and Dodder, and Water-vole? Perhaps after all they had made a mistake to come on this trip; a lot might have happened to Cloudberry in all those months which had passed since he went away. And truth to say, there was something a little sinister in this gloomy evening, and the chasing ripples and sighing wind seemed heavy with foreboding.

The next instant his heart gave a bump, and all these sentimental thoughts had gone in the instinct of self-preservation. For downstream, threading its way close to the water, was the lithe brown form of one of their most dreaded of enemies, Stoat! He was puzzling on their scent. Unknown to them he had followed them for a long way along the Folly bank. Now the scent was getting stale and he was almost on the point of giving up.

With a lightning-like movement both gnomes were on their feet, for both had seen their dreaded enemy almost at the same instant. There was no chance of climbing up inside the willow, for the barrel of the tree was not hollow. They must make a break for it while there was time. To be cornered inside the root would be disastrous.

Each had the presence of mind to grab his stick and bundle. They slipped out of the tree, keeping it between them and their pursuer, and made their way as fast as they could up the stream. Not far distant it took a wide bend to the left and the bank was clothed with thick bushes, but stoats can climb bushes with agility.

Their safest chance lay in a tree up which they could climb. Unfortunately, as you may have noticed, few trees have branches very low to the ground which would have given them a start, and, anyway, there was not a tree in sight save some elms across the meadow. The gnomes might have made a dash for these, but if the stoat was really hot on their trail, he could overtake them. When in a hurry the little devil in brown can move like lightning.

One point was in their favor, they had a good start, and stoats do not as a rule hunt by sight until they are very near their quarry.

The gnomes ran as fast as they could up the shingle; now and again they glanced over their shoulders. Stoat had gone inside the willow stump and was smelling around. Perhaps he would find the heads and bones of the perch which might delay him, but it was a forlorn hope. Such things happened at the Oak Pool, but they were never far from the old tree, and when chased could simply run inside and bar the door.

For the next ten minutes they ran as fast as their short legs could carry them. Baldmoney led, but after a while began to get a little puffed. Sneezewort, in better training and lighter build, began to make the running.

They reached the bend and the next moment their pursuer was hidden from view; perhaps he would give up the chase and content himself with exploring the willow root. Both gnomes were now puffing and blowing; their little anxious faces, always red at the best of times, were deep crimson and beads of sweat rolled off them. The heavy bundles hampered them in their flight, but they contained all they possessed and would not be abandoned unless things became very hot indeed.

"I can't see him," gasped Sneezewort, looking back.

"Don't stop running," puffed Baldmoney, "he's very likely still on our trail."

Round the bend there was a fallen log which lay almost across the stream. The water gurgled and swilled round the end of it, deep and swift, but it was jumpable. They scurried across the log and landed safely on the far bank, though Baldmoney, tired and spent, wet his right leg to the knee. They found themselves in a dense sedge-bed. The ground was miry and black, but they plunged in among the reeds.

A startled water-vole plopped into the stream and a reed-bunting flew up, excitedly flirting his white-edged tail and looking about on all sides at the shaking reeds.

Had you or I been standing on the bank we should have thought a rat or mouse was rustling through the water-plants, for the gnomes were quite hidden, only the sedges quivered. At last, the reeds thinned and in their place a forest of sturdy dock plants, with stout and hairy stems, raised their broad umbrellas overhead. It was fine cover, but no cover in the world avails a gnome or rabbit when a stoat is once on the hunting trail, so they pushed on.

Then the docks thinned and they could see the light once more and the brown Folly open to the sky, crinkling in a thousand catspaws over a wide shallow, and beyond, a deep pool. They crossed the shallows to their original bank, hoping that the stoat would lose the scent in the running water. They were now utterly spent and must find some sort of hiding-place. Leaning over the pool was a willow branch, its main stem half awash, and the slender rods grew straight up in a thick palisade. Right at the end the gnomes caught sight of a moorhen's nest; it might have been one of the many "rest" nests that the cock bird builds as rafts for his babies when they are hatched. You will nearly always find two moorhen's nests belonging to the same pair of birds.

They would have liked to have gone farther, but both were blown, and this was the only possible cover in sight. They crept out along the half-submerged branch, squeezing in between the willow wands until they reached the nest, and into it they tumbled, one on top of the other.

The nest, which contained three handsome eggs (quite cold, for the hen had not begun to sit), was substantially built, but very damp. They made themselves as small as possible, squeezing in between the eggs and taking care not to break them, and lay peeping fearfully down the stream.

Below them the brown water slid and hissed, strings of bubbles showed far down under the surface and the gnomes could see shoals of little silver minnows, a whole school of them, passing like a cloud.

"Is he following us?" whispered Baldmoney when he

had got his breath. "I can't see a sign of anything."

Sneezewort did not reply. He was breathing so fast and his heart was a-hammering so quickly he could hardly see.

Downstream they could just discern the log where they had crossed to the far bank; beyond that, the bend and the steep sandy bank hid everything. There was nothing to be seen save an old rook flying across the rim of the meadow. He came oaring his way along and alighted on the shingle at the shallows where, after a quick look round on all sides, he began to hunt for mussels. Rooks and crows love freshwater mussels.

He waddled about in the shallow water and along the edge of the reed bed, turning over some old empty shells which he found lying about.

A large spot of rain came plop! into the pool, then another and another. They rattled on the leaves like bullets, the falling drops making little tents in the water. As the minutes passed the heavy breathing of the gnomes quietened and they began to feel secure. The rain, lashed by the wind, increased in violence and the gnomes began to shiver.

Up by the reed bed the rook had at last found a mussel and he flew away with it over the fields. The vista downstream showed no sign of life.

"I think he's given up," whispered Baldmoney. "He hasn't come any farther than the willow."

Sneezewort, knowing the ways of stoats, was not so

sure. It all depended whether the stoat was hungry.

As the gnomes lay in the bottom of the nest with their chins on the rim of it, it occurred to them what a fine meal the eggs would make. A big black water-boatman came up from the depths of the pool and lay on the surface with his oars outspread. And close to the nest a whole crowd of tiny silver beetles were weaving about on the surface of the water; they moved and glistened like minute racing cars.

Then the gnomes saw Stoat. He was puzzling up the bank, quartering the ground like a hound. He went along the log and stopped, for it was a big jump for him, and he did not like the look of it. At other times it might have been interesting to watch the little hunter at work, but it was no fun when the quarry was yourself, and Baldmoney and Sneezewort trembled with apprehension. Stoat ran back along the log and began coming up the bank on the other side. Then the gnomes realized that they had made a mistake—that they should not have recrossed the brook. Had they remained in the reed bed they would have been safe. But Stoat now had nothing to guide him. He came along slowly with frequent pauses, showing his yellowish-white chest as he sat up in the grass. When he ran, his body was arched in a hump, the black-tipped tail held high. Nearer and nearer he came, and the poor little gnomes crouched lower in the nest.

Stoat was now not more than thirty paces from their

tree, and the next moment was at the shallows where they had crossed. He must have struck their scent then, for he came on at the hunting run with his muzzle fairly low.

Neither gnome spoke, but each loosened his knife in its leather sheath in a meaning sort of way, as though he meant to sell his life dearly.

Stoat reached the log; the watching gnomes could now see every detail of the cruel flat head, the sharp muzzle and the primrose-yellow chest. They could see the whiskers, like needles, and the working nose. He reared himself up on his hind legs with his front paws on the end of the willow branch, and the next moment was looking in their direction with cruel little button eyes. Then he began to come along the tree, threading the willow wands with lithe purpose.

Baldmoney and Sneezewort waited until he was almost at the nest before acting. Perhaps they were hypnotized by the deadly little beast. Had they been rabbits they would have simply sat back and squealed. But not so the gnomes. As Stoat came almost within springing distance they dived over the edge of the nest like young moorhens, one on one side, and one on the other, down into the brown water, taking their bundles with them.

Stoat chittered with rage, displaying a sudden row of ivory needles. A foot away was the unhappy Sneezewort's head, drifting downstream with the current, and a little to the left, Baldmoney's, both swimming as gracefully as frogs.

For a second Stoat was inclined to follow, for stoats swim with ease. And then he saw the three smooth eggs lying in the cup of the nest. In a moment the gnomes were forgotten. Here was a far greater delicacy, EGGS!

Stoats love a nice fresh egg; every year thousands of birds lose their precious clutches to the little brown robber. He climbs the blackthorn to get to the nest of blackbird and thrush, finch and blackcap, and not only eggs fall to him but baby birds as well.

In a second or two he was breaking open the moorhen's eggs, greedily sucking the contents, and then, when he had eaten them all, he curled round in the nest and went fast asleep like a full-fed dog.

Meanwhile the two gnomes, believing that they were still being followed, let the current take them far down until they reached the willow where they had spent the night. There they landed and shook themselves like wet birds.

There was no sign of Stoat following them so they collected their fishing lines, which they had abandoned in their flight. The hollow under the tree reeked and they did not tarry long. It was still raining heavily when they started out again. They did not follow the stream at first, intending to give it a wide berth, for they had no desire to run into Stoat. Leaving the Folly on their left, they struck across the fields; walking through the long grass was hard work and they were soon wet to the waist. Since their swim there had been no chance of drying their clothes; anyway it did not matter, for they could not be any wetter.

They struck the Folly again a quarter of a mile above the moorhen's nest and walked hard all night, covering quite a mile of ground. After a while the rain ceased and the wind died away. The stars came out and the sough of the wind sank to silence. With exercise they soon became warm and dry again, and by the time dawn began to break, the scene of their adventure with Stoat was far behind. But they could not help glancing back now and again; it was easy to imagine things in the half-darkness, and once or twice the gnomes thought they saw the sinister brown form coming after them through the grass.

As detail began to grow in the dawn they saw they were now in different country. The low water meadows had closed in on either hand and the Folly was running much more swiftly, with here and there miniature waterfalls which rattled merrily over the flotsam of the floods. Dark trees grew on the banks, and soon they found that they were entering a steep valley. Bub'ms were everywhere; they had drilled their holes in the steep slopes and the ground was honeycombed, and splashed with orange earth.

It was difficult going, for thick bushes (brambles and holly) grew right down to the stream edge, and silver birch, conifers, and sapling oaks formed quite a wood. Soon they came to a wire fence which barred their way, for it was composed of fine-mesh netting to keep out the Bub'ms. A glaring notice nailed to a tree announced in staring black letters "Trespassers Will Be Prosecuted." Beyond the wire they saw a dark mass of firs and pines, a gloomy and rather sinister place, with the Folly gushing over a miniature waterfall.

"Do you think this can be Crow Wood?" whispered Sneezewort.

"It looks very like it to me," replied Baldmoney. "I think we had better find a place to sleep."

There was no passage through the wire save by way of the stream which ran under it. A mass of withered rubbish almost blocked the Folly, for the floods of winter had swept it on the wire mesh. After some searching they found a small hole against the bank and slipped through. It was Crow Wood without a doubt, and their hearts began to hammer.

Masses of red dogwood, guelder-roses, and privet hemmed them in, whilst overhead the dark tassels of the firs almost shut out the greying dawn. Not far from the stream, sprawled down the bank, was a giant Scots Pine. It had torn up much of the bank in its fall, and the roots appeared in the half-darkness like the limbs of some long-dead monster.

They crawled right under the trunk, next the root, through a perfect jungle of fern and nettle, and there they found a cozy hollow where they could hide and rest. Lulled by the Folly water, which sent back an echo from the dark tunnel of the trees, the gnomes soon fell fast asleep, and the music of the stream was a comforting lullaby, one that was familiar, and which had always been part of all their sleeping and waking life. Even in this strange and somewhat sinister place it sang as sweetly as ever, and soon the eventful night was quite forgotten in dreamless and untroubled slumber.

The clouds blew away, the sun climbed higher in the sky, and soon little spots of sunlight pierced the thick foliage, shining redly on the rough bark of the pine. Insects, warmed and full of new vigor, began their busy day. Two wood-wasps sat on the pine trunk and combed their antennae, next to a beautiful, burnished, greenfly which shone as brightly as a kingfisher. You would never have guessed two very tired little gnomes were tucked away behind the ferns; even the little sharp-eyed wood-mouse never saw them when it came scurrying along the ground close to the root.

# CHAPTER 7

# Crow Wood

THE GNOMES SLEPT WELL, and without any undue dis-
turbances, in their green and secret hiding place. They
awakened late and found to their astonishment that the
afternoon was well advanced. The sun was out, dappling the
nettles round the tree, though it was a green under-waterish
kind of light which seemed rather curious.

As they had gone to sleep in the early dawn they had
not been able to note their surroundings clearly, and they
had also been deadly tired. But now they were able to take
stock of the dreaded Crow Wood of which they had heard
so much from the other animals. It did not seem so terrifying a place after all; they both came to the same conclusion
as they sat side by side on top of the pine log, swinging their
legs, and looking about them.

Overhead, the trees formed a green canopy, and as far as
they could see up the course of the Folly were more trees,
trees everywhere, on either side, stretching away and away.

There was rather an exciting "adventury" look in the dark shadows between the boles, and the spots of sunlight on the branching bracken fronds; and everything smelt so fresh and beautiful after the rain.

"I think this isn't at all a bad place," said Baldmoney in a relieved tone of voice.

"Nor I, in fact I think it's a wonderful wood; I've never seen so many trees before."

The truth was the gnomes were unfamiliar with woods and had never known anything bigger than the little copse below the Oak Pool. The more they looked about them and sniffed the sweet smell of the leaves and bracken, and watched the play of dappled sunlight, the more they liked it.

"We must explore this wood very thoroughly," said Baldmoney at length. "We must make friends with the Bub'ms (all rabbits were called Bub'ms by the gnomes), "wood-pigs" (hedgehogs), "birds and fern-bears" (badgers), "and find out if any other gnome has ever been seen in Crow Wood. You may depend upon it," he added wisely, "if Cloudberry really *did* come up here, even though it was so long ago, the animals would remember it, for the story would be passed down from family to family. And then, of course, there's sure to be some relation of Ben's here, and he's bound to be very old—owls always are, I don't know why. I've never met a young owl except the owlets. I've only met owlets and very old owls. Funny, isn't it?"

"That's true, I never thought of that," replied Sneezewort . . . sniff! sniff! sniff! "Oh, how good the wood smells! Do you know, Baldmoney, I'm just beginning to enjoy myself for the first time this trip! I somehow feel things are going to be better, and you can't deny we've had some shocking bad luck one way and another, what with losing the *Dragonfly* and then Stoat coming after us. Perhaps things will look up now; we deserve a bit of good luck."

They sat for a long time on the log chatting until their stomachs reminded them of breakfast.

"Oh dear," sighed Sneezewort, "it makes me mad to think of all that lovely food that went down with the *Dragonfly*; it isn't going to be easy living on the country. I'm tired of fish."

"Never mind, let's stew some of these nettle tops and dig for pig-nuts. I'm sure there are pig-nuts somewhere around; it looks the sort of place one ought to find them."

They got off the log and climbed away from the stream, up the steep slope of the wood.

"Don't let's go too far away from the Folly," said Baldmoney in rather a shamefaced whisper. Somehow they felt they ought to whisper.

"By the good god Pan, do you notice something?" ejaculated Sneezewort, suddenly gripping Baldmoney's arm.

"No; what?"

"There are no birds singing!"

While they had been close to the Folly they had not missed the song of the birds, for the rattle and music of the stream had filled their ears; now they seemed wrapped in a great quiet. Far below, the tiny voice of the Folly rose to them through the trees, but not a single bird note was to be heard—not even a pigeon cooed up in the thick tree-tops, or a blackbird warbled from the underwood, never before had they been in such a silent place.

Why wouldn't the birds sing? Were they scared of something? Two little shivers crept up two little spines; Sneezewort looked at Baldmoney and pursed his lips to whistle a tune, but something made him keep silent. Somehow, even talking seemed a sacrilege.

Gnomes possess courage and perseverance, and though they may have felt fear, neither thought of turning back. Instead they did the most sensible thing—they began to search about for some friendly wild creature who perhaps could give them news of Cloudberry.

Working their way along the steep side of the bank they came at last to a warren, and it was with a great feeling of relief that they saw a fat doe Bub'm sitting, sunning herself at the mouth of her hole.

"There's Mrs. Bub'm, let's go and talk to her," said Sneezewort with unmistakable relief in his voice.

She had five baby Bub'ms with her, and they were

having a great game on the sandy bank round the warren. The gnomes approached with caution and the old doe never saw them as she had her eyes half closed. Baldmoney stepped out from behind the tree.

With a rush the tiny babies scampered for the hole, where they all sat up like little question-marks. Mrs. Bub'm was so startled she jumped round, her eyes wide with fear. But when she saw they were only gnomes she was obviously relieved. "My! You did make me jump," said she. "I thought at first I heard Giant Grum coming down the bank!"

The gnomes exchanged a meaning look. So it *was* true about the Giant after all!

They wished her good afternoon, and, being tactful little people, admired her family. Like all mothers the world over, the old doe was pleased and for some time they had to listen to all her domestic matters, how the wet weather was so trying for a growing family, and how poor the bark had been during the winter. (Rabbits eat a lot of bark during the cold weather and grow fat on it.)

"And Stoat, Bub'm, I hope he has not paid you a visit?" inquired Sneezewort.

"Stoat, did you say? Huh . . ." (Here Bub'm shuffled her pads into a more comfortable position.) "Stoat, did I hear you say? Why, we never see *him* in this wood—he daren't come anywhere near."

"Indeed," answered Baldmoney, interested, "is that so?

*Dodder, Baldmoney and Sneezewart exploring Crow Wood*

What a splendid place you have chosen for your family!"

"There has not been so much as a smell of him for many a long year. Giant Grum sees to that."

This was the first time the gnomes had heard a good word said for the ogre; he couldn't be such a bad ogre after all. Baldmoney said so.

The old rabbit seemed very astonished at this last remark.

"*Not so bad! Not so bad*, did I hear you say? Why, you must be mad! He will kill anything, except that spoilt and vain creature he pets and guards so jealously; that stupid, chicken-headed bird with tail feathers as long as himself, that Chinaman with a white neck-ring and spurred legs."

Neither gnome could make head nor tail of what Bub'm was saying, but they did not wish to appear ignorant.

"Do you think he would kill *us*?" asked Sneezewort in a very small voice.

"Kill you? Kill you? Why, of course he'd kill you!"

"He'd have to catch us first," said Baldmoney with some spirit.

Bub'm shook her head slowly. "Oh dear! You poor gnomes, you have such a lot to learn, you have indeed. I can see you have never been to Crow Wood before and don't belong to these parts. Giant Grum doesn't have to *catch* you; he can kill you if he's standing as far away as that pine-tree over there."

She indicated a tree which was far up the bank, almost on the crown of it.

"She's only trying to scare us," whispered Baldmoney in Sneezewort's ear. "Don't take any notice. Ask her if she's seen any sign of Cloudberry."

"I suppose you don't happen to have heard of one of our people coming up the stream, a long time back, or you haven't seen a gnome in Crow Wood before?"

The old rabbit sat for a while in silence and the gnomes began to think she had not heard their question.

"No, I haven't seen a gnome in Crow Wood all the time I've been here, but I've heard stories now and again."

"Stories?" they said together. "Stories? Do tell us please."

"Well," began Bub'm, "last year I heard . . ." Suddenly she stamped her leg twice, thump, thump!

The gnomes knew what *that* meant, so did the babies. In the twinkling of an eye Bub'ms and gnomes dived down the hole without waiting to see what was the matter.

They ran helter-skelter down the burrow, the old mother Bub'm leading and the two gnomes bringing up the rear. They pushed and jostled, one of the babies fell over, another tripped Sneezewort so that he fell headlong on the loose sand of the burrow floor and had all the breath knocked out of his body. You never saw such a panic in your life.

The hole led downwards for a space, then turned right

again, and finally sloped upwards until they found themselves in quite a roomy underground chamber.

Though the gnomes did not like to say so, it was rather
stuffy, and they thought it would be better for a window,
and it isn't much fun sitting in the dark.

When all were in the chamber, no one said a word, the
only sound was the rather heavy breathing of the gnomes.

"What is the . . ." began Baldmoney. "Shhhhhhhhh!"
hissed the rabbit. "Not a word—listen!"

Both gnomes listened with all their ears, and the baby
Bub'ms did too; the gnomes thought they seemed very
frightened.

Then they became aware that something was shaking
the earth, a mighty hammer beating, some distant battering
ram . . . thump, thump, thump, on the earth outside! Nearer
it drew until they heard it pass overhead and die away in the
distance. Then, far away, a sullen explosion was heard, far
down the wood.

"Giant Grum, I'll be bound," said both gnomes
together. "Wasn't he awful?"

"You're right, gnomes," said the old doe, "it was the
Ogre himself; he hasn't been this way for some weeks now.
I wonder which of the Wood People has been killed now.
Perhaps it was Squirrel or Jay. Jay's a cunning one though,"
she chuckled. "He leads him a fine dance and no mistake.
He sucks the eggs of that impudent Chinaman and plays

high jinks with the rearing-pens. You must go warily if you meet one of those Chinamen; if you aren't careful he'll go and sneak to Giant Grum that he's seen you in the wood and then the Giant will come after you with his club that roars. Uh! How I hate those vain birds!"

"Well, well," said Baldmoney, after a bit, "you do seem to live in a funny way in this wood! Why, down our stream, where we come from, all the animals live together on very good terms; you hardly ever hear an ill word said."

Bub'm sniffed. "Uh huh! I've never been outside the boundary; few of our people have. It doesn't interest me very much how other folk live; by all accounts this stream of yours must be a funny sort of place, and no trees, you say? Well, I shouldn't like that."

"What's higher up?" asked Baldmoney. "Outside the wood, I mean."

"Don't know, don't want to know," said the rabbit in rather an offhand manner, "this burrow is good enough for me and my children. All I ask is to be left in peace and no White Stoats."

"White Stoats?" queried the gnomes. "White Stoats? What do you mean? I thought you said you never saw Stoat in this wood!"

"Not *Stoat*, but another just as bad. He's in the pay of Giant Grum, and in return for board and lodging he comes and kills our people. But it's all right, it's all over now until next autumn. Then the fun begins." (Bub'm meant ferrets.)

"Well, well," said the gnomes again, "this *is* a queer sort of wood." And then they remembered the true object of their journey. In the excitement of the Giant's footsteps they had quite forgotten.

"You were telling us, Bub'm, about a story you heard about another gnome who came up the stream," Baldmoney reminded her.

"Oh! Yes, to be sure I was, when that dreadful THING came along. Well, mind you, it was a long time ago, but I remember my parents telling me about a gnome who came up the Folly and lived for a time in the wood. He made a lot of friends among the animals, I believe, and left a very good name behind him. I don't know what happened to him; whether he was killed by Giant Grum or not I can't tell you, but there are all sorts of legends about him. He told everyone he was looking for the Folly Source, why, I can't imagine! Now gnomes, if you don't very much mind, I want a sleep."

"And we want some breakfast," said Baldmoney. "Come on, Sneezewort, I'm terribly hungry, and before we do anything else we must get some food."

"I'm only sorry I've nothing to offer you," said Bub'm apologetically. "I never keep food in the house, it smells so. Anyway, what's the point, when it's growing on your doorstep? You will find plenty of nice young grass, higher up the bank, and I can recommend the ash bark this year—it's delicious!"

"Bark! Grass!" snorted Baldmoney, as the two gnomes made their way down the passage to the open air. "Whatever does she take us for, Bub'ms or cows? Bark! Grass! The very idea," and he sniffed indignantly.

"I don't like that old Bub'm much," confided Sneezewort. "She's always sniffing and superior. She seems to think a lot of this beastly old wood, but if you ask me, all the animals seem at loggerheads. Give me the Oak Pool any day."

"Wasn't that Giant perfectly awful—the sound, I mean?" said Sneezewort. "Did you ever hear anything so horrid as those bump, bumping footsteps? Why, he must be ENORMOUS! And that awful thunder club, did you ever hear such a noise in all your life? It was as bad as a thunderstorm."

They came out of the hole and stood for a minute or two listening. Baldmoney nudged Sneezewort and pointed to the loose sand round the burrow mouth. He said nothing, he just pointed.

Sneezewort saw the prints of an enormous hobnailed boot imprinted in the red earth and farther on they stumbled over a cylinder of purple cardboard, a cartridge case. It was like nothing they had ever seen before and smelt of gunpowder. The copper cap on the end might be useful, for gnomes are passionately fond of bright metal. They cut the cardboard off and Sneezewort put the metal cap in his pocket.

They were just on the point of going down the bank again to the stream when a small stick struck Baldmoney on the top of the head, making him jump yards.

"Good gracious, by the great god Pan, what was that?"

They looked up and saw a grey squirrel scolding them from a fork in a pine tree. He was saying quite a lot of rude things, fluffing his tail, and throwing sticks at them.

"What a rude squirrel," exclaimed Sneezewort. "Really, the animals here *are* impolite."

"Hullo! Gnomes, looking for gold? You're the first gnomes I've seen; what funny little things you are, to be sure!"

Baldmoney waggled his beard disapprovingly. "You rude thing, throwing things like that. You've forgotten your manners. That's the worst of these grey foreign squirrels," he said in an aside to Sneezewort. "You wouldn't find a red squirrel doing that sort of thing."

"Hi! Squirrel," Baldmoney called, "stop throwing things at us and come and make friends. We want to meet you."

The squirrel looked rather shamefaced and came down the tree head first. He didn't seem to bother which way up he was. He bounced onto the pine needles and looked at them rather impudently.

"Why, bless me, what funny little creatures!" He shook with laughter and seemed almost doubled up. Ignoring his rudeness, the gnomes still tried to be polite, though both their faces were a trifle redder than usual; nobody likes to be laughed at. And after all, you must remember that the gnomes were so much older than Squirrel and so much more English; indeed they were the most English things in England. And Grey Squirrel was only a foreigner and had not been introduced into this country very long. He came from America, which accounted for the boisterous, hail-fellow-well-met manner; yet, despite the stick-throwing incident, he was an excellent fellow at heart.

The gnomes told him everything, and when he had heard their story to the finish, right up to their meeting with Bub'm and the terrible footsteps of the giant, he made a very sensible suggestion.

"Well, gnomes, after all that, it seems to me you must want one thing more than any other at this moment, and that's some breakfast, or is it supper? The best thing you can do is to come up into my drey in the top of the pine there and have a meal. You will be out of the way of giants and can get a fine view from the top—in fact, it's the best view in the wood," he added proudly.

The gnomes thanked him profusely, but did not quite see *how* they were going to get right to the top of the tree; it would take such a long time to climb. But Grey Squirrel soon overcame a little thing like that. "Climb on my back and put your arms round my neck and we'll be up in a jiffy!"

Baldmoney went first and then Squirrel came down for Sneezewort, and the next minute all three were safe and snug in the stick nest in the tree top. It was quite roomy inside, lined with soft leaves, and not a bit drafty. The squirrel told them to make themselves at home and then searched about for some food.

"I hope you like nuts, gnomes," he said, "because I've got some extra good ones put away at the foot of the tree; name your choice—pig, hazel, walnut, or beech, you can have which you like; or shall I bring you some mixed allsorts?"

Gnomes are passionately fond of nuts, for they form the staple food of the little people in the autumn.

"We don't mind," said Sneezewort politely. "It all sounds very nice."

"Very well, good-bye, gnomes, I won't be long," and he disappeared down the tree.

"What a nice person," said Baldmoney after he had gone, "he improves a lot on acquaintance, much better than old Bub'm."

While Squirrel was away they had time to admire the scenery. There was no doubt about it, Squirrel had chosen a very nice view. In one direction the gnomes could look out along the tops of the pines and oaks which stretched almost as far as they could see. What was rather curious, however, was that some of the trees were above them and some below, for the pine was on the steep side of the hill. In a gap in the needles they could see the gleam of the Folly, though they could not hear it, and away on the other side of the valley were green fields and more trees. A tiny thread of blue smoke was rising up on the evening air from the center of some dark pines.

Sneezewort pointed it out to Baldmoney. "There must be a house there," he said in a puzzled tone. "What a funny place to have a house, right in the middle of a wood. We must ask Squirrel about it. . . . O dear! I wish he would be quick, I'm so hungry!"

"And so am I," said Baldmoney, rubbing his little tummy ruefully. "Perhaps he won't be long now."

But they waited and waited, and soon they saw the red sun sinking lower over the far hills until it dipped down behind them, seeming to get larger, as it caught the trees and to move more swiftly. Away over the wood, the west was duck-egg green, flecked with gold cloudlets. Darker and darker it grew, and still no Squirrel appeared.

Baldmoney looked out of the drey, right down, down, to the wood floor. It seemed such a long way he felt quite dizzy. At last they felt the tree shake a little and the next moment Squirrel appeared, very shamefaced and apologetic.

"Really, I'm most awfully sorry, but my store of nuts seems to have gone; I can't find it anywhere."

"Oh! You squirrels," sighed Baldmoney, "you are all alike: you gather your nuts and hide them and forget where you've put them. The red squirrels are just the same."

"Perhaps one of you would like to come and help me look, though it's getting rather dark," said the squirrel after a rather awkward pause. So Baldmoney went down the tree with him and in about five minutes both were back with all the nuts they could carry. Baldmoney had soon smelt them out, though they were under another tree a long way from where Squirrel thought he had hidden them.

So they had a fine meal, and when all was finished they tucked themselves up in the drey and talked long into the night. The stars came out one by one, and then the moon (which was now getting quite big) cast a curious silvery greenish light over the tops of the trees.

Squirrel talked incessantly about all kinds of things, chiefly of the American woods where his forebears came from, and about strange things called chipmunks, bobolinks, summer yellowlegs, and all kinds of little people of which the gnomes had never heard. He spoke almost as if he had been there himself (though, of course, he hadn't; it was only what had been passed on from squirrel to squirrel). He told them of Crow Wood, and the Giant, and the cruel things he did, and how the Wood People hated him. But he knew nothing of Cloudberry, and could not help the gnomes at all. Still, it was all very pleasant to have this new companionship, and already the gnomes felt very much better and more refreshed. They decided to sleep the night in the drey and explore the wood next morning.

The smoke they had seen ascending through the trees apparently came from the Giant's Castle. It was not a very big castle, not nearly so big (so Squirrel said) as another castle on the other side of the wood. Squirrel had never been there and didn't even know if a Giant lived there too, but he didn't think so. As far as he knew, there was only one giant, Giant Grum, and he seemed quite enough to go on with.

At last the gnomes could keep awake no longer, the sough of the wind in the pines was so soothing. It was such a lovely sound, almost like the long rollers which break gently on a beach in hot summer weather, delicious and sleep-making. And the scents of the pines contributed to making them drowsy.

No wonder they were soon fast asleep, rocked in their lofty cradle in the pine-tree top. It did not matter what fearful things prowled below in the moonlight, or what ghastly giants walked abroad with clubs that roared like thunder, and killed you half a mile off. Nothing could touch them in their cozy little house, and soon Crow Wood, Giant, Stoat, Bub'ms, Squirrel, Cloudberry, and the Oak Pool were all forgotten.

# CHAPTER 8

# Giant Grum

THE GNOMES WERE EARLY astir the following day. The sun was streaming into the drey, and dew sparkled on every twig and leaf. Squirrel was already up and out and nowhere to be seen. So the gnomes had to climb out of the drey by themselves and make the perilous descent to the ground, a task which took them some while. By the time they reached the foot of the tree and dropped lightly into the bracken they were black and dusty. Pines are easy enough to climb, but are shockingly dirty trees, as many of you may have found out for yourselves.

As there was so much cover in the wood they decided to spend a few days exploring it, and making friends with other animals.

"You know," said Baldmoney, as they walked among the bracken fronds. "I like Crow Wood. It isn't nearly such a terrible place as a lot of people make out. If we can keep clear of Giant Grum we shall be all right."

"I quite like it too," said Sneezewort, in a cheerful voice, "especially on a lovely summer morning like this, but I wish the birds would sing."

They stood still and listened, but all they could hear was the voice of the Folly talking away in its steep bed below them.

"I wonder what poor old Dodder is doing now," mused Baldmoney as they continued on their way. "Fishing, I expect, or pottering about in his coracle. Perhaps he's asleep. I wish he were with us!"

"So do I," agreed Sneezewort heartily, "it would just make everything perfect. Still, we shall have some rare tales to tell him when we get home."

Their way now led them down a narrow grassy path hedged on either side with tall bracken. It had not yet reached its full stature for the tips were still curved over into little shepherds' crooks. It made a fairy avenue of green on either side of the track, for the path they were following was only an animals' "runway." It wandered here and there, under brambles, round the stumps of trees, under fallen branches, in and out beneath dense blackthorn, and under the winding tendrils of wild honeysuckle. You or I could never have followed it. Deep green moss was everywhere, and on some of the big smooth boles of the beech trees, mossy coverlets stretched some way up the trunks.

The gnomes swung along, taking deep breaths as they

went, and both felt very happy and contented. Suddenly, on rounding a bend in the path, they came face to face with a most gorgeous bird, one of the most splendid creatures they had ever seen. He was almost as beautiful as the King of Fishers. His head was bottle green with a hundred glancing lights upon it, as though it were made of mail, and his breast was the color of beaten copper. Instead of an ordinary tail he had a long pointed one, as long as his body, barred with cross marks of blue black. On either cheek were scarlet wattles and on his head two eared horns of green and blue feathers. And to complete the vision he had, on either leg, a sharp pointed spur.

The gnomes stopped in amazement. They never imagined such a gorgeous creature existed. He surveyed them with an arrogant air as though they were beetles.

They wished him "good morning" very politely, but were only answered by a cold and disdainful stare. The pheasant (for it was he) looked them over from head to toe. It is never pleasant to be looked up and down in this way, but the gnomes were not abashed, though secretly each felt a tiny anger mounting within him.

At last the pheasant spoke. "What, may I ask, are you two persons doing in my wood? Who gave you permission to come here? Don't you know it's private property?"

"Private property?" queried the gnomes. "Private property? There's no such thing as private property in Nature!

The woods and fields belong to the earth, and so do we. We don't know what you are talking about!"

The pheasant strutted forward in an aggressive manner, waggling his wattles like an enraged turkey. "Now, I don't want any impudence. This is private property and you're trespassing, be off, both of you, and don't let me catch you here again." And fluffing out his gorgeous feathers he crowed a long crow, Cock! cock! cock! cock! cock! so that the woodlands rang and the gnomes were deafened.

"What a rude creature," said Baldmoney, in a quiet tone to Sneezewort.

"How vain," said Sneezewort. "And he called us *persons*."

"I'm waiting," said the pheasant in a steely voice, looking over their heads.

"Well, you vain insolent creature, you can wait! We're not going out of this wood for you or anybody else!" replied Baldmoney hotly.

"Then you will be prosecuted," snapped the pheasant. "It says so on the notice boards all round the wood, and it'll serve you right. Now, are you going, or are you not?"

"Emphatically NOT," said the gnomes with some heat, "and we advise you to let us alone and not to interfere with us. We shall go where we please, and do what we please, for we're older than you, and you're nothing but a foreigner, in short, an utter outsider!"

The pheasant, now he had had his say, and finding the

gnomes were not in the least impressed by his appearance, or in awe of his grand manner, looked rather foolish and confused. "Well, you have been warned," he said, with his head in the air, as he stalked away with all the dignity he could muster. "Giant Grum shall hear of this; he'll come and shoot you, and hang you up on the gibbet, with the hawks and owls and weasels, where you belong. We won't have vermin in this wood, and that's what you are, VERMIN!"

Gnomes are good-natured little people as a rule and rarely lose their tempers, but the last remark of the pheasant's roused Baldmoney to white fury, which, however, he sensibly controlled.

"You arrogant creature," he called after the retreating figure, "we shall meet again and you will remember that insult. Make the most of the sunlight and the green bracken. We shall meet again!"

And so saying the gnomes turned their backs on the pheasant and made their way down between the trees towards the Folly. Its friendly chatter was comforting, quite like old times, though its character seemed very altered. It was noticeably smaller and shallower; here and there at bends and corners deep black pools opened out, unstarred by water-daisy or lily.

"Baldmoney! Baldmoney! Look what I've found, quick!" Sneezewort bent down and picked up something which was lying among a drift of old leaves close to the water's edge. It was a rusty pocket-knife with two blades.

"Don't you recognize it?" said Sneezewort excitedly. "It's Cloudberry's. Don't you remember the knife he found in the Willow Meadow, and how proud he was of it?"

Baldmoney took the knife and examined it closely. The blades were so rusted they would not open, but without a doubt it was Cloudberry's knife. How long it had been lying there it was hard to say, but from its condition, many months.

What a stroke of luck! It seemed at last they were really getting "hot." One thing at any rate was certain, Cloudberry must have passed this way. Perhaps the knife had dropped out of his pocket when he jumped over a log near by. Apart from its associations, this find was a very real one to the gnomes; their flint knives were poor things compared to this real knife of steel.

\* \* \*

"Cloudberry must have been in an awful hurry to drop his knife," observed Baldmoney that evening. They were back again in the squirrel's tree-top house (the latter had obligingly extended his invitation to them to stay for as long as they were in the wood) and again he had helped them up the tree: in truth he was very glad of the gnomes' company, for he was the last squirrel left in Crow Wood, all his relations having been killed by Giant Grum long ago.

"Yes, that's true, Baldmoney; perhaps something was

chasing him. Giant Grum, perhaps. And what a bother he would be in without it, he thought more of that knife than anything he had." Sneezewort was scraping away the rust from the blades and very soon had them clicking sweetly and as bright as new. "We must explore the stream tomorrow; this fine weather isn't going to last, if you ask me."

Baldmoney peeped out of the entrance of the drey. "It's very quiet tonight, not a breath of wind."

"Yes," said Squirrel from the corner, where he was hunting for imaginary fleas, "this fine weather is breaking up; I smell rain."

Out over the valley the sky was inky black, piled with large clouds of a reddish color like brick dust. It was hot in the drey, the gnomes were glad to sit at the entrance, watching the wood below and the dark pine-tree tassels outlined against the sunset. Far away something muttered and growled like a great beast. A whitish glare ran along the horizon and was gone. Then it flickered again. Not a breath stirred the trees, the sound of the Folly was sharp and distinct. Owls hooted. Then the rumble came again, louder this time.

"Cock! cock! cock! cock! cock!" The ringing crow of a pheasant broke the stillness. Squirrel spoke from the darkness.

"There goes the Chinaman, scared to death of thunder; it reminds him too much of October when the Big Bangs begin!"

"Yes," chuckled Baldmoney, "we met him down the wood this morning and he tried to turn us off, *us*, if you please, who were here in England before he was thought of!"

"That's the Chinaman all over," said Squirrel, "he thinks he owns the wood. Anyway, he isn't wild, he's as tame as a chicken. You should see the pheasants up in the rearing-pens, pampered spoilt things!"

A vivid flash lit up the interior of the drey in a dramatic fashion. In that instant glare the gnomes could see each other's eyeballs glint, and the grey form of Squirrel hunched in the corner. Nobody spoke; like humans, they were still in awe at the power and majesty of the heavens in tumult. The following crash seemed to shake the wood, and even the gnomes crouched low in the darkness. Another flash followed, lighting up momentarily the wooded slope and the far hills. And then the silence was broken by the pattering of rain. Sudden puffs of wind arose and sang in the pine branches, hissing away to silence. The rattle of rain gathered power. Soon it was drumming down, sending a mist of drops rebounding from the twigs. The drey rocked in the tree top, the fir tassels whipped and roared in a sudden great wind. How relieved were the gnomes to be in the cozy shelter of Squirrel's drey!

"I'm glad we're not down in the wood," said Sneezewort, cuddling up to Baldmoney. "I shouldn't like to be up the Folly now. I wonder what poor old Dodder is doing."

"I can give a pretty good guess," chuckled Baldmoney—"snug in the old root with the door shut to, I'll be bound."

"And a fire going," added Sneezewort.

"*And* old Ben and his family tucked up out of the storm," said Baldmoney, feeling suddenly homesick.

"And Cloudberry, what's he doing now, I wonder?" Baldmoney looked out through the dim entrance.

Somewhere yonder, away up the Folly, through the dark wood perhaps, in the unknown and uncharted country, was their long-lost brother. Something made them shudder. It was dreadful to think of anyone being out on such a night. A mystery is always fascinating. Would they ever find him?

Flash followed flash, the heavenly artillery thundered and crashed, the woodland creatures cowered in their holes under the fury of rain, wind, and thunder.

Squirrel told them tales of past tempests, and old legends connected with his native land across the sea, until the storm went growling away over the hills and all was silent save for the drip, drip of the rain in the dark wood. And oh! The sweet scents which arose in the warm night, of thirsty earth no longer thirsty, and the moist steaming leaves!

\* \* \*

Crow Wood was still steaming next morning, when, after a breakfast from good Squirrel's store of "mixed allsorts," the gnomes set off again to explore the wood. By mutual consent they had decided to make Tree Top House their base of operations until they were quite satisfied Cloudberry was not anywhere in the locality.

After the storm the wood had rather a beaten look, for the rain had been very heavy. It had washed off all the bud casings from the trees and bushes and scattered them on the ground. When they reached the bank of the Folly they found it discolored with flood, and sticks and leaves were floating down.

Baldmoney put his lines together and caught some fat minnows; the fish would make a welcome change from a vegetarian diet. After he had caught six fat fish he put them in his bundle and they went on up the stream.

Beeches and oaks were fewer and soon there was nothing but endless conifers: larch, beautifully arrayed, looking like fairy torches in their new green (which is one of the loveliest greens in Nature), and tall firs which shut out most of the light.

Close to a bunch of hazel which grew half in the stream, forming a dense thicket, a tearing screech brought the gnomes to a halt. The next moment a cheeky-looking bird with a high crest and blue wings came bouncing down onto a hazel twig. It was Blue Jay, a handsome rascal with a merry china-blue eye, full of fun and mischief.

"Hullo! Jay!"

"Hullo! Gnomes!"

"You're just the one we wanted to see," said Sneezewort.

133

"We think you can help us."

"Well, I'm always only too pleased to do that. Crow Wood seems popular with the Little People these days. But you're playing with fire, you know; this isn't exactly a safe place for gnomes."

"We're not living here," explained Baldmoney, "we're just passing through and having a look round. You see, we're looking for Cloudberry."

"Cloudberry?" queried the Jay, cocking his head and wiping his bill.

"Yes, our brother, you know. He's up here somewhere we feel sure, and we found his knife yesterday farther down the stream. I suppose you haven't seen another gnome up here at any time?"

"Yes, I have," said Jay in a matter-of-fact tone. "I saw one yesterday."

"What!" screamed the gnomes together. "You saw *another* gnome YESTERDAY?"

"Yes, the funniest sight I've seen for a long time. He was sitting on Otter's back and they were coming upstream!"

The gnomes could not contain themselves for joy.

"Tell us, tell us, which way did they go? When did you last see them?"

"Oh, they were just going upstream, yesterday afternoon."

The Jay seemed to treat the whole thing in a very casual manner.

"Come on," exclaimed Sneezewort, "we must follow them; they may be miles away by now."

Without more ado, and hardly a word of thanks to Jay, they went on up the stream as fast as they could, stumbling over sticks, forcing their way through brambles and clambering over fern-clad banks. The wood grew darker and thicker until they seemed to be in a green twilight, and then, on rounding a bend in the stream, Sneezewort suddenly laid his hand on Baldmoney's arm, pulling him down into the bracken.

"Look! Smoke!"

Upstream behind a hazel thicket there was a faint mist of blue.

"Someone's lit a fire," whispered Sneezewort. Baldmoney sniffed. "Someone's cooking fish!"

"It's Cloudberry, I do believe," said Baldmoney in an excited voice. "Fancy daring to light a fire in Crow Wood!" They crept forward through the bracken and hazel bushes and the next moment they saw a sight which surprised them.

Behind a large stone close to the water, arched over with hazel bushes and branching bracken fronds, was a gnome. He had his back to them and was busy frying something over a little fire. On a shingle spit beyond was Otter eating a perch.

"Cloudberry! Cooeee!" shouted the gnomes, but the roar of the water drowned their voices. At any rate neither Otter nor gnome looked round.

They ran along the shingle and then the gnome suddenly turned his head. It was Dodder!

"Dodder!"

"Baldmoney! . . . Sneezewort!"

"However did you get up here?"

Dodder indicated Otter, who, having finished his perch, was cleaning his whiskers.

"I couldn't stick being alone," growled Dodder; "I thought I might as well join you two. It wasn't much fun down by the Oak Pool, and I thought the change would do me good."

The gnomes were so pleased they hugged each other.

"We never thought you'd come after us," said Baldmoney at last, rather out of breath. "We've often talked about you, wondering what you were doing with yourself. But how, by the great god Pan, did you get up here?"

"Well, after you'd gone, I came after you, but couldn't make much progress with my lame leg. Heron gave me a lift up to the mill, and then I saw your boat. I thought you'd both been drowned, but when I couldn't see any sign of you I guessed you'd gone on up. I was just thinking of turning back when who should come along but Otter, and the rest was easy. He said, 'Leave everything to me; we'll find the others if we have to swim up to the source,' and he meant it too. That's what I *call* a friend. What happened to you?"

The gnomes told Dodder of their own adventures, starting from the breaking of the *Dragonfly's* paddle and the incident with Stoat, finishing up with the finding of Cloudberry's knife and their good friend Squirrel.

"It's a pity about the boat, though," said Sneezewort sadly. "She went down with all our gear; we only got away with what we stood up in."

"The boat's all right," said Dodder with smug pride; "when Otter came along we salvaged her and found she was not holed. And what's more, most of the provisions were still on board."

"What!" exclaimed the gnomes together. "You managed to save her?"

"Oh yes—at least Otter did, *and* I came up in her, towed by our good friend. We came up in fine style, and we left her under the fern just inside the boundary. Naturally we couldn't get up the waterfalls."

Here was splendid news. The gnomes danced for joy, and made a tremendous fuss of Otter, whilst Dodder turned the fish over in the pan (a cocoa-tin lid which he had found).

"My! That fish smells good—quite like old times," said Sneezewort gleefully, rubbing his hands.

The spitting fish *did* smell good, and Baldmoney soon dived into his bundle and fetched out the others he had caught that morning.

The blue smoke from the fire drifted away through the bushes as they all sat round watching the little fishes jumping in the pan like crickets.

"You know," said Baldmoney with his mouth full, "it's mighty risky lighting a fire in Crow Wood. We've heard the giant once, it was *awful*—he must be perfectly enormous."

"Pooh," said Dodder, "we can't go in fear and trembling of Giant Grum. I've heard him too. Soon after I came into the wood I was talking with some Bub'ms near the Folly and suddenly they all rushed away. I peeped round a tree but could see nothing because it was so dark under the branches, but I could hear something big moving higher up the wood. All the animals seemed panic-stricken and there wasn't a sign of anyone; I suppose they had all gone to ground. I must admit I did feel a little scared. After a bit the sounds died away and they all came out of their holes and we went on talking as though nothing had happened. But Giant Grum isn't going to worry me. I'm going to enjoy myself. I haven't had a decent holiday for years. Even if we don't find Cloudberry this trip is going to do us good. What do you think, Otter?"

There was no reply. Otter had gone as silently as a shadow.

"Don't worry," said Dodder, "he's about somewhere; he's always doing that, slipping off without saying a word. He'll turn up again. I expect he's gone upstream fishing. He says the fish are better here than lower down. Smaller of course, but a better flavor."

There was a movement in the bracken on top of the bank and a scarlet-wattled face peered down at them. Cock! cock! cock! cock! cock! The sudden explosive sound made the gnomes jump in all directions. Dodder and Baldmoney whisked into the bracken and Sneezewort dived under the hazels.

"Picnicking isn't allowed in Crow Wood," shrieked the pheasant, beside himself with rage. "I tell you I won't have this trespassing. Cock! cock! cock! cock! cock!"

"Dash the bird, he'll let everyone know we're here." growled Baldmoney. "Shut up, you noisy brute!"

"Shut up, did you say, shut up? I'll soon shut you up! If my master hears me calling he'll very soon shut *you* up. Cock! cock! cock!" he shrieked again at the top of his voice.

"Sounds like an old motor horn," hissed Sneezewort. "Never heard such a noise!"

"Put that fire out," said the wise Dodder. "If the giant does come he'll smell the smoke even if he doesn't see it."

Then the sneaking pheasant rose out of the bracken like a rocket and went off through the trees, still "cocking."

"What a noisy, unpleasant person!" said Dodder. He hobbled across to the fire and scattered the embers with his foot and stamped out the sparks. Then the quiet of the wood was shattered.

BANG! And then, after an instant silence in which even Dodder's presence of mind seemed to forsake him and he stood as if turned to stone, BANG! again, close at hand. It was an awful moment. Then the gnomes dived for cover, and not a thing was to be seen but one little red spark which burned and glowed among the stones. They were right among the bracken on the water's edge.

"I never knew Giant Grum was so c-c-close," stuttered Sneezewort in Dodder's ear.

"Shhhhh!" hissed Dodder. "Listen!"

Up the wood a stick crackled. "Oh, dear, he's coming, we shall be seen," whimpered Sneezewort.

"You'll be heard if you make all that noise," growled Dodder. "Shut up, can't you?"

They lay trembling in the thick cover. The sounds were drawing nearer. There was a snuffling noise and they heard a big gruff voice say "Seek him, Jet, seek him!" Splashings and cracklings. "Oh, dear, he's got a dog," moaned Sneezewort. "He's got a dog."

"Shut up, and lie still!"

A line of bubbles passed down the stream. They saw for an instant the face of Otter, a very different animal from the sleek, contented, friendly beast which a moment before had been eating a fish beside them on the shingle. He was swimming with difficulty and a dark cloud showed in the water of his wake.

"Oh, dear! Otter's been shot," moaned Sneezewort—
"poor Otter!" And he began to cry.

"You'll be shot too, in a minute, if you don't keep quiet,"
growled Dodder. "Do you want us all to be killed?" But
Sneezewort saw tears in Dodder's eyes too. They lay with
beating hearts as the sounds of cracking sticks drew nearer.

Suddenly a big black retriever came pushing through
the bracken close to them. Its slavering muzzle and staring
eyes were framed in the green bracken fronds within a foot
of them. The dog was for an instant taken aback when he
saw them. Its hackles rose and its lips wrinkled back. Then
he charged like a buffalo.

Three little plops, "Plop, Plop, Plop!" in the brown
Folly, and the gnomes were gone.

"Seek him, Jet! Good dog, seek him!" A huge hairy creature in velveteens with a gun under his arm pushed through
the hazels, looking about him with wide-open bloodshot
eyes and half-parted mouth. "Seek him, good dog!"

But all he saw was a slight disturbance in the water and
three dim forms, like frogs, swimming under the far bank.

"Water-rats," he snorted. "Where the devil's that otter?
Seek him, Jet, good dog!"

Giant Grum stopped, puzzled. Down on the shingle,
close to the root of the hazels, were the marks of a tiny fire;
one little ember still glowed. Lying about were the heads of
at least a dozen minnows and a few bones. He bent down

*Dodder hears the approach of Giant Grum and
the Wood People run for cover*

and examined the shingle and the soft sand. "What the . . . ?"
he muttered. "What the . . . ?" He was absolutely non-
plussed. For fifty years he had been keeper in Crow Wood
and knew the spoor of every wild animal and bird. Never
before had he found anything like this. The otter was forgotten in this amazing find. A fire, tiny footmarks, like the
prints of human feet. "Jet! Jet! Come here, *good* dog!"

The retriever came pushing back along the stream.
"Here, Jet, here!" The black muzzle went "wuffle, wuffle"
over the sand and the man saw the short hairs bristle along
its spine. Then the dog was called off and Giant Grum went
up the bank. He lay down in the bracken and told the dog
to be silent. For a full hour he lay watching the stream. But
all he saw was the crinkling water and the nodding of the
green hazel leaves.

# CHAPTER 9

# The Gibbet

IT WAS A JOLLY REUNION that night in Squirrel's drey, though somewhat marred by the death of poor Otter. Their good-natured host did not seem to mind how many people shared Tree Top House, and he had helped them up one by one, taking particular care of Dodder and his game leg. They took off their wet things and hung them up on the pine twigs to dry, cuddling down in the dry leaves and grass lining of the drey close to Squirrel.

They were soon as warm as toast. Truth to say, Squirrel was quite enjoying this unaccustomed company, for he had got tired of living alone. There was so much to talk about and discuss and Squirrel made many helpful suggestions.

Dodder agreed with the proposition to make Tree Top House their headquarters for the next day or two, while they thoroughly explored Crow Wood. If Cloudberry was not discovered, then they would go on up the Folly, to the source. If he were not to be found there, then they must give up the search and return to the Oak Pool. They talked long into the night, hearing many tales from Squirrel of the wicked doings of Giant Grum and the Wood People generally.

"You must meet the Wood-pig" (hedgehog), said Squirrel. "He's always poking around in Crow Wood at all hours of the night; you never know, he may have come across Cloudberry, or at any rate had some news of him. And the White Owls, they should be able to help; we ought to go and see them. They live in the beech at the other end of the wood; they've been there for as long as I can remember, in spite of Giant Grum. We'll go and see them sometime."

*   *   *

The first thing the gnomes did the next morning was to go down the Folly to the boundary of the wood and portage some of their belongings from the boat. Sneezewort and Baldmoney were overjoyed to see the *Dragonfly* again, for they had spent so much labor in building her. They found the boat drawn up in the bracken, so cleverly hidden that the sharpest eyes would never have seen it. They carried away all the food they could, including some watercresses which Dodder had collected on the way up the Folly. Squirrel obligingly made many journeys up and down the pine tree, dumping all the food inside the drey; it was wonderful how roomy Tree Top House proved to be. Their moleskin sleeping-bags and change of clothes were welcome too, for the last few days the gnomes had been "living rough."

Squirrel thought it advisable to see the wood-pigs and the white owls later on, as these creatures sleep during the day and it would have been a breach of good manners to disturb them; anyway they would have been too sleepy to talk or give any coherent account of anything.

When all this was done, Squirrel went off to play in the wood and the gnomes found themselves at a loose end for the rest of the day, so they went off into the bracken to explore.

Early in the afternoon, as they were poking about the roots of a fallen pine digging for pig-nuts, Baldmoney made a discovery.

Down among a thicket of dead green nettle close to the root he suddenly saw a rounded brown object speckled all over with light spots. He was puzzled at first until he saw it was a hen pheasant. She was sitting on her nest and was fast asleep! He tiptoed back to the others and told them of his discovery.

"Mrs. Chinaman," exclaimed Sneezewort, "what a find!" All three crept through the nettles to have a look at the sleeping bird. Sneezewort put his finger to his nose, and his toothless mouth cracked into the semblance of a grin.

"Here's our chance to get even with that sneaking

pheasant," he whispered. "We'll steal her eggs, and won't we have a feed! You keep *cave* for Giant Grum and cock pheasant and leave the rest to me!"

He stole up close to the unsuspecting bird and, making no more noise than a mouse, he removed first one egg and then another without waking her. She only shuffled down lower on the nest and half-opened one eye. As he removed each large greenish egg he passed it back to Baldmoney and Dodder, who were waiting at his elbow. He worked with such skill that the hen pheasant never suspected anything. Soon they had seven eggs lying in the bracken and the gnomes carted them back to the foot of the pine.

"What a feed we shall have," chuckled Dodder, "and how mad the birds will be when they find their eggs have gone!"

When the hen awakened she found her mate standing by. "I've had such a funny dream," she said. "I dreamt my eggs had hatched, and I felt our babies creeping between my thighs!" The vain cock bird strutted round. He was inordinately proud of his wife and family.

"I'm afraid it will be a long time yet, my dear, before they hatch; you haven't laid the full clutch yet."

Suddenly the hen let out a shriek. "They've gone, they've gone!"

"What are gone?"

"My eggs, stupid, someone has stolen them!"

"Nonsense!"

"Look for yourself!"

She got up and surveyed the empty nest with horror. "Not an egg! Someone must have stolen them while I was asleep!" He came running to her and together they surveyed the empty nest.

"I know who it is!" shrieked the incensed cock. "It's those gnomes, I know it is. Giant Grum shall hear of this!"

Cock! cock! cock! cock! cock! and he went blustering away through the wood followed by his tearful wife.

\* \* \*

That evening, when the sun had gone down and the moon, nearly full, was climbing over the dark trees, the gnomes and Squirrel, after a royal feed of fresh pheasant's eggs, set out to find Wood-pig. They found him rooting down by the Folly.

"Allow me to introduce Dodder, Baldmoney, and Sneezewort," said the squirrel, "friends of mine who are staying with me."

The hedgehog blinked. He had the quaintest little face, rather like a tiny pig, with a long snout and wee eyes, which, however, were very sharp and did not miss much.

All three gnomes bowed politely and Sneezewort and Baldmoney took off their skin caps.

"We thought you might be able to help us," said Baldmoney. "We're looking for another gnome, a brother of ours, Cloudberry, who came up the Folly some time ago and never returned."

Wood-pig snuffled. "Oh yes, now you come to talk of it, I *do* seem to remember my mother telling me of a gnome she met by the Wood Pool."

"That must have been him," said the gnomes excitedly, "that must have been Cloudberry. No other gnomes live on the stream."

"Let me think," said the Wood-pig. He sat wrapped in thought for a long time. "Yes, I remember now. He told my mother he was looking for the Folly Source, and asked her whether she had ever been up as far. When she said she hadn't he went on up the Folly. That's all I know."

"Where's the Wood Pool?" asked Baldmoney, turning to Squirrel.

"Oh, that's right in the middle of the wood, not far from the Giant's house."

"Let's go there," said Dodder, "we might find some trace of him."

Squirrel was sleepy, he did not like being out at night, so excusing himself, he returned to Tree Top House and the gnomes went on alone to find the Wood Pool.

It was the most perfect night, so still and starlit, with the calm light of the moon making strange shadows from the trees.

Following the Wood-pig's instructions, they struck up

the bank, leaving the stream and plunging deeper and deeper into the heart of the wood. Dog-roses glimmered in the dusk and honeysuckle scented the air. On all sides the tall pines rose straight and still, and once or twice they saw the form of a roosting pheasant on the lower branches, with its long tail hanging down behind. Then the first thinned and ash poles began, tall slender poles green with moss. There was considerably more light here, for their branches were thinner and let through the rays of the moon. Sometimes they saw the black bundle of a pigeon's nest with a tail sticking over the edge, sometimes the form of a roosting pigeon beside it. And then they came to a well-trodden track, winding between bushes of box and holly. Baldmoney bent down and examined it carefully. There were marks of big hobnailed boots in the soft soil, many marks!

"Giant Grum walks here," whispered Baldmoney. "Perhaps this path leads to his house" (the gnomes always spoke in whispers—somehow, in the wood, it was the natural thing to do). Once or twice they came upon a faded cartridge case and they cut off the brass cap carefully.

At last, far away, they heard a faint, soft murmur. Running water!

They came suddenly on the pool. It was a lovely spot, hedged round with thick rhododendron bushes, and with the moon's reflection on the still surface. Water-voles were swimming about and, at the far end, two mallard. The murmur of water came from a hatch at one end of the pond where the overflow ran through an iron grill covered with moss. Dodder made a discovery.

"This must be the Folly," he whispered. He was right. The stream ran into the pool at the far end and, after by-passing the hatch, fell in a tinkling waterfall down the steep bank.

The ground was soft and miry near the edge of the pool, black with rotted leaves. Some large fish jumped out in the center, sending shaking rings outwards which broke up the moon's reflections.

It was a most attractive place to the gnomes. They made a circuit of the pond, disturbing the waterfowl. The ducks got up, quacking loudly, and flew away over the trees.

"Just the sort of place Cloudberry would like," whispered Dodder. "He always loved ponds and messing about with water." (As a matter of fact all gnomes love messing about with water, which, after all, is very understandable.) But they found no trace of Cloudberry and, after searching for a little longer, they decided to follow the path which led past the pool into the heart of the wood. The murmur of the waterfall died away behind them and everything became very still.

The ash poles gave way to oaks, fairly young trees, and sallow bushes grew everywhere. Then the trees opened out into a clearing and in the moonlight they saw a grisly sight.

A split ash pole had been nailed to two oaks and from it hung a long line of things which at first appeared to be rags. They stole forward to get a better view, their shadows black in the moonlight.

"Ugh! How *horrible*," gasped Dodder, covering his face with his hands, "how perfectly *horrible*!" And indeed it was. For what appeared to be rags were the bodies of birds and animals nailed by the neck to the pole. Some were long dead, nothing but skeletons, to which a few scraps of fur or feather still adhered; owls, hawks, stoats, and weasels, and even the harmless birds like blackbirds and thrushes. No wonder birds were scarce in Crow Wood! A long dark shadow hung at the far end, the latest addition to this grim gallery.

When they saw what it was the gnomes wept unrestrainedly. It was all that remained of poor Otter. Dodder was more upset than anyone, for had it not been for him, Otter would never have come to Crow Wood at all. Woodpigs were there too, their pathetic little spined jackets rustling in the passing breeze, and two fern-bears (badgers). On the right-hand end of the pole was a handsome magpie. It must have been freshly killed for it was in beautiful plumage; the colors shone, even in the moonlight.

Dodder began to search about in the long grass under the gibbet. The others wondered at this ghoulish occupation and watched him picking up a bone here and a feather there and examining the skull of a weasel. Then it dawned on them what he was doing. He was looking for the remains of Cloudberry! They helped him then, hardly daring to glance at the gruesome array above them. But they found nothing more than the skeletons of birds, crows, and squirrels.

"I've had enough of this place," said Baldmoney suddenly. "Let's go, I feel quite sick."

So after one last look (the gnomes are thorough little people) they left the clearing and retraced their steps to the Wood Pool. Another path led over the hatch which they had not noticed before and this they followed. The surrounding trees threw black bars across it, and now and again they came upon signs of Giant Grum—a cigarette end tossed away, another cartridge case, an empty match-box.

Something began to squeal in the thick bushes ahead of them. It was the throttling agonizing squeal as of an animal in distress. Keeping to the shadow of the bushes, the gnomes went to investigate. They found a Bub'm caught by its neck in a snare. It was struggling violently and strangling itself. But in a minute the gnomes had it free, loosening the cruel wire, which Dodder put in his pocket. Poor thing, it was terribly frightened, and lay for some time with staring eyes and heaving sides. When it could speak it gasped its thanks.

"Oh, that *dreadful* giant," exclaimed Sneezewort. Dodder was looking very grim. His face was rather less red than usual and he spoke through his teeth.

"We must pay Giant Grum back for this, for Otter . . . everything. I don't know how, but we will, before we go back to the Oak Pool. I owe it to Otter and his family, we owe it to the Wood People. The birds must come back and have no fear, the trees shall again hear their morning songs."

"Please go away from Crow Wood," sobbed the Bub'm, who had now recovered from his ordeal. "He'll only kill you too and hang you on the gibbet. What can we do? We are so small and weak—*please* go!"

Dodder was silent, and for some time afterwards the others could get no reply to any of their questions.

"What you said is all very well," remarked Baldmoney. "We came up here to find Cloudberry. I'm not sure that the Bub'm isn't right—there's not much we can do, you know. I say, let's find Cloudberry first, and then, if you like, we'll try and do something."

"Well said," agreed Sneezewort, "that's what I think. We are little and weak. Giant Grum is strong and big—the odds are all against us!"

But still Dodder did not reply. In silence they trudged back past the Wood Pool and saw the dawn greying in its wan face. They met Wood-pig going back to his daytime retreat under the bracken. They told him of their night's adventures.

"Ugh!" he snuffled. "Ugh, ugh! You must expect to see

things like that in Crow Wood. Anyway, I'm glad you didn't find Cloudberry under the gibbet; I thought you might, though I didn't like to say so. If you take an old wood-pig's advice, gnomes, leave this place and go up the Folly. I can't see you are going to do any good by stealing pheasant's eggs (though I can't blame you for that—I often do it myself) and letting rabbits out of snares, lighting fires, and upsetting things generally. The end will be that Giant Grum will get really nasty. It's no good running into a wasps' nest—you'll only get stung," and so saying, he trotted off into the bracken, looking like a big wood-louse with pink legs.

When the gnomes got back to the tree it was quite light and Squirrel had just awakened. He hoisted them up into the drey and tucked them up paternally. Then he went off into the wood to get his breakfast.

It was some time before the gnomes could get to sleep, so they lay talking.

"I wish we could *do* something," insisted Dodder. "If *only* we were as big as the giant. Supposing we were to have a meeting of all the Wood People and talk the whole thing out?"

"How can we do that?" said the practical Sneezewort. "How could we let everyone know?"

"Tonight is Midsummer's Eve," said Dodder after a while. "In the old days it was a great night for our people, almost as important as Hallowe'en; even the humans kept indoors in fear of us. If only we could have a meeting tonight! There must be some way. Can't you think of something, Baldmoney?"

But I regret to say that all the reply he had was a snore!

# CHAPTER 10

# The Gathering of the Wood People

T HAT EVENING, WHEN twilight fell, Baldmoney and Sneezewort were all for continuing the hunt for Cloudberry. But Dodder had set his mind on a meeting of the Wood People, and nothing they could say or do would turn him from his purpose. He always was stubborn, and now he had this new bee in his bonnet.

They made a large meal of beechnut cakes, two dried mushrooms each, some smoked perch (a new experiment in the culinary line discovered by Dodder on his way up the Folly), and a handful of nuts which Squirrel brought them.

When this had been disposed of Baldmoney and Sneezewort felt in a better frame of mind; besides, it was Midsummer's Eve, and for the Little People to fall out on such a night would be dreadful—it would be as bad as children quarreling on Christmas Eve.

They humored Dodder, agreeing with everything he said. But how were they to begin to call the Wood People together? That was the question. Squirrel offered to visit all his friends, but it would take too long. Give him a week, he said, and it might be done. But no, Dodder insisted it must be that very night. The truth was, the death of Otter weighed heavily on his conscience and he felt it must be avenged. They talked and argued as the sun went down and the frog-like nightjars came out, hawking along the ridings, whirring their spinning wheels from every ferny shadow, and precious minutes slipped away. Then Dodder got up slowly and strapped on his leg.

"Where are you going?" asked the gnomes and Squirrel.

"I want to be alone," Dodder replied. "You must not follow me. I am going a little way into the wood," and with the help of Squirrel he climbed down the tree.

The others were alarmed. This was unlike Dodder and in a curious way they were awed. They stood round the base of the pine and watched the little hobbling figure vanish among the fern, saw the nodding bracken come to a standstill, and heard faint rustlings dying away in the wood.

The moon (full now) climbed into the heavens, and millions of white moths wavered and clicked among the honeysuckle and fern brake. Far away an owl hooted, a solemn ghastly sound.

Midsummer's Eve in the woods! The magic of it! Cannot you picture the scene as I see it? The somber trees, so still, so grave; the million exquisite scents of leaves, grass, and bracken; the sweet half-sickly smell of honeysuckle and faint spicy odor of the dark pines? And under Tree Top House the two gnomes and Squirrel, waiting, listening, with an ever-growing uneasiness which they found hard to explain.

We will not follow Dodder or pry upon him, we will stay beneath the pine with Baldmoney, Sneezewort, and Squirrel.

\*　\*　\*

It needed but an hour to midnight when the fern rustled again and the halting figure of Dodder in his batskin coat came through the wood. His face seemed transfigured, as though a great weight had been lifted from him; the others stood dumbfounded. This was a new Dodder and they felt embarrassed.

Nobody spoke, the silence of the forest wrapped them round.

"Let us sit here a while beneath the pine," said Dodder in a whisper, "and let no one speak."

Baldmoney and Sneezewort obeyed, resting their chins on their knees. They noticed that Dodder was trembling and continually stroking his beard, a habit he had when excited; the atmosphere was electric. Even the animals and birds of the night seemed hushed, not an owl hooted, not a nightjar whirred. Was it their imagination, or did even the tiny dancing ghost moths cease to weave among the ferns and bushes? Never before was such a silence anywhere. Time was not, only the shadows of the trees moved as the big pale moon swung across the heavens.

And then far, far away, from the heart of the forest, they heard a SOUND! At first so faint as to be hardly audible, but growing with each passing moment. Was it the song of some insect in the fern, the wind in the tree tops? Nearer it seemed to come, and then they knew it was pipe music, surely the loveliest music ever heard. It seemed not of this earth; yet in it was all the song of birds, of the wind passing over the meadow grasses and through slender reeds, the song of insects at the heat of noon, of trees in tumult, the voices of secret streams and broad rivers and of the eternal seas.

With a sudden impulse the gnomes stood up; Squirrel sat up too like a little grey rabbit with his paws hanging against his whitish tummy. And then they began to walk towards the music, threading their way among the bracken stalks and under the brambles, not looking where they put their feet, walking like blind things or automata. And it seemed too that the whole wood was moving; if the trees could walk they would have done so, for even they began to shiver their leaves, though there was no wind, as if they were striving to move their fast-bound feet. Everywhere, all around, there was a quiet controlled pattering.

Then the gnomes knew it to be the People of the Wood;

wood-pigs, bub'ms, fern-bears, wood dogs, tiny mice and squirrels, weasels, bats, snakes—yes, even snakes—frogs and wild roe-deer, all the woodland birds, even those of the day as well as of the night; the jays and magpies who should have been asleep, the hawks and little birds; tree pipits and tree creepers, wrens and wagtails, though alas! There were few small birds, for as you know, the songsters were scarce in the wood of Giant Grum.

All were moving forward through the wood, all converging on the clearing where the gibbet stood. At ten minutes to midnight the great gathering was complete. Baldmoney, Sneezewort, and Dodder found themselves standing once more on the edge of the gibbet clearing. The gibbet still stood there in the moonlight, with its dangling array of draggled victims, but before it was a wondrous Being, his cloven feet in a circle of glow-worm light. The gnomes knew who he was, as did all the great concourse of the Wood People, jostling shoulders with each other in a great hollow square. There was no enmity now between beast and beast, hawk and bird; weasel and mouse stood together, owl and field-vole, gnome and fox, all those animals that had survived Giant Grum were there. Hundreds upon hundreds of eyes made a continuous band of faint light all around the clearing. The rustling of footsteps still continued as late-comers arrived. Dark wings lapped silently across from tree to tree, bats with hurried noiseless flight came to rest up in the oaks, faint snappings of sticks were heard on all sides. But as the seconds passed these sounds grew less and less until all was silent once again save for the faint sweet reed music which sobbed and shook, holding the animals and birds under its magic spell. At last that too died away as Pan slowly lowered his his pipes and laid them on the grass, where they seemed to burn in a row of lambent flames.

Utter silence then, not even the rustling of the leaves was heard. It was midnight on Midsummer's Eve! Everything seemed to listen, the trees, and grass, insects, animals, and birds. Then Pan spoke, and his voice was as sweet as the Folly music and the beating pulse of summer seas.

"People of the Wood, one of you has called upon me. I have come! What is it that you want of me, O People of the Wood?"

For an instant no one replied or stirred. Then into the broad moonlight of the clearing hobbled Dodder. His head was bowed and his back bent. The animals watched him but said no word. He passed with halting tread across the dewy grass and stood before Pan, the god of all the wild things. Then he spoke clearly so that all could hear.

"O mighty Pan, we thought you must have gone, so long have we called upon you and had no answer. The swallows have been many weary times since last we saw you; even I, the oldest thing alive in the woods and fields, thought you had gone with the Others. I prayed that, if you were still indeed among us this Midsummer night." He paused, overcome with awe at the majesty of the Woodland God. "Speak on, Dodder," said Pan gently (he knew his name, you see). "What is it that you want? I have come back once more to you all . . . once more . . ." Pan paused, and in the silence not a foot moved or a wing rustled, "and then I shall indeed be gone until that day when we shall all return, yes, all, gnomes and wild forgotten things alike, to the land where once we lived."

"We want," said Dodder, "this one thing, O good god Pan, that Giant Grum should die."

Pan answered not for a while, but sat looking at the hundreds of tiny eyes weaving and glinting in one continuous chain all around him.

"That is a terrible thing to ask of me," he said at length, "a terrible thing, that the Giant should die. But" (and Pan slowly turned and looked upon the gallows behind), "I need not ask why this Giant should die. I know everything, I know how he has used your People. But I must hear from you all, yes all, that you desire that the Giant should die. I ask you now, in this solemn hour, is Giant Grum to die?"

A strange murmur seemed to sweep across the clearing, to meet like two great invisible waves, which meeting, melted away. "Yea! Yea!" Silence fell again.

Then Pan spoke. "There are those among you who did not say 'yea.' Let them stand forth!"

From the dusky swaying ranks moved nearly five hundred pheasants. They did not walk with their heads upraised, but with low and creeping carriage, and stood in a timid semicircle round the good god Pan. An angry murmur arose from all the animals, but Pan held up his hand for silence. "Let their spokesman speak," he said. The gnomes recognized the proud cock pheasant, whose eggs they had stolen, strangely altered and no longer proud.

"O Lord Pan, if the Giant, our master, should go, then so shall we. He it is that feeds and tends us. The Wood People steal our eggs. For us these woods were planted. If the Giant goes we shall starve."

Again an angry murmur came from the hollow square, but again Pan silenced them with a gesture.

"The woods were here before man walked the earth, though he can tame the trees and work his will upon them, even as he has tamed you, O pheasants."

And the pheasants turned and crept away, the silent ranks parted to let them through, thousands of eyes watched from tree and fern and grass.

When they had gone Pan spoke again. "Your wish is granted, the Giant shall no longer walk Crow Wood. Come, venerable gnome, to me."

Dodder advanced, eyes still downcast, and stood at Pan's

cloven feet, where, had it not been for his leg, he would have humbly knelt. Pan stretched up his hand to the oak tree close by and plucked six leaves, giving them to Dodder.

"Take these leaves, venerable Dodder, they shall rid you of Giant Grum for ever." Dodder took them, trembling. "Tomorrow at noon, go to the Wood Pool, and you shall know what to do, and you shall see what you shall see."

"How can so frail a thing as a leaf avail us against the Giant," whispered the doubting Baldmoney in Sneezewort's ear. "There is no magic left in England now!"

"Only have courage and faith," continued Pan, taking up his pipes, "and the death of your brothers will be avenged."

And so saying he stood up to his full stature, the pipes again at his lips, and slowly he seemed to dissolve away. The sweet music, so haunting and compelling, seemed to rise up among the trees, floating mysteriously to and fro, now loud, now faint, but all the time dwindling and dying, until it was heard no more and there was no trace where Pan had been, only the moonlit clearing and silent gibbet hung with bones.

Far away a farm cock was crowing, and the paling east showed dawn as near. With its coming the great concourse melted like hoarfrost in the rays of the sun, the rustlings and the clickings died, and dew winked wet upon the grass.

\*   \*   \*

Giant Grum had no appetite for breakfast and his wife was worried. All night he had tossed and turned in his sleep, muttering, groaning. His wife wanted him to stay in bed.

"You have the flu, I'm sure; lie you still and let me send for the doctor."

But he would not. "No, the fresh air will do me good; I must go down to the pens. It's fresh air I want. Perhaps this hot weather has got me down a bit."

He took his gun from the corner and, whistling Jet, went out into the glorious morning. Soon the little half-timbered cottage among the trees was hidden by a bend in the path. He strode along with his dog at his heel. Two hundred yards from the house was a clearing and here the pheasant pens were ranged row on row. At intervals were poles from which were suspended the bodies of crows, jays, and magpies, who came to rob him of his precious chicks. As soon as he came within sight of the clearing he stopped short. Something was wrong, not a pheasant was to be seen! Usually they came running to him like chickens to be fed, but the place was deserted. He went from pen to pen, all were empty! He looked about him at the trees and bushes— nothing! Was this a dream? Yes, he must be really ill: a pulse beat in his head.

A little rest under a tree, down by the Wood Pool. It was cool there. He would sleep and wake and find all was well. This flu played tricks with one, to be sure. He went back down the path, past the cottage he strode, unheeding his anxious wife, down the checkered sunlit path.

Ah! There was the cool water; how peaceful it looked under the trees! Trout were rising, dimpling the surface; here was the place to rest, to sleep! He threw himself down among the fern, close to a pine tree, laying his loaded gun beside him. Just a little nap, only a short one, and then he would wake. All would be well, he would see clearly again . . . all would be well. He closed his eyes and the dog, sitting by his side, kept watch, its ears pricked.

How still his master lay, he hardly seemed to breathe! A dragonfly passed down the glade, zooming up into the sunlight and, turning swiftly, repassed. The dog heard the click of its jaws as it caught an insect. Bees passed, and up above, in the cool shadow, flies jigged. Now and again yellow streaks flashed by, seeming to leave a continuous line against the background of sallow and fern. They were wasps and they had a nest in the bank below the Wood Pool. Soon the dog felt sleepy too. He looked again at his master and then, hunching his back with his eyes on the ground, and smelling the fern, he turned round and round until he had made himself a comfortable couch. Then, with a big sigh, he closed his eyes and, like his master, fell fast asleep.

\* \* \*

The cool shadows across the forest path moved as the sun moved. A lovely tawny gold fritillary, newly hatched, came by, hovering over the bushes, passing on. Then a banded White Admiral with gliding, graceful flight. Man and dog slept; the sun, gathering power, made the moist fern steam. The hum of insects filled the air, the summer song of the woods.

Then the fern rustled and a face peeped out, a tiny bearded face, crowned by a batskin cap with the ears left on. It was Dodder.

There before him lay Giant Grum, all the hairy length of him, all the sweaty man-smell of him, fast asleep! This giant killed Otter, Otter of the gentle eyes, whose joy was the running water and spotted shingle.

The sides of the sleeping dog went in and out gently, the hind legs quivered in an uneasy dream, dream barks came from him and the half-opened eyes showed white with sleep. Dodder moved through the fern to where the heavy gun lay among the crushed bracken fronds. A ladybird was crawling up the blued barrel. It reached the end and wavered uncertainly. Then a bumble bee came droning through the fern forest. It found the head of a purple knapweed and clambered on it, bending it right over until it touched the gun stock. Dodder saw the polished grain of the wood and the worn smooth appearance of the steel barrel where the giant's sweaty hand held it when firing.

He put his fingers into his pocket and drew forth the leaves, the six oak leaves which Pan had given him. He crept to the muzzle of the gun.

\* \* \*

A tiny pine twig dropped from the tree above. It struck the giant on the nose and he sat up stretching.

Ah! He felt better—that terrible ennui had left him. Nothing like a nap in the open air. The dog was still asleep. What had awakened him? He scratched his nose and looked about him. This would never do. Supposing his master had caught him sleeping, he might get the sack!

Ah! What was that he had been dreaming? Something about his pheasant pens. He chuckled, what silly things are dreams!

Pat! Another stick fell. He looked up into the tangled dark branches above him. A squirrel was it . . . something. He got to his feet, peering up, his sharp eyes searching, searching. And then he saw Dodder, perched on a branch thirty feet above him. The dog was awake too, the hairs bristling along the ridge of its back, its eyes staring upwards.

\* \* \*

Giant Grum groaned and passed his hands over his eyes. Oh dear, still seeing things! He looked again. Yes . . . yes . . . a tiny man in a batskin cap and coat sitting on a pine branch. Beside him was a grey squirrel.

But these things *can't* be; after all, one must be practical. The squirrel, yes . . . but that other thing . . . there weren't such things as gnomes . . . it was impossible. It must be a new kind of bat! And then, as he watched, the vulgar little gnome leaned forward and spat! The tiny spot of white came swiftly down like a plummet and hit him in the eye. Giant Grum let out an oath.

*     *     *

The gun came up, a cracked finger with a black nail crooked round the trigger. A gnome was it! Well, we would see! Neither Dodder nor Squirrel moved, the tiny face was actually grinning at him.

Giant Grum's right thumb pushed forward the catch on top of the gun, hiding the one tiny word "safe." He pressed the trigger and then . . . something went "pouf" at the giant, blowing him out like a candle.

*     *     *

"It was simple," said Dodder to an admiring ring of animals who had gathered round Tree Top House.

"I pushed the leaves down inside each barrel, and then Squirrel and I went up the tree. He was fast asleep and we threw things on him to wake him. Then he stood up and aimed his club that roars. I knew Pan was with me, I wasn't even afraid when I saw those two black mouths pointing at me, I knew the leaves would burst the gun. Then he fired, there was a great noise and the giant went backwards into the bracken. I think he was dead; I was glad to come away. Listen!"

And then they heard birds singing—blackbirds, thrushes, willow warblers, wood wrens, blackcaps, white throats, tits, chaffinches, greenfinches, and the glorious voice of the nightingales. The birds had come back to Crow Wood at last!

\*   \*   \*

*Author's Note.* It is not generally known that a slight obstruction, if some inches from the muzzle of a gun barrel, is sufficient to burst it when the cartridge is fired, especially if the gun is much worn.

# CHAPTER II

# The Animal Banquet

DODDER THE GIANT-KILLER was feted by the animals; he was acclaimed the Hero, the Savior of Crow Wood.

A truce was declared and the gnomes asked all their friends to a great celebration by the Folly Falls, below Tree Top House, as many as cared to come. All the next day there were comings and goings, excited whisperings among the fern, rustling of oak leaves, and flappings of wings. It was amazing how quickly the news spread, bird told bird (they were the chief messengers).

Wood-pig was rootling for worms up the brook when he was surprised to see Chaffinch, "spinking" at him from a hazel twig. "Are you coming to the Animal Banquet," it asked him, "down by the Folly Falls tonight? Nearly everyone's going to be there. Dodder the Giant-Killer and his two Brothers, Squirrel, and the rest—it's going to be a wonderful time; bring your own grub!"

Wood-pig would have liked to spend the evening quietly,

for he was a shy little spiny person, but he agreed to come. Fern-bear, asleep deep in his fortress far under Crow Wood, was awakened by a wood-mouse tickling his whiskers. "What! Ugh! Ah!" He awakened rather testily, sneezing and coughing.

"Animal Banquet by the Folly Falls, Wood People welcome—tonight! And bring some food with you," squeaked the mouse and vanished.

Fern-bear poked his snoring family with his snout. "Animal Banquet tonight at Folly Falls, Wood People welcome," and then he went straight off to sleep again.

From beak to beak and from muzzle to muzzle the word was passed round, "Folly Falls tonight, bring your own grub!"

As soon as the sun was down the animals and birds began to arrive. They were amazed to see a big fire burning, with flames leaping high into the air. Even the trees seemed to crowd round, bending their heads to join in the fun. Birds of every description were there, the bushes and fern bent with their weight. But it was noticed that the foxes, stoats, and pheasants had not been invited.

Wood-pig brought a ball of worms in moss (and other things which didn't smell very nice); the nervous little roe-deer, their eyes big with wonder, hovered in the background, too shy to come into the circle of light. Crowds of bats hung upside down under the oak boughs and kept getting in everyone's way, for the fire mazed them and they flew about in the smoke, cheeping excitedly. The gnomes had spent the day catching fish: minnows, perch, and three whopping trout from the Wood Pool, so there was plenty for everyone.

Squirrel had found, quite by accident, a perfectly enormous cache of nuts under one of his trees, and Fern-bear, rather tactlessly, brought some fresh-killed meat which looked suspiciously like infant Bub'ms, but as Bub'ms have far too many babies, everybody pretended not to notice. He also brought what appeared to be a plucked pheasant, but *he* said it was fowl.

There was no other drink but the Folly water; if the gnomes had been nearer home they would have provided many rare wines, well matured, such as elder and nettle, but it was too long a journey back to the Oak Pool to fetch them.

Dodder had every excuse for a swelled head, but he modestly took no credit for what he had done.

When all had feasted they gathered round the glowing fire, watching, enthralled, the tiny brilliant sparks shooting up, to wander way like fairies among the leaves of the oaks. Every time the fire burnt up brightly the velvet blue-black sky seemed to darken, and all the while the Folly kept up its happy song.

They took it in turn to tell stories. Even the shy roe-deer sidled nearer and listened with their great ears. I regret to say that some of the bats, overcome with the effects of a large meal of insects and half suffocated by the wood smoke, kept dropping off their leaves into the fire; only a few were rescued with difficulty. Wood-pig was disgustingly sick from eating too many worms. I am also ashamed to say that the gnomes, too, ate far too much, and while Bub'm was in the middle of rather a long and dreary story of "why Bub'ms wore white cotton-tails," Baldmoney's belt parted with a loud snap and his skin jacket split all down the front!

As animals have practically no sense of humor nobody laughed or even noticed it, but Dodder and Sneezewort were secretly convulsed. The fire burnt low and the flames ceased to leap and jump. Instead there was a cozy red glow which turned all the animals and birds a rosy pink. As the night wore on the day birds became terribly sleepy. They tried hard to keep awake, but one by one they tucked in their heads and puffed themselves into woolly balls.

Of course the owls and nightjars were in high spirits and kept everyone enthralled by their tales of banshees and bogies. White Owl told an eerie story about a churchyard until he had all the animals peeping over their shoulders at the strange dark shadows among the trees, for some could not believe that Giant Grum was now really powerless to harm them.

The baby Bub'ms (who should have been left at home tucked up in bed) had a high old time, scampering about between people's legs, and pulling Fern-bear's whiskers. That sly gentleman looked very foolish and uncomfortable, as well he might.

Squirrel excelled himself. He told them stories of American wild life and the vast pine woods of the North; even the bouncing Bub'm babies had to listen.

At last when he had finished, Sneezewort touched Dodder's sleeve. "Now we have all the Wood folk here, why not tell them of our quest?" he whispered. "They might give us some news of Cloudberry."

Dodder nodded. He put on his bone leg and stood up. Everyone was respectfully silent. He told them of their journey up the Folly, of how they came to be in Crow Wood at all, and how he had killed the giant. And then he asked them for news of Cloudberry.

"This is the object of our journey," he said. "Midsummer is past, the year is drawing on. It will not be long before the trees are yellowing and their life draining down deep within the earth, where all life sleeps. We must find Cloudberry before the winter comes, for then we shall have to return to the Oak Pool and you will not see us again. If any have news of him, or have seen him, speak," and he sat down.

Then the White Owl spoke from the oak above.

"I remember him, gnomes—I remember your lost brother. He was dressed like you in skins and came up the Folly two years ago looking for the source. He stayed two days in Crow Wood and then he went on towards the big lake. I never saw him after he left the wood. Whether or not he found the source I cannot say."

"How far is it to the Folly Source?" asked Dodder.

"I cannot tell you," the White Owl answered. "I have never been, nor have any of the Wood People, but it is a long way. You will never reach it by walking."

"We must get the boat," said Baldmoney eagerly. "We must go on by boat!"

"There are no falls beyond the wood," said the owl. "At least, I do not think so. But the Folly gets very narrow and the water shallow."

"Never mind," said Baldmoney, "the *Dragonfly* will get along all right. With three of us we can travel at a fine pace. Let us start tomorrow!"

Dodder rose to his feet again. "Well, People of the Wood, we must say good-bye. We start tomorrow to go on up the Folly. Perhaps you will see us on our way down, when the leaves are turning. If I have been able to do some service for you I am glad, but it is our great god Pan who must have your gratitude and thanks."

The fire was now a welter of white ash and glowing sparks, a tiny chill wind blew them hither and thither, the blue-black gloom of the wood was all around. And then it seemed that the night wind in the tree tops began to sing a lullaby. The dark pines moved gently, their tasseled branches swinging and swaying, the oak leaves rustled together, forming music and words, music and words, dreamy, haunting, and unbelievably lovely. And this is what they seemed to sing:

# THE CROW WOOD LULLABY

*Music by* WALTER PITCHFORD

Sleep, sleep, Deep sleep, Lit-tle ones come to rest,

Nothing shall harm you, Pan-pipes shall charm you, Safe in your wood - land

nest: Sleep, sleep, Deep sleep, The breath of the night grows

chill, But stars in the sky Will fade by and by, Lit tle wild ones, be still.

So one by one the tired animals dropped asleep where they sat; the rabbits nodded, the birds rolled themselves into tighter balls, the mice cuddled into Fern-bear's long hair for warmth. Only the owl remained awake, looking down at the ring of sleeping wild things below him. And there he kept watch, smiling a little, perhaps, to see this trusting pathetic little band at the foot of the tree. He stood very upright, looking like a white goblin, as he turned his huge eyes this way and that.

Dodder lay on his back, an infant hedge-pig under each arm, Sneezewort's pockets were full of shrews, and three baby dormice had made a warm nest under Baldmoney's beard. They slept until cock-crow, and when at last dawn broke there was nothing to show of the high revelry and feasting but the cold grey ashes blowing on the banks of the Folly.

\* \* \*

Bright and early next morning the gnomes went down to the wire with Squirrel. They found the *Dragonfly* still safely tucked up under the fern, and Baldmoney and Sneezewort went over her carefully and examined the broken paddle. They found that the rowlock had broken under the strain, and the wire of the paddle was badly bent. Still, it could be repaired, and Baldmoney had another idea.

"How would it be to make a mast and a sail? We might get a favorable breeze upstream and it would help us along a lot."

"That's an idea," said Sneezewort excitedly. "I wonder we didn't think of that before."

So they looked about for a suitable mast. Squirrel soon found one—a stout pine twig. They bored a hole in the decking with Cloudberry's knife and wedged it firmly in, damping it with water to make the wood swell. Then they searched for a sail. "What could be better than a dock leaf?" suggested Sneezewort.

"No, something stronger . . . I have it!" exclaimed Dodder, who was now as proud of the boat as if he had made it himself. "We can use one of our sleeping-bags."

"The very thing," said Baldmoney, "the very thing!" They lashed a cross-piece to the mast and, making two small holes in either end of the moleskin, threaded the stick through, tying it firmly to the top of the mast with twisted grass rope. The only thing that worried Baldmoney was the fact that it would be difficult to furl the sail in an emergency, but Sneezewort pointed out that the cross-piece could be untied.

With the help of Squirrel they carried the boat up the bank, for they could never have got her up the rush of the falls. It was hard work and they had to stop frequently to get their breath, but at last they reached the head of the swift water and paddled the boat up under the nut bushes to the Wood Pool. There was a faint westerly breeze aft and the sail was rigged up. To their delight they found that the boat moved well, right up the center of the pool. This was a very different business to sweating at the paddle handles; now they only had to paddle occasionally to steer her. They had a trial run right up the pool, tying up to an overhanging nut bush at the far end.

"Splendid!" crowed Baldmoney, rubbing his hands. "I never knew sailing could be so delightful." In a very short time all was made ready and it was time to say "good-bye."

"I wish I was coming with you," said Squirrel rather wistfully. "But if I got aboard I'd sink the boat. If only I were smaller!"

"Never mind, Squirrel, you've been a great help to us, and we owe you a lot. Without you I don't know what we'd have done, letting us sleep in Tree Top House and everything. We'll soon be back, Squirrel, and I hope Cloudberry will be with us. And you must come and stay with us at the Oak Tree Pool."

"Mind you find yourself a wife," shouted Dodder as he climbed aboard. "There's no excuse, Squirrel, now the giant has gone! Remember us to the Bub'ms, wood-pigs, and all the animals! Good-bye! Good-bye!"

Squirrel gave them a push off and the *Dragonfly* slowly turned her bow towards the open water of the Wood Pool.

Looking back, they could see the grey form of Squirrel sitting on the bank, now and again shaking his tail at them, getting smaller and smaller. At first they could see his face clearly, his pointed ears and bright eyes, but soon these melted and dwindled until he was a mere grey blob, appearing rather pathetic, against the background of trees.

The breeze freshened, and while Dodder looked after the sail and paddles (which had been mended by Baldmoney) the others busied themselves with putting the deck into some semblance of order. The steering of the boat was soon mastered, though at first Dodder had to keep on shouting "left a bit," "right a bit," "hard left," and so forth.

It was surprising how well the *Dragonfly* sped through the water. Soon they were right out in the middle of the pool. The water chuckled under her with each puff of wind and the bow dipped downwards in quite a professional manner; considering she had not been built for a sailing-boat she went extraordinarily well.

Dodder, sitting back in the boat puffing at his pipe, revelled in it.

"Why we never built a sailing-boat before I can't think," he said. (Their frogskin fishing-boats were nothing compared to the *Dragonfly*.) "This sailing business is the most wonderful thing in the world! Hard left!" he shouted as the *Dragonfly* yawed dangerously round.

"All right, all *right*," said Baldmoney testily; "I know what I'm doing." (As a matter of fact he didn't; he was not nearly such a good helmsman as Dodder.) "Tell Sneezewort to get on with tidying up the deck!"

The latter packed their belongings neatly together, the sleeping-bags in one corner and stores in another, fishing-lines coiled round the mast. Soon all was shipshape and they settled down to enjoy themselves.

The Wood Pool was nearly half a mile long, a beautiful sheet of water, hedged round with trees. Water-hens scuttled away, showing a silver comb of spray from their dangling legs, and a blue dragonfly settled on the mast. After a little while the breeze softened and the boat ceased to forge ahead, and when they turned a corner of the pool and the screening trees took their wind, they were becalmed.

Sneezewort and Baldmoney took the paddles, and Dodder the helm, and the *Dragonfly* went steadily on towards the head of the pool; chunk, chunk went the paddles, and the gleaming ripples parted before her bow.

"Easy does it," shouted Dodder, peering under the sail; "we're coming into the narrows."

The banks crept nearer, trees hung over, trailing their branches in the water, and soon they were in the Folly again. It flowed slowly, for the Wood Pool dammed it up so that paddling was easy. Dodder trailed his fingers in the water; the coldness of it was delightful.

"I'm glad I came," he said dreamily. "You fellows could never have got on without me."

"Yes," said Baldmoney, "do you remember how angry you were when we said we were coming up the Folly? We never thought you would come."

"If it hadn't been for me, we shouldn't be sailing up the Wood Pool," said Dodder with some truth, "with Giant Grum about we shouldn't have dared to show our noses."

The Folly now seemed to pass under a long tunnel of trees; it might have been a stretch of African river. The water was deep and black and almost without movement. Here and there bleached and rotten sticks like crocodiles protruded from the surface and they had to guide the *Dragonfly* with care. Tall branching ferns came right down to the water's edge, bending gracefully over their reflections. They were more delicate and finely cut than the bracken fronds, and they heightened the effect of a tropical river.

It needed little effort to propel the boat, for the current of the Folly was still lost in the dammed-up stream. Dodder lay on his back gazing up at the ceiling of green, watching the caterpillars swinging on invisible thread from the thick foliage. Then the stream took a sharp right-handed turn and at the far end of the tunnel they saw an ornamental stone bridge.

"I don't like the look of that," exclaimed Baldmoney, ceasing to paddle and shading his eyes with his hands. "It smells of giants to me."

The bridge must have been very old, for the stone was weathered and covered with moss and one or two of its babistrades were missing. They paddled on with caution, only turning the paddles now and then. The boat glided along very slowly. All around willow warblers were singing; their song was like a musical waterfall, very small and sweet. A chiff-chaff (which is very like a willow warbler in appearance) kept up a continuous monotonous song: "chiff chaff! chiff chaff! chiff chaff! chiff chaff! zeet, zeet, zeet, zeet!" as it hopped about among the dense foliage.

The bridge drew nearer. They saw a stone shield over the central arch with an incised monogram SC and 1732 below it in quaint figures. Water-voles, unused to the boat, dived from their galleries in the peaty soil of the bank and would not stop to talk. They were like savage tribes fleeing at the sight of a white man.

"Silly things!" said Dodder. "Why won't they stop and make friends?"

"It's the boat, I expect," whispered Baldmoney. "They don't know what it is."

At last they drifted under the stone arch, and Baldmoney brought the *Dragonfly* scraping gently against the stonework. Ivy creeper was draped in long festoons on the far side of the arch and a wagtail's nest was built among the hairy cables of the main ivy stem. It was full of fledglings which stepped over the rim with round and frightened eyes.

The mayflies were hatching; over the grass thousands of them could be seen dancing up and down; some, locked together, fell down among the meadow flowers. Others dropped into the water and were borne away, gyrating feebly, to be sucked down by waiting fish. Now and again all the insects ceased to dance and not one was to be seen. Perhaps they were resting. But in a few moments they would be a-dance again all along the banks of the stream.

"We will tie up here for a bit," whispered Baldmoney. "I don't like the look of this place. Mrs. Wagtail may be able to give us some news." The gnomes tried to talk to the fledgling wagtails, but they were either too frightened or too shy to reply. They cowered down in the nest, and one was so nervous it let fall a tiny white spot into the water.

"Leave them alone," said Dodder. "They are scared of us; wait until their mother comes back."

All was in shadow under the arch of the bridge and they were well hidden. They watched the wavering light bars ripple along the stonework and the silver water-beetles skating and weaving. All around them the birds sang and the chiff-chaff kept up its monotonous refrain.

# CHAPTER 12

# The Storm

THE RIPPLES, LAPPING UNDER the bridge, were like olive-green fish scales. They ran along the old stonework, making it glisten. For many years they had washed the stone until it was a darker color and green with moss. Here and there, protruding from crevices in the wall, were green hart's tongue ferns, and a snail was crawling on one of them with a black-and-yellow banded shell upon its back.

Upstream the sky seemed lighter, for the trees were not so numerous, though close to the bridge was a large horse-chestnut; its handsome splayed leaves, spread like fingers, hung over the water. The rotting candles had long since been stripped of flowers and were withering; earlier the tree had been a mass of glorious bloom. In October this would be a wonderful place to hunt for "conkers" . . . those gloriously polished mahogany balls, like precious stones in their leathery white pulp settings!

The gnomes used conker skins for pipe bowls and cabinet-work; Baldmoney had made Dodder a wonderful smoking cabinet for his pipes with them. It stood in the corner of the oak root at home and was greatly admired. But it was many weeks yet to "conker time," and much might happen in the meanwhile; they might never see that lovely conker cabinet again, or the Oak Pool!

"Chissick, chissick!" A pied wagtail came dipping up the stream close above the water. She flew with undulating switchback flight, up and down, up and down, her bill wedged wide with a bundle of juicy mayflies.

In the nest the babies heard the gladsome sound and a forest of unsteady wagging heads upraised, five red trumpets opened. She fed them carefully, dividing the flies as she did so. Every year she had built under the bridge.

The sound of the mother-bird's arrival awakened Dodder. He could not at first remember where he was as he had been in the middle of some fantastic dream of giants and gibbets, boats and fish. He rubbed his eyes and for a second or two lay staring at the stonework, collecting his thoughts.

Yes, of course, now he remembered everything, the start from the Wood Pool, the bridge and the wagtail's nest! He raised himself on his elbows. Baldmoney was curled up on the sleeping-bags in the stern, making funny whistling noises through his beard.

"Chissick, chissick!" Dodder stood up unsteadily, for his one good leg had gone to sleep.

"Mrs. Wagtail! Hi! Mrs. Wagtail!"

The mother wagtail was sitting on the edge of the nest with her black-and-white back turned towards the boat; she had not noticed the *Dragonfly* and her crew.

"Goodness! How you made me jump!" she said, hopping an inch or two into the air and half preparing to fly away. "Why! It's the gnomes!" She recognized them, for with the other Crow Wood people, she had attended the meeting in the gibbet clearing.

"Whatever are you doing up here?" she asked when she had recovered her composure.

"We are on our way upstream to find our lost brother. Can you tell us what lies ahead; is the water rough, and are there any falls?"

"No," she replied, "as far as I know there are not any waterfalls. It is still water for a long way, right past the gardens. Then you will come to the big lake."

"Big lake?" asked Dodder. "Gardens? What *do* you mean?"

"Oh! Don't you know? This is Clobber Park. It's a beautiful place and there's a heronry on Poplar Island in front of the house—at least there used to be," she added, "but Lord Clobber talks of having the nests pulled down because the herons take his trout. You will have to be careful on the lake, you know," she added, "with that little boat of yours.

Sometimes the waves are very big."

"What a bother!" exclaimed Dodder. "I thought there was nothing but wild country above Crow Wood. We don't want to be seen, you know—it would never do."

The wagtail could tell him nothing about the Folly above Clobber Park, and after Dodder had admired her family she excused herself, for the babies were getting hungry and clamoring for food.

Dodder awakened the others and told them what the wagtail had said.

"It's a nuisance, but it can't be helped. We shall have to risk being seen. I don't fancy going up the lake in the dark, and if we wait for the moon to rise it will mean we can't make a start before morning. The best thing we can do is to have some supper and then start."

Evening had come and the rain had stopped. The lowering sun shone right in their eyes, making the water a blaze of gold which dazzled them. The mayflies no longer danced. Everything smelt beautifully fresh and raindrops still fell from the thick masses of the overhanging chestnut just beyond the bridge.

"I'm jolly hungry," said Dodder. "I don't know about you fellows, but some fried minnows would go down rather well."

"Don't you think it's risky to light a fire?" asked the wary Sneezewort. "You never know who might be about."

"Pooh! Let's chance it." The truth was that since Dodder

had disposed of Giant Grum he had become rather cock-sure, and quite indifferent as to whether anyone saw them or not. He was tired of skulking about, hiding, and living in fear of the mortals; why, they could be killed by a tiny oak leaf!

So they landed on the bank close to the bridge and Baldmoney and Sneezewort hunted around for firewood. Dodder busied himself with preparing supper, cleaning the fish and arranging them head and tail in his frying-pan. This frying-pan was really rather ingeniously made. You will remember they had saved all the copper cartridge caps they found lying about in Crow Wood and by hammering out three or four of these and combining them they made splendid little frying-pans. True, they only held a few minnows at a time, but when the little fish were cut up they went in the pan easily. The mussel shells were never satisfactory (though they held more) for the heat of the fire split them.

In a few moments the gnomes returned with some dry firing, stalks of gix (wild hemlock), dried leaves, and grass, and it was not long before a thread of blue smoke arose on the evening air and the delicious smell of cooking fish was wafted to their minute noses.

Dodder was so hungry that little dribbles ran down his beard. Sneezewort went off again into the trees and returned in a short time with his hat full of wild strawberries. What a feast they had!

Everything seemed rosy that evening; the Giant had been disposed of, the weather had cleared up, they had their beloved *Dragonfly* back again, and now it only remained to find Cloudberry.

Gnomes do not eat with knives and forks, but in the good old primitive way, that is, with the fingers. The fish were taken up and held by head and tail and the backs were bitten out, the way Otter ate his fish. No bones troubled them, and, after all, this is a very good method of eating a fish, piping hot from the pan. If you don't believe me, try it for yourself!

"My! I feel better," said Dodder at last, wiping his greasy fingers on his beard and popping the last strawberry into his mouth. "I'm ready to start at any time. We can't wait until the sun goes down—it will be hours yet."

Baldmoney got up and walked forward to where the boat was tied. He jumped ashore and was fumbling with the grass rope when his eye, wandering carelessly over the stonework of the bridge under the ivy creeper, caught sight of some scratches among the grey lichen. He looked more carefully and this is what he saw:

These scratches would have conveyed nothing to us, but in gnome language it meant this: "Cloudberry, cuckoo time."

Do not imagine that the gnomes wrote as we do, they have their own ciphers and alphabets. The cloud and bunch of berries was Cloudberry's way of signing his name, and the bird with the inverted V in front of its beak meant April (cuckoo time).

"Dodder! Sneezewort!" The others were by his side in an instant, for they had seen him looking intently at the stone under the ivy.

"Look! Look what's written here! It's Cloudberry! He must have scratched that!" Sure enough, though the scratches were very faint, they were just decipherable.

"We're on the right track," said Baldmoney excitedly, "we shall find him. What a piece of luck we just happened to tie up by the bridge!" They danced about and hugged each other, and Dodder very nearly fell backwards down the bank in his excitement. Then, all at once, he subsided like a pricked bubble. The color drained from his face and his eyes were staring, staring upwards to the stone balustrade above them.

The others sensed something was wrong and they followed his gaze. There above, looking down directly at them, was a small boy with red hair. His hands were clasped over his ears, his elbows rested on the parapet, and he was smiling all over his freckled face.

What happened next you can guess. Plop! Plop! Plop! and the gnomes shot over the side like corks. They came up under the arch and hung on to the stonework. They were too frightened to say a thing, they just dumbly stared at one another in horror.

At last Dodder found his voice, though it was nothing but a husky whisper. "Now we've gone and done it!"

"It's all your fault," hissed Baldmoney. "We should never have lit the fire!"

As luck would have it, the *Dragonfly* was under the creeper and well hidden. There was just a chance the boy would not see it. How long they remained there I do not know. It seemed ages to them. Unfortunately their fire was still smoldering and the copper frying-pan still among the members. At last they felt the bank jarring. Two stout legs appeared under the arch, very scratched legs, without socks, the feet in grubby tennis shoes. The boy was bending down, looking at the fire. He took up the little copper pan and dropped it quickly for it was still hot. It rolled down the bank and fell into the stream. This was a piece of luck for the gnomes.

Then he came and peered under the arch. But the gnomes only had their heads above water and in the shadow the boy could not see them; besides, the light was going.

"I wish he'd go away," whispered Sneezewort. "I'm getting cramp!"

They hung on to the brickwork until their fingers began to ache dreadfully, but still they clung. Dodder's teeth were chattering.

"It's the last t-t-t-time I light a f-f-f-fire in the d-d-day-time," he stuttered. "I'll be glad when we're c-c-clear of this place. This is what c-c-comes of being over-c-c-confident."

Boys on the whole are not very patient, and Robin Clobber was no exception. It was not long before he tired of looking for them; soon a voice was heard calling "Robin! Robin!" and he ran off across the grass. It didn't seem very amazing to him that he had seen three little men, cooking their supper by the old bridge. After all, he was only seven years old, and he took everything as a matter of course. He had always thought that the old bridge was the sort of place where one *might* see gnomes, though his idea of the Little People was based on the absurd creatures pictured in his story books, ridiculous beings in tinsel frocks with gold stars in their hands and with gauzy wings sticking out of their backs, pictures which of course are very pretty but are not like fairies at all.

That night, when his father came to say good night to him as he always did, Robin decided that he would say nothing about what he had seen. But after his father had kissed him good night and was just going out of the door he changed his mind.

"Daddy!"

"Yes, Robin?"

"Fairies don't have wings, do they?"

"All the ones I've seen hadn't, Robin."

"Oh! So you've seen fairies too, have you, Daddy?"

"Yes, quite a number. But they are fickle creatures, Robin; when you grow up don't have anything to do with them."

"Oh! . . . Where did you see your fairies, Daddy?"

"I can't remember now—in all sorts of places, abroad mostly; why, have you seen a fairy?"

"Well, I saw three little goms—and goms *are* fairies, aren't they?—down by the bridge."

"Goms?" queried his father, puzzled.

"Yes, goms."

"Oh! You mean gnomes, Robin." (Robin's father could not help laughing.)

"No . . . I mean *goms*," maintained Robin stoutly.

"All right, goms, then; and what were your goms doing, may I ask?"

"Cooking their supper on the bank of the Folly."

"Oh, they sound rather jolly goms, much better fairies than mine. What were they cooking, Robin?"

"Little fishes."

"I hope they weren't cooking my trout," said his father seriously. "I've only just restocked the lake."

"Oh no, the fish were too small for trout; I don't know

what they were. When the little goms saw me they dived into the water and went under the bridge. Don't tell Purkis, will you, Daddy—he might shoot them."

"Purkis has gone away on a long holiday, Robin, and I . . . well, I don't think he will be coming back."

"I'm glad, Daddy; I didn't like him."

"Well, Robin, you must go to sleep; good night, and sweet repose!"

"Slam the door on the doctor's nose," answered Robin, and fell fast asleep.

Like all grown-ups, his father didn't believe Robin had seen the "goms," which, under the circumstances, was perhaps a good thing, and he was glad of the opportunity of breaking the news that the keeper had gone.

\* \* \*

When all was quiet the gnomes came out from under the bridge and took off their clothes. It was lucky for them they had a change of dry things in the boat.

"Come on, let's go," said Baldmoney. "The sooner we're away from here the better, and we've lost a perfectly good frying-pan. *I'm* not going to dive for it."

"Nor I," said Sneezewort. "*I* think Dodder ought to, it's all his fault; he'll have to make another now! A nice mess we should have been in if that boy had found the boat."

Sneezewort untied the grass rope and they pushed off. The sun had gone and the evening hinted at a storm. Black clouds came hurrying over and the rain began to fall again. They hoisted the sail and soon the bridge was hidden by a bend in the stream. They glided past the shaven lawns and terraces of Clobber Court.

"There's the lake!" called Baldmoney from his lookout forrard. In the grey dusk they saw a sheet of water which seemed like a vast inland sea.

You must bear in mind that the gnomes were very small and their surroundings consequently much bigger than they would have appeared to a grown-up person. Not only that, a day to a gnome is like a week to us; not only scale but time as well was magnified to them. That is why the older one becomes, the bigger one grows, time seems to fly by more quickly, and it is also why one's old home seems so much smaller if you visit it again in later years, when you have grown up. Though it was only two months since they started on their adventure, it seemed to be two years to them.

As they drew towards the open water the breeze freshened. In a very short time they lost sight of land; it was only a blur in the fading light, and soon even that vanished and they were all alone, right out on the open water.

There was no need to steer with the paddles, indeed, after a while, on Dodder's orders, they detached the paddles and lashed the sail to the two paddle uprights as it was more secure and "drew" better. But the *Dragonfly* began to rock alarmingly.

Dodder was the first to feel a queer sensation in the pit

*The* Dragonfly *runs into heavy weather on the Big Sea: far across the tossing waves can be seen the trees of Poplar Island*

of his diminutive stomach.

"Oh dear! I do feel queer. I hope those fish were all right," he groaned. This reminded the others that they too there feeling rather uncomfortable inside.

Splash! A wave broke over the side of the *Dragonfly*. Splosh! Another broke over the bows.

"Down with the sail," shouted Baldmoney. And indeed their situation was becoming terrifying. For the further they got out into the middle of the lake the bigger the waves became and the worse they felt. The whole truth of the matter was that they were seasick, and that is a dreadful malady.

On all sides were the tossing grey ripples crested with foam, there was no trace of land, and the *Dragonfly* was shipping more and more water. Unfortunately all the gnomes were now feeling so ill that they could not stir a finger to reef the sail, and the harder the wind blew, the faster the boat went along, and more and more water came over the side.

"Bail! Bail! For Pan's sake," groaned Dodder, "or we shall be shipwrecked." He threw them some of the empty cartridge cases, which made excellent bailers, and, ill as they were, they began to bail for all they were worth. Water was now swilling about on the bottom of the boat almost to their knees, and the *Dragonfly* quivered drunkenly, waterlogged and unmanageable. As fast as they threw the water out, more came in, and the wind, charged with spray, tore at the sail.

I don't know what would have happened had not the sail been carried away. The binding to the cross spar broke, and sail and spar went overboard; she was driving under "bare poles," as the old mariners used to say. Utterly exhausted, the gnomes had to give up. They rolled about on the bottom of the boat, soaked through, with the water breaking over them. They felt so ill that they didn't mind if they *were* drowned. In the darkness and the howling wind the *Dragonfly* tipped and ducked. Then a faint grating sound came from under her keel, the forward movement stopped abruptly, she was aground.

Baldmoney was the first to recover sufficiently to realize that they were no longer tossing on the open lake. He crawled to the side and was violently sick. Then he felt better. Overhead dark trees were whipping in the night wind, and the *Dragonfly* was bump, bumping on hard stones.

He scrambled over the side and, feeling for the rope, feebly made her fast. In the darkness it was impossible to tell where they were. He helped the others out of the boat and they crawled up the shingle and lay under some bushes.

\* \* \*

All night the roar of the surf sounded in their ears, and with teeth chattering violently they saw the east begin to grey.

With the coming of the dawn the wind showed no signs of abating and the waves were as huge as ever. They saw the far bank; sloping fields dotted with pheasant coverts, round spinneys of fir, and pleasant parkland. All their fishing tackle had been swept away and their stores washed overboard, but their sleeping-bags were intact (with the exception of the third sleeping-bag, which had done duty for a sail) and these they carried up the shore.

They were feeling far too ill to do anything more. What with the thrashing of the trees and the roaring of the surf on the shingle they were quite mazed. After a while, as the light increased, the effects of the night's ordeal wore off and Sneezewort, who was a better sailor than the others and the first to recover, at last pulled himself together and ventured out from under the bushes.

He soon made the surprising discovery that they had not, as he had first thought, been driven aground on the bank of the lake. They were on Poplar Island, and nearly half a mile of storm-tossed water separated them from the mainland. Unless the waves and winds subsided they would have to stay there for the rest of the day. So he went back to the others and fell fast asleep again, which, under the circumstances, was the best possible thing to do.

# CHAPTER 13

# Castaways on Poplar Island

THE ISLAND WAS NOT very large, the gnomes could have walked all round it in half an hour. Ground ivy was everywhere and hid the earth, there was very little grass. Bushes of all kinds grew thickly, chiefly dogwood and red willow, and here and there thick holly clumps.

Five big black poplars grew in the center, and high in the upper branches were the herons' nests, seven of them, huge stick structures three times the size of rooks' nests. The herons are early breeders—they lay their eggs in late February and March—so that the young birds had flown. But there were signs of the departed fledglings; droppings splashed all over the place, broken eggshells (great blue-green shells, larger than ducks' eggs), old fish-bones, and dried frog-skins.

Islands, however small, are fascinating places, as many people have found. There is a primitive sense of satisfaction in the knowledge one is surrounded by water. If you live on an island you know you are secure from wild beasts, for very few animals would dare to swim across from the mainland.

The wind was still blowing hard from the nor'-east, driving the grey waves on to the shingle, where they broke in white foam. Storm-bound swallows hawked up and down on the lee side of Poplar Island, and some settled all a-row on a willow branch for a rest. Insects were to be found in the calmer air, and this is why the swallows had congregated at this spot.

The graceful little birds sat out of the wind on the willow branch, which now and again dipped gently into the water as a gust found its way through the bushes, chattering in language unintelligible to gnomes, of Africa and hot lands by the Nile. Perhaps the stormy weather put them in mind of their coming journey and the joys of sunny Natal and Cape Colony, where most of them wintered. It was their chattering which awakened Dodder. The little gnome was stiff and cramped from the night's ordeal, and for some time he could not move. He lay gazing out from the ground ivy at the grey ripples chasing past and the rough water beyond. In the lee of the island the ripples, though uneasy, were not unduly rough, though, looking left, he could see, just off the point of Poplar Island, the main thrust of the storm driving the breakers on to each others' backs. Three coots bobbed up and down like corks; he could only see them when a larger wave than the rest lifted them up—they appeared exactly like little fishing smacks riding at anchor.

Dodder awakened the others and suggested breakfast. They bemoaned the loss of the provisions now at the bottom of the lake, and also of their fishing-lines and tackle. Fortunately Dodder always carried with him a spare line and hook (the real hook, he had found by the Folly) and with this he tried to get some fish. Grubbing among the ground ivy he found the earth was dry and powdery, for the leaves had sucked up most of the rain of the night before, and soon all hands were turned to looking for worms. At last Dodder found two small brandlings under a stone. For some reason worms like lying under stones and can be often found there when other places are drawn blank.

He baited up his hook and crawled along a willow bough (rather a risky proceeding with one leg) and began fishing. But for some reason not one would bite; perhaps the wild weather had driven them away, or perhaps there were no minnows in the lake. Whilst thus engaged he heard Sneezewort, who had gone down the bank to where they had left the boat, come running back through the bushes. From his haste Dodder guessed something was wrong.

"It's gone!" he gasped, throwing himself down among the ivy quite out of breath. "It's gone, it's gone!"

"What's gone?" asked Dodder testily.

"The boat! It's been washed off the shore, the mooring rope is broken!"

"Now we *are* in a fix," said Baldmoney, appearing from behind a tree. "We're marooned and here we shall have to stop. All our stores gone and only one fishing-line! Something's got to be done!" Baldmoney never said a truer word, something *had* got to be done, but what?

"The fish won't bite either," said Dodder, gloomily casting in his line again. "I don't believe there's a fish round the place."

Sneezewort, gazing out over the grey ripples which were rising and falling off the island, uttered an exclamation.

"There she is! There's the *Dragonfly*!"

"It isn't, it's a bird!"

"'Tisn't; it's the boat!"

"Yes, you're right."

Far out, showing only now and again on the crest of a wave, they saw the ill-fated *Dragonfly* heading up the lake. Even as they watched it a larger wave than the rest broke over her and she slowly settled down. The bow cocked up and in another moment she went under.

"There she goes," said Baldmoney, "there goes the *Dragonfly* . . . the fruits of all our weeks of work, our only hope of reaching the Oak Pool alive."

\* \* \*

Dodder fished and fished, but never once did the tiny quill float show any sign of diving under. It bobbed up and down merrily, but not a fish showed itself. In despair Dodder hauled in his line and came off the willow.

It was indeed a gloomy morning—everything seemed to be working against them. Instead of the wind abating, it seemed to be increasing in violence, and the far shore and trim plantations were shut out in grey curtains of driving rain.

The gnomes found some shelter in a hollow of one of the black poplars, and there they crouched together for warmth, huddling together like storm-bound wrens.

"We can't stay here for ever with nothing in our bellies," said Sneezewort. "As far as I can see, we're here for keeps."

"If the boat had been tied up properly it would never have come adrift," muttered Dodder, scowling at Baldmoney.

"It's no good blaming me," returned that worthy. "We were all so dead beat, we couldn't do anything much last night; and, anyway, we couldn't have started this morning with this wind—no boat could live in it."

"I wish the herons hadn't gone," said Dodder at last. "If Sir Herne was here he'd help us, he gave me a lift up to Moss Mill, and I know he nests here on Poplar Island 'cos he told me so."

"Oh, it's no good wishing he'd turn up," said Baldmoney. "After their young are hatched they go off to the rivers and the coast. They wouldn't stay around here."

High above them the wind roared through the black poplar, and it seemed to be trying to tear the leaves from their hold. Nobody spoke, they just sat and listened to the storm and the continuous fret of waves on the shingle.

There was a woodpecker's hole in the trunk above them, but it did not look new. The bark was blackened round the lower edge. Sneezewort, idly looking at it, saw something stir on the rim. It was a draggled wild bee. It seemed to be creeping there for shelter. Poor thing! Perhaps it thought the summer had gone.

"This can't last for ever," said Baldmoney, as he gazed dolefully out over the tossing waters. "The sun will shine again; all storms blow over. Help will come in some way or another, you mark my words."

"Next time, let's see the boat is properly made fast," growled Dodder.

Then they began to quarrel, each trying to blame the other. The truth is they were all irritable because their little tummies were empty, and nothing makes a gnome (or a man for that matter) more irritable than to have nothing inside him.

The storm blew itself out by late afternoon and miraculously the sun suddenly burst forth from behind the clouds. The poor gnomes had had nothing to eat all day; they had crouched in the hollow under the trunk and gone to sleep.

But as soon as the sun came out, making every twig and leaf sparkle with a million diamonds, they felt renewed hope.

As the wind died away and the warm rays set everything

steaming (including the gnomes) a humming began up in the woodpecker's hole. First one bee appeared and then another, and soon a constant procession was going in and out. Baldmoney was the first to notice it.

"Look Dodder! . . . Hey! Sneezewort! . . . A wild bees' nest! Honey! Honey! Honey!"

Now there is nothing gnomes like more than honey. Every summer they go into the banks and hedges looking for wild bees' nests, which they raid as efficiently as fern-bears.

It did not take Baldmoney long to make up his mind. It was an easy tree to climb, with plenty of branches. He took off his skin coat and, with Cloudberry's knife in his teeth, he went up.

To cut through about three inches of bark and wood is no easy matter, but from long practice Baldmoney was almost as skillful as a woodpecker. He worked away for all he was worth and the bees didn't seem to mind. They did not perhaps realize what he was doing; anyway, he was so small, perhaps they thought he was a bird.

As Baldmoney worked, the chips fell rustling down among the ground ivy where the others were standing, looking up.

"You're working very hard, gnomes. . . ." A tiny reedy voice sounded in his ear, and a humble little bird, very like a mouse, with a thin, needle-like bill, slightly curved, and a curious serrated tail which she used as a prop against the trunk of the tree, came sidling round. It was Treecreeper.

"Hullo, Treecreeper," said Baldmoney, scarcely looking up, "sorry I've no time to talk, but we're simply starving. We're marooned, our boat's washed away, and we've lost our fishing-lines," and he went on cutting away at the rough tree trunk.

Buzz! Buzz! Buzz! Several worker bees, returning laden with pollen in their little honey bags, flew angrily around. There was too much activity outside their nesting hole and they were beginning to be suspicious. The guards at the entrance to the nest began to get wary, but that didn't worry Baldmoney as gnomes are as impervious as badgers to bee stings.

More and more bees began to gather; the humming grew. Treecreeper retired somewhat hastily when two bees settled on her spotted back. How hard Baldmoney worked! The sweat dripped off him and ran down the tree, then Sneezewort came up and took a turn. At last they were through and there came a hollow booming from within. There was a great turmoil in the camp.

Dodder could hardly see Baldmoney and Sneezewort for bees; they came out in such a swarm they were like a black whirling dust storm round the entrance to the nest. Baldmoney got his hand in at last and broke off pieces of the crisp, papery comb, full of lovely amber treasure. He put them in a dock leaf and Sneezewort passed it down. Baldmoney was black with bees. They crawled all over his head and hands, and some got inside his jacket and down his neck, and some became entangled in his beard, and they stung and stung and stung, but Baldmoney didn't mind a bit!

"There's always been a bees' nest in the poplar," said Treecreeper to Dodder. The little bird had again crept round the tree in a spiral, making Dodder jump. But Dodder did not answer, for he was so hungry and the smell and sight of the honey were almost too much for him. He was dribbling like a hungry puppy.

"Oh! *Do* be quick, Baldmoney; I'm *so* hungry," he called.

"Coming!" came the answer from above.

Down came Baldmoney and Sneezewort, the former with a dock leaf between his teeth full of honeycomb. It made an awful mess, for the sweet stuff oozed out of the leaf all over his jacket, but he was too hungry to notice it.

They ate the honey among the ground ivy at the foot of the tree, whilst the angry bees roared about the wood-pecker's hole overhead. The gnomes soon had honey all over themselves; it matted their beards and glued up their fin-gers; some of it ran down out of the corners of their mouths onto their skin coats; but wasn't it good, wasn't it a feast! All their past troubles seemed to be worth while. Poor bees!

\* \* \*

In a very short time there was very little honey left and barely a scrap of comb, but several wasps arrived and rather worried the gnomes by settling on their beards to suck the remnants of the feast, and they had to keep them off with a ceaseless winnowing of sticks.

After they had finished and washed the sticky stuff from their persons they set to work to make themselves a hut. After great deliberations and argument it was finally decided to build it in a tree; as Sneezewort said, "Let's have it up a tree; we don't know what wild animals live on the island, and anyway a house in a tree is much more fun than a house on the ground." Which after all was a very sensible remark (for Sneezewort).

So they set to work, collecting sticks, moss, and leaves, and gathering all the material at the foot of a spindly pine tree, the only one on the island. They chose the pine because usually it is an easy tree to climb, with plenty of branches.

As gnomes are observant little creatures, you may be sure they picked up some tips from Squirrel as to house-building in the tree tops. Of course Dodder, with his game leg, couldn't do much save gather sticks, and he left the actual building to Sneezewort and Baldmoney.

They found a branch fork about seven feet up which made a natural platform on which to lay the foundations, and the hut (or rather nest, because when finished it looked exactly like a very large wren's nest with the opening at the side) soon began to take shape.

They had to make a ladder to help Dodder up, for of course he could not climb as easily as the others. By dusk the house was completed and the gnomes were quite exhausted, for it had been hard work. How it brought back the old days in Crow Wood with Squirrel! They wished he was with them, life would have been so much jollier.

From the hut they could see out over the grey lake and look down into the dark, dark water, for even close to the island it was deep. They could see all the little pebbles on the shore and the ivy leaves far below. When the wind blew it played a song among the fir tassels just as it used to do in Squirrel's house in Crow Wood, a beautiful soothing sound.

If there had been plenty of food on the island all this would have been tremendous fun, for there's no fun quite like making huts, whether up in trees or on the ground.

By the look of things they would be on the island for some time, unless some kind friend should chance along. But as all the herons had gone away for their annual holiday, this was unlikely.

Next day Dodder, hunting about on the south foreshore, made a discovery. In the shallow water he found a small bed of freshwater mussels, huge shells which were almost as much as he could carry. With this glad news he hurried back to the others. He found them putting the finishing touches to the tree house.

"Food! Food!" he shouted. "As much as we want!"

Sneezewort and Baldmoney came running along the shore and very soon they were carrying the big shellfish up to the pine tree, stacking them against the trunk. This was indeed a piece of luck because Dodder's efforts with the fishing-line had still proved useless.

As dusk fell, Baldmoney, with some difficulty, got the fire going, for the sticks were damp, and soon a bright little blaze was burning at the foot of the pine, and Baldmoney drew out his knife and began opening the mussels.

"Did you ever taste such beauties?" said Dodder with his mouth full. "I do believe they are better than the Folly mussels. It's a pity Poplar Island isn't a little nearer home." (They had long since exhausted all the mussel beds near the Oak Pool.)

Sneezewort smacked his lips as he took a steaming morsel from the frying-pan. "I think this little spell will do us good; after all, we've been on the go since we left home, killing giants and Pan knows what." They were beginning to feel quite cheerful again.

When they had eaten all they could hold they lay round the red embers gossiping. It was this hour by the dying fire-light that the gnomes loved more than any other time. It was then they talked of so many things.

"Funny how a fire makes you want to stare and stare at it," said Dodder reflectively, blowing out a cloud of tobacco smoke and watching the glow of the red fire's core. "Men are just the same, so the hobgoblins used to tell me. There was a hobgoblin in the old farmhouse which stood where

Lucking's farm now is. He told me they sit, just like we do, staring into the embers. Of course, it is understandable in man, because a fire is the only bit of wildness left in his house; his surroundings are artificial, but a fire makes him think of the days when he lived as we do, out in the open with nothing but caves and hollow trees to shield him from the weather."

*   *   *

And so they chatted on and on. It was only natural that at last the conversation should turn to the real object of their journey.

"I know it's all very good fun living in a house in a tree on a desert island," began Baldmoney, "but we can't stay here indefinitely. We've got to build another boat. It's too far to swim to the shore and no animals live here who can help us. This really *is* an uninhabited island, except for the birds, and they can't help us much."

"That's true," replied Dodder, sucking his teeth, "we shall have to build something. But I've an idea. There are a lot of frogskins lying around, thanks to our good friends the herons. It won't take us long to build a coracle like our fishing-boats at home, and then we could choose our day when the sea is calm" (the lake was so vast to them that they called it the sea) "and then we can get to the shore. Of course, we can't build another *Dragonfly*—we haven't got the wood for one thing, and it would take too long."

"Supposing we *get* to the shore," said Sneezewort, "what then? Do we try and go on with our coracle?"

"No . . ." Dodder thought a minute. "We shall have to start for home. The journey won't take us long because we shall have the current to help us down. Let's have a look at the map, Baldmoney."

Baldmoney took off his waistcoat and spread it on the ivy leaves in the light of the fire and studied it carefully. It was beautifully drawn; the Oak Pool, Moss Mill, the rapids and waterfalls, Crow Wood, and Wood Pool, even the Gibbet Clearing, all were there.

"The Oak Pool is about four days' journey from here," said Dodder at last. "It should be an easy trip down; we will probably be able to shoot the rapids—we'd be back in no time."

An owl hooted at the far end of the island, and in the silence they could hear the low talk of water lapping on the south shore. "If only Owl would come and chat to us, he might help," said Sneezewort dreamily. Full of mussel and warmed by the genial glow of the fire, he was nearly asleep.

Far away a fox barked from the fir coverts on the shore. The gnomes could not suppress a shudder; it was like hearing the cry of a wolf. Again and again they had heard the distant howl of a fox during their trip up the Folly; always there came a creeping fear, which was instinctive.

"It's a good thing we're on an island," said Baldmoney.

He was putting the finishing touches to a little drawing of their hut in the tree. "I don't much fancy this country; it smells of wood dogs."

Slowly the fire died away; nobody spoke. They lay on their backs warming their toes and watching the trembling stars high above and the dark rustling crown of the black poplars etched against the velvet sky.

"It's a pity we couldn't have found the Folly Source and Cloudberry," said Baldmoney. He had put on his waistcoat again and was looking out through the opening of the hut at the dim obscurity of the vast water. . . . "That writing on the bridge, it did give one a little encouragement."

"Perhaps it's all for the best," replied Dodder. "Anyway, even if we don't find Cloudberry, this trip will have been worth while."

Some diving bird called across the water and in the pine tree the wind rustled softly, blowing the sparks about in the dying embers of the fire. Tiny stealthy noises came from all around them, faint rustlings and clickings, the night noises of the wild.

What did the future hold for the three little gnomes, what adventures, what joys, what sorrows—who could tell?

❧

# CHAPTER 14

# The Shark

WHEN THE GNOMES SET TO work to make the frogskin coracle they had some difficulty in finding the right wood for the job. It had to be pliable and easily bent and there were few willows on the island. But after a day or two it began to take shape.

At first they thought of fitting paddles like those on the *Dragonfly*, but that idea was abandoned after a few experiments. The craft was too frail to stand the strain and it was decided to use sail alone.

It took a long time to scrape the frogskins clean and make them pliable. This was done by soaking them in water and steaming them by the fire. They worked hard, for time was against them. Bar the mussels and the honey (which would soon be exhausted) there was nothing to eat on the island, and despite persistent efforts by Dodder to catch fish with the last remaining hook and line, all his efforts were of no avail.

This was very curious. Dodder was an expert, and there

must have been fish round the island, indeed he had caught a glimpse of several nervous shoals of roachlings, but they all seemed extremely shy and would not look at his bait. And then one evening, about ten days after they had been cast away, Dodder suddenly found the cause.

He was fishing as usual from his favorite perch (a branch which overhung the water) and as he gazed down into the clear depths below he was aware of a vast dim shape, slowly rising under the log. It was quite a second or two before he realized what it was, a monstrous fish quite three feet long, barred like a giant mackerel and with a cruel shovel mouth. Its wicked little eyes swiveled this way and that and its barred fins trembled ever so slightly. It rose from the dark depths exactly like an airship and at last came to rest about a foot below the surface, its pale gills blowing slightly as it hung poised in the water.

It was a monster pike, the shark of fresh water! Dodder was so horrified, he was incapable of movement; he just sat rooted to the log not daring to lift his line. He could see the red worm impaled on his hook wriggling frantically, but he dare not lift it out.

Then there was a sudden "boil" and the rod was torn from his grasp. Away it went, hook, line, rod, everything, and Dodder fell off the stump backwards, landing by the merest chance on the very fringe of the water, among the ground ivy.

He gathered himself together and hurried away, as fast

as his game leg would carry him, towards their camp.

He found the others bent over their task.

"Oh, dear, I've had such a scare," he gasped, flinging himself down among the willow chips and scraps of skin.

"What is it, Dodder?"

But poor old Dodder could only lie and gasp. Baldmoney sprang to his feet, drawing his knife and glaring into the shadows under the trees.

"What is it, Dodder . . . a wood dog?"

"No . . . a shark, a perfectly enormous shark, as big . . . as big, as . . ." Dodder was at a loss to give them any comparison. He stretched wide his arms, but that was not wide enough, he looked about him but there was nothing large enough to demonstrate the length of the pike. At last he gasped, "Well, it was the biggest fish *I've* ever seen; it could swallow us all up, *Dragonfly* as well, and then have room for more!"

The others shuddered.

"*That's* why we can't catch any fish here; *that's* why even the water-hens won't come near us. It's the shark, that's what it is!"

"And something else has happened," added Dodder, nearly on the verge of tears: "he's gone off with my rod, line, hook, and everything; we're sick to death of mussels and we have finished the honey. Unless we can get away soon we're going to starve!"

Baldmoney looked at the coracle. It was nearly completed, it only needed drying in the sun and one more willow strut adding. The mast was fitted, it should be ready soon. One thing was evident: if they did get safely away from Poplar Island they must turn for home. To continue the journey provisionless and without fishing-tackle (which would take too long to make) was a risky proceeding. Besides, the new boat would not sail so well as the *Dragonfly*, and it would be impossible to tack up the Folly with so small a mainsail.

No, there was nothing for it, once safely away they must turn for home and let the current carry them back downstream. It was disappointing, bitterly disappointing, but there it was. They must acknowledge defeat with a good grace. After all, they had had good fun, one way or another, and their adventure in Crow Wood alone was worth all the perils they had survived so successfully.

\* \* \*

Two mornings later Baldmoney announced that the coracle was finished.

A slight breeze was blowing from the west and the sky was overcast.

The gnomes were not sorry to leave. The diet of mussel had little nourishment in it and they wanted a change of food. A little after sunrise they pulled the craft down the bank and pushed it into the water. It floated well, though it was a ticklish business getting aboard, for coracles are easily upset. There was calm water close to the shore, so they had to paddle with sticks.

As they drew slowly away they looked back at the island, which they fondly hoped they were leaving for good. Gradually the land receded. They could see the tree where they found the wild bees' nest, and the marks of their camp fire among the stones, and they felt no regretful pangs. They could see also the lone pine where they had built their house, but they were not sorry to see the last of it, either.

A string of duck passed across, slanting down in a long line. They were the first ducks the gnomes had seen since they were cast away. On all sides were signs and sounds of autumn. Rooks cawed lazily, climbing round and round in an immense spiral, high in the sky, a habit they have in fine autumn weather. Mist lay over the land, but as the sun rose it began to clear and there was the pearly prospect of a glorious day.

The coracle sailed well; Baldmoney and Sneezewort were proud of their handiwork. And indeed, the little craft was beautifully constructed, completely watertight, and it rode the ripples splendidly. As there were no seats the gnomes had to sit on the floor, all together in a bunch. It would not have taken much to capsize the whole affair and Dodder remarked it was a good thing that they were heading for home. Once clear of the island they felt the breeze and Baldmoney gingerly hoisted the dock-leaf sail.

When they were about forty yards out from the island, Dodder, who was helping to steer with the aid of his paddle, went hot all over, and his eyes nearly popped out of his head. Three little heads swiveled round, six little eyes bulged, two beards bristled.

"The shark!"

"Where? Where?"

"Behind us; it's following us—we're lost!"

Looking closely through the little clear ripples which were breaking over one another in tiny bubbles under their wake they saw the ghostly shape of the giant shark. It was coming after them without effort, seeming never to move a fin, just steadily gliding along like a submarine.

"Don't splash the paddles," whispered the terrified Dodder. "When we get into the breeze we may draw away."

But after a second or two it looked as if the pike meant business. He was coming closer and they could see the wicked green head, shaped like an enormous boot, with two little holes which might have been his nose.

And then the worst happened!

The wind, which had been quite fresh, suddenly dropped, and the coracle, slowly spinning round, came almost to a standstill—becalmed!

Baldmoney and Sneezewort snatched up the paddles. They were still only a short way from the island and it was a *very* long way to the mainland—they could hardly see it for mist. Dodder shuddered when he thought of the deep deep water below them and only the thin skin of the coracle between them and the dark ocean and rows of devouring teeth!

Splash! splash! went the paddles as the coracle began to head back towards the island which they so fondly hoped to have left for ever. Better starvation than to be eaten alive by a shark! Yes indeed! But they were still many yards from the shore, and Sneezewort, getting panicky, began to "catch crabs," which meant he was dipping his paddle too deeply under the surface.

The coracle began to rock like a cork. But they were working their way back by degrees. First it was fifty yards, then thirty, then twenty. Nearer and nearer came Poplar Island; they saw the comfortable solid look of the stones, the ground ivy, the thick bushes, and the tall trees.

Meanwhile the pike, who was still following, saw his prey escaping. He did not know exactly what the thing was which scurried in front of him, but it moved swiftly and looked uncommonly like the round body of a duckling, and he was hungry.

With one stroke of his broad tail he dashed in, so quickly the eye could scarcely follow, and the next moment the coracle, Dodder, Sneezewort, and Baldmoney disappeared in a swirl of bubbles!

\* \* \*

By some merciful chance (perhaps Pan was taking care of them) all three gnomes were flung clear when the pike attacked them. And more fortunate still, the mast of the coracle became wedged across the cruel mouth, with its fearsome array of needle-like teeth, gagging the hideous monster.

He would have liked to swallow the three gnomes, but he could not; he lashed and threshed like a huge whale, his glaring eyes rolling, and his barred tail churning the water, sending the spray flying in all directions in spasms of impotent rage.

Meanwhile, Baldmoney had got Dodder by the collar and was pulling him ashore. Sneezewort had already scrambled out unhurt and all three were none the worse for their adventure. But it had been a narrow shave.

Not far away the water still continued to swirl and boil, for the monster fish was vainly endeavoring to rid himself of the sharp gag which wedged his cruel jaws apart.

But the gnomes did not wait to see what happened to *him*. They scurried away among the ground ivy and a few seconds later were back in their old camp.

\* \* \*

"Well," said Dodder rather grimly (they had got the fire going and were now dry once more), "here we are, back on this beastly desert island, and here, if you ask me, we shall stop. The only thing we have is our sleeping-bags" (these had floated clear when the coracle overturned), "and we've no fishing-lines—even if we had it wouldn't be much use, we've no boat—no honey, all we've got to eat is mussel, and I'm sick at the sight of the stuff. If we eat much more we shall get scurvy; all mariners suffer from scurvy. I've never known such a barren, beastly, uninhabited island. Unless Heron or somebody comes along we're in a nice mess," and Dodder kicked savagely at a stone with his good leg.

"*I* think we ought to be jolly glad we aren't inside the shark," remarked Baldmoney in a relieved voice.

"Well said," squeaked Sneezewort. "We must be thankful for all small mercies. Something will turn up, you mark my words." But Sneezewort didn't really hold much hope in his heart of hearts.

"We'll be here until the first frosts, if you ask me," growled Dodder, "and then we shall die of cold."

"Well, the lake might freeze over," remarked Baldmoney brightly, "and then we could walk ashore!"

"Oh yes! And walk all the way back to the Oak Pool, I suppose," sneered Dodder, "with no food, no warm clothes, and no place to sleep at night, save in the snow—*very* sensible!"

It was obviously no good arguing with Dodder while he was in this mood, so the others kept wisely silent.

All they could do was to wait and hope that something

would turn up, or some kind friend carry word of their plight to the otters or the Stream People. The gnomes knew that the Stream Folk would move heaven and earth to save them, were they told of the state of things.

Next day they made a thorough exploration of the island in search of some hidden source of food. Had it been earlier in the year there would have been birds' eggs, but nearly all the feathered folk, even the treecreeper, had gone away and there was nothing left but empty nests.

A few young swallows still haunted the willow, but they were so taken up with their coming journey they wouldn't even deign to notice the gnomes.

Truth to say, things were looking very black indeed. The continued diet of mussel was making them all ill, and Dodder was so weak he could hardly get about. He lay all day inside the house, rolled up in his sleeping-bag. There wasn't even a blackberry on the island. Sneezewort, exploring the southern end, found a few unripe nuts, but they were soon eaten.

*     *     *

The golden autumn weather seemed to be making amends—the sunlight was different, hazy, and more silver than gold.

Quite miraculously spiders' webs appeared on every leaf and bush, like silver hammocks slung to catch the morning dew, beautifully fashioned and anchored by long silken cables to stick and leaf. The tall poplars began to burn with spots of yellow, and from the distant shore came the clatter of binders in the cornfields. The gnomes could see little figures working among the sheaves, stooking them up in neat rows in readiness for the carts.

A foolish red robin haunted the island for a week. The gnomes implored it to take a message to the Stream People, or Heron, but it was either too stupid or too lazy to do so. It just sat on a yellowing sprig of dogwood and sang melancholy piping songs all day long until the gnomes threw stones at it. They needed cheering up, anyway.

If only the King of Fishers would come along! He would do all he could to help; but why *should* he come along? There were no fish to be caught by the island.

I don't know what would have happened had not Sneezewort, walking one evening round the shore, found the body of the shark washed up on the shingle. It was quite fresh, though rather thin. The gag of wood, which was the mast of the coracle, was wedged firmly in its jaws and it had starved to death. Pike live on small fish or, indeed, anything they can catch and master, but they catch their prey with their deft snapping jaws. This monster had been powerless.

There was not much meat on the long rakish body, and luckily the water-rats had not had a chance at it, otherwise there would have been little left.

But for the first time for days they had a good square

meal and felt new gnomes after it.

Now that the shark was dead, perhaps the little fish would come back, though the gnomes had no hooks and lines to catch them with. It is true they could soon make more hooks, but on the island there was no horsehair which they could use for gut, and the hook alone would be useless.

Perhaps they could build another boat. But they had used up all the frogskins, and they had not the heart to build another wooden boat, or, for that matter, the strength. For these poor little gnomes were really slowly starving to death. But while there is life there is hope, and perhaps the finding of the pike marked a new turn of events and meant that their luck had changed.

Dodder remembered the night in Crow Wood when he had prayed to Pan to deliver the Wood People from Giant Grum. He would pray again.

He went off alone under the dark bushes and was gone for an hour. Perhaps Pan would hear them and send deliverance. But prayers are not always answered by return of post, so to speak, or in the way we think they should be answered.

When next morning no Heron appeared, or the sleek and friendly head of an otter did not bob out of the mistwreathed water, Dodder thought that Pan had not heard and that he had forgotten his children. Perhaps Pan willed them to die; after all, they had lived for a very long time.

How fast the summer was going now! It was sad to see the leaves falling. They drifted in colored rafts upon the quiet waters, so solid that you might have thought you could walk upon them! They lay all over the island among the ivy, and sometimes a puff of wind made them whirl and dance round and round as though they were alive.

One by one the swallows departed until there were no birds left at all; even the gloomy little robin (useless bird) went away, and the only song was the wind in the trees and the melancholy lap, lap, of ripples on the barren stones.

# CHAPTER 15

## The "Jeanie Deans"

THE TWENTY-NINTH OF September was Robin Clobber's birthday, and what a day to look forward to!

You know what it is to go to bed on Christmas Eve, or some other important "eve," and think "Tomorrow is the great day: I'm going to do so and so!"

So it was with Robin. He couldn't for the life of him go to sleep. He tossed and turned in his little bed, his mind would give him no rest.

It was a cozy little room, this bedroom, with white walls hung with gay John Hassall prints, a toy cupboard full of lead soldiers, model tanks and airplanes, kites and I don't know what. Some boys might have been spoilt, but Robin wasn't. He was a sensible boy for his age.

Now, what would Daddy and Mummy give him for a birthday present? Not a bicycle—he had one at Christmas; he didn't want any more tanks, though he could do with some "Valentines" to complete his collection, and a Spitfire wouldn't come amiss, one that really flew (all his others were model ones which couldn't fly a yard). A gun ? No, he wasn't quite old enough; he'd like to have a new .410 double barrel, the one in the red Army and Navy catalogue downstairs.

A knife? No, he had a good knife. He couldn't think what it would be but it was sure to be nice.

\* \* \*

On the wall was a cuckoo clock with fir cone weights. When it struck the hour a little blue-and-white bird came out of its house and bowed, and one of the fir cones rattled down quickly, swinging against the wall. "Tick tock, tick tock!" Robin thought on. A fishing-rod? Well, that was a good guess, a fishing-rod would be nice. He might go down to the bridge on the lake and catch some trout with it. He would fry them in a pan like the little men he saw that day by the stone bridge. Robin wondered where they were now, what they were doing; he would like to see them again.

"Tick tock, tick tock." Robin's eyes slowly closed. "Tick tock, tick tock!"

\* \* \*

On the breakfast table was a heap of parcels and letters, all for Robin. A scribbling diary from the maids, complete with pencil, which fitted neatly in the back, a fountain pen from Jarvis the butler, chocolates, books, a Spitfire from Uncle Ernest (but it couldn't fly), a big box of peppermint creams, and then . . . this long, heavy parcel from Daddy and Mummy.

It was wrapped up in brown paper and tied securely with string and it had a Basset Lowke label. Good omen! He saved this parcel until last, then, with trembling fingers undid the string.

Two layers of paper, one thick and one thin, and then a big white cardboard box.

Off came the lid. . . . Tissue paper carefully wrapped round something heavy, long, and hard. What could it be? When Robin unwrapped the heavy thing he was quite dazed for a minute with delight.

It was an exquisite model of a coasting steamer, the *Jeanie Deans*, smelling of spick-and-span enamel! It had a proper hold, full of little hooped wooden barrels and sacks, two derricks which really worked with chains and hooks, lifeboats slung on working davits, heavy iron anchors which were just like real ones, a funnel, black and red, portholes, and coils of rope neatly stacked on pine decking, a cozy cabin with a companion-way, little pictures on the walls, and a proper fo'c'sle, with a door which opened and shut. It even had a wireless aerial. Was there ever such a thing made as this wonderful ship? You wound it up by a key inside the funnel. This was not as it should be, of course, but you couldn't have everything, and anyway you would never have noticed it, so cleverly was the mechanism concealed, and there was a spare winding key which was kept in the fo'c'sle. Robin gazed at the wondrous ship in a trance.

Mummy showed him how it worked by winding it up inside the funnel (as if Robin didn't know!) and after breakfast they went down to the lake, Robin clasping the ship in his arms (it was all he could do to carry it). Mummy insisted on showing him how to hold the red propellers under the stern. As she wound the engine up she didn't notice the little lever close to the stern which locked the propellers, but ladies aren't really very mechanically minded! Robin was afraid something would happen, the spring would break, or the barrels would drop out of the hold. Then he remembered that on her first voyage she should carry some sort of cargo. The little sacks were filled with sawdust—that was silly. The barrels were empty, that would never do—she must carry a cargo. Robin had an idea. The *Jeanie Deans* should be part of a convoy, carrying food across to Britain, with the U-boats and the German dive-bombers after her, and the lake should be the Atlantic. A wonderful idea!

So before she was launched, Robin decided he would fill the little sacks and barrels with food. Close by was a big bramble bush covered with juicy blackberries; they would do for oranges. Everyone likes oranges, and blackberries were nearly as nice. He collected a hatful (Mummy helped him) and packed them neatly away in the barrels. Each barrel held three juicy blackberries and there were fifteen barrels in the hold. Then he put his hand in his pocket and brought out a handful of peppermint creams. He packed the sweets away in the bags (there were eleven sacks), and then, her cargo complete, and fully laden, the *Jeanie Deans* was ready for her first perilous voyage.

Robin only hoped that some sneaking U-boat commander was not watching him through his periscope!

The *Jeanie Deans* was put carefully into the water, and Robin, who was now holding the propellers, which were straining to go against his fingers, gave the ship a gentle push. Away she went, steaming bravely from the shore on her first voyage, fully laden with barrels and merchandise, a brave sight!

The sun shone, the water sparkled, the reeds bent in the wind, and the leaves fell all around.

Ahead of the *Jeanie Deans* was a mass of leaves, and Robin thought she would stick fast in them. But the powerful engine made light of the matter and she got safely through.

Why was it that Mummy had not altered the rudder before putting it in the water? Robin began to feel nervous.

Out and out into the lake went the little ship, tiny wavelets breaking against her painted bows, but her master and mate did not steer again for the shore. The *Jeanie Deans* was evidently bound for Britain, and no thought of coming back to port. Why should she? It was a glorious morning, just the weather for a long sea voyage, so on she went, out into the shining dazzle of the water.

Robin began to run along the bank; Mummy, too, was anxious—how silly of her to forget the rudder! Just like a woman! Surely the spring would soon run down and the ship would drift back to shore! But no, on she went, getting smaller and smaller on the dazzling expanse of the lake. Robin began to cry . . . his lovely boat, the loveliest birthday present he had ever had! His joy was turned to sudden bitterness, his birthday spoilt.

"It's all right, Robin; we'll get it back in no time. . . . I'll tell them to get the punt out." (She did not know that the punt, which was kept in the boathouse at the far end of the lake, was too leaky to float, from long disuse.) "Don't cry, Robin; it's bound to come to the side."

The *Jeanie Deans* was now only a tiny speck far out on the breast of the shining ocean. Robin flung himself down on the grass and wept bitter tears.

\* \* \*

The 29th of September found the gnomes in a bad way. Despite the glorious sun and sparkling water, and the brilliant colors already showing in the leaves of the island trees and bushes, the gnomes were in no mood for admiring the beauties of the lovely autumn morning.

Dodder was definitely weaker, and the others were in an even worse state. All through the day they lay in the hut, feeling too feeble to move.

When the sun began to sink and the breeze, which all

day had been blowing off the land, dropped, Dodder got up and hobbled unsteadily along the shore. He was in a desperate frame of mind. In some ways he felt responsible for the expedition.

You will remember he was the oldest gnome of the three and the wisest. He had urged that the voyage be continued, and he now heartily wished he had persuaded the others to turn back after killing the giant in Crow Wood—surely that feat was enough to go on with!

He hobbled along over the stones, following the curve of the beach. In one sheltered bay he came upon web footmarks in the soft sand and some grey feathers. Dodder knew the feathers of every bird that flew. He recognized them at once as goose feathers. That was curious . . . they had seen no geese, tame or wild, on the lake. It was just possible wild geese did rest here on their spring and autumn migrations, for it was a large sheet of water, and the feathers had lain there a long time, so he thought no more about it. Everything was so peaceful and beautiful. The lake was just like a huge polished mirror and the atmosphere so clear that he could see the far shore with its thick woods and, rising over the trees, a thin mist of smoke from the chimneys of the big house.

He sat down on a stone and lit a pipe. At this rate they couldn't last out much longer. If only the herons would come back, or poor Otter's brothers pay them a visit. But he knew why they shunned the place. It was the lack of fish. Even the frogs kept away because of the herons.

Over the water danced a cloud of midges, up and down, up and down; a wonderful night for fishing, if only he had his hook and line. Already there were signs of more fish about the island; now that the shark was no more, they were returning. But they could not be caught without fishing-lines. He hid his face in his hands.

Well, there wasn't much else he could do. He had prayed to Pan, and Pan hadn't heard him; perhaps he was busy elsewhere in another part of the country, looking after his big family of animals, and had no time to bother with three castaway gnomes. If his prayer was meant to be answered, surely it would have been by now?

Dodder got up and wandered on. Everywhere bare stones and bushes with not a berry on them, no mushrooms here because there was no grass, truly a barren wilderness. He was thirsty and remembered that Baldmoney had told him of a little spring farther along the shore. At any rate they did not lack water, and both gnomes and men can live for days on water alone; it is the lack of it which kills quicker than lack of food.

He soon found himself in a part of the island he had never been before. The trees came right down to the water's edge, overhanging it, and here and there were massive boulders and, of course, the interminable ground ivy.

At last he heard the distant tinkling of running water. It must be the spring! On climbing over a large fallen tree he came upon it, bubbling fresh and clear out of a little natural basin in the rock. He knelt down and drank greedily, wetting his beard. The water was delicious and he took long draughts. Then he felt better.

As he raised his eyes, he saw something sticking over the top of a large stone a little way down the shore, something painted black and red. *Whatever* could it be? He rubbed his eyes and looked again and then, seeing it did not move, he cautiously approached it, crawling through the ground ivy.

Slowly the object came into view . . . a big red-and-black funnel, quite seven inches high! Another squirm and he peeped round the rock and he was so flabbergasted he lay quite still. It was a huge steamer, a beautiful craft, with not a scratch on her paintwork. There she lay with her bows on a little spit of white sand, quite motionless. No smoke rose from the funnel and there was no sign of life on board; it was far too small to carry a human crew. A thought flashed through his mind—could it be Cloudberry's? It might be. By some strange chance he might have built the boat, though it seemed unbelievable. For a long time he lay watching for any sign of life on deck, then he boldly crept closer until he was right under her bows. He saw JEANIE DEANS; in big gold letters painted on either side of the bows and the heavy anchors hanging down. She flew no flag, but her paintwork gleamed as spick and span as a silver roach. There was a little ladder made of tarred rope hanging over the side and, despite his game leg, Dodder managed, after a struggle, to reach it. Rung by rung he hauled himself up until he was standing on the pitch-pine decking.

His heart beat wildly. Supposing someone was on board! He stood for a long time listening and then very cautiously peeped in at the saloon door. Inside was a table with a little lamp hanging over it, and four bunks let into the walls, empty and without bedding. At the far end of the saloon was a picture of King George VI and Queen Elizabeth and the two Princesses. So she was an English ship! He went inside, examined the bunks, admired the pictures and had a good look round. Once he thought he heard steps outside and crept under the table, but it was only his imagination. In one corner of the cabin was a cupboard let into the wall. Inside he found six small tin plates, six large ones, a carving knife, forks and spoons, and a little copper stew-pan.

He came out of the cabin and then began a thorough search all over the ship. He lifted the covers off the two lifeboats. Inside each was a pair of oars and a coil of rope. Everything smelt of paint and clean, new wood.

He went into the fo'c'sle and there found a bright hollow object with an oval ring at one end. He lifted it up and blew down it. He thought it might be some sort of musical instrument. Perhaps the captain played it, or could it be the bos'n's pipe ? No, it was too big (he did not know it was the spare key). He scratched his beard and took off his cap, but he couldn't make head nor tail of it. Then he went along the deck to the hold and peeped fearfully in. There was a little ladder which let down the side. He could see rows of barrels and in one corner a little pile of sacks.

So the *Jeanie Deans* was carrying a cargo. Perhaps it was food. Food! Dodder's mouth began to water. He was suddenly aware that he was very hungry. He climbed down the ladder and gingerly approached the barrels. When he took the top off the first one he could have cried with joy. It was full of the loveliest, juiciest blackberries he had ever seen! But he didn't take one—he remembered Baldmoney and Sneezewort back in camp, starving and weak and hardly able to stand.

Next he opened the mouth of one of the sacks; large round white things, like sugar engine domes, were inside—whatever were they? Gingerly he broke off a piece. OOOO! but it was good! He had never tasted anything so delicious in his life as peppermint creams!

So Pan had not forgotten them after all.

* * *

As darkness fell, three little gnomes, carrying bundles, might have been seen picking their way among the stones towards the stranded steamer.

Dodder had returned to camp with the staggering news, and it was decided to return to the ship with all haste. Food was there, and there also seemed to lie their only chance of ever getting away from the island.

After Sneezewort and Baldmoney had toured the ship (as delighted and amazed as Dodder with this wonderful answer to their prayers), they forgathered in the cabin to talk things over.

The rising moon cast an eerie light through one of the portholes and in the half-darkness could be heard the sound of juicy suckings, for they had brought some peppermint creams and blackberries up from the hold to ease the pangs of hunger.

The first thing to be considered was the problem of getting away from the island.

Dodder, having finished his meal, wiped his mouth on his sleeve, squeezed the juice out of his long beard and lit his pipe. Then he began:

"Now, Baldmoney and Sneezewort, we've got to do a lot of thinking. First, the ship is aground, and it isn't going to be easy to get her off, and once off we've got to find how she works. Below, in the engine-room, there are levers and cogs, springs and bolts, which I don't understand at all. But, gnomes" (and here Dodder brandished his pipe), "we've got to move with the times. I have no doubt, if we think long enough, we shall find a way out of this difficulty and discover the secret of how the engine works. We must all use our heads and be intelligent. Pan wouldn't have sent us this boat if we couldn't sail it.

"Here we are, in a brand-new spanking steamer, but as she stands she's useless. It's true we've got food now to last us for a week or two, but that isn't going to last for ever, and the sooner we get busy the better.

"Who knows? The owner of this ship might come along and find us here; we should be arrested and thrown into prison, because, really, it does not belong to us at all!

"It may belong to some other gnomes. Remember, we have always lived by the Folly, in the Oak Pool, and never stirred from the place. I see now, that was a mistake. We thought we were the only gnomes left in England . . . well, perhaps we were wrong. Cloudberry may have met some other gnomes—they may even have built this boat. After all, what would humans want with a ship of this size? Her owner and crew may be even now on the island; they may return at any moment!"

The gnomes sat in the moonlit cabin, listening. After Dodder's last remark they began to imagine things. Baldmoney went out on deck and looked about.

It was a serenely calm night. The moon, half full, rode in a clear sky, the trees rustled softly. Something fell with a faint splash not far away and he saw gleaming rings widening on the still water. But it was only a leaf which had fallen from one of the bushes.

In the moonlight the *Jeanie Deans* seemed even more imposing, with her huge funnel slightly slanting against its background of stars, her gleaming bridge, whity-green in the moonlight, and dark shadows lurking in the hold. But, beyond the faint noises of the night, the wind amongst the trees, and the occasional splash of a falling leaf or stick, all was still.

The gnomes began once again to explore the ship, but after about an hour they were no nearer the solving of the difficulty. What power on earth could move the silent hulking vessel which, so perfect and amazing, lay like a heavy sleeping monster on the white sand of the little bay!

Baldmoney climbed on Sneezewort's shoulder and peeped down the funnel. He saw the vertical steel rod inside, but it was inexplicable as everything else about the ship. Then Dodder remembered the bright thing in the fo'c'sle. He brought it along and showed it to the others. Baldmoney, perched on the funnel, had it passed up to him. He turned it over and over and then, a sudden idea occurring to him, he pushed it over the rod inside the funnel; it fitted perfectly!

Perhaps this was the secret. But when he tried to turn the key (for, of course, it *was* the key, not only to the engine, but to all their difficulties) it would not budge an inch. Then Dodder moved the locking lever against the side. Nothing happened! He twiddled the spokes of the steering wheel, still nothing happened, save that the rudder moved, making a little slapping noise in the water.

The gnomes pulled their beards and talked in low voices. No . . . that bright thing that fitted in the funnel *must* be something to do with the engine! Sneezewort climbed up and tried to turn it, then they both pushed and pulled. Dodder passed them up his stout cudgel stick which he always carried. They put it through the bow of the key and tried to make it work as a lever.

"Push," hissed Baldmoney to the struggling Sneezewort.

"Pull," groaned Sneezewort, little beads of sweat forming on his brow.

Strange clickings started, and from the interior of the engine-room came a sudden whirring sound, as of a caged monster, which scared them out of their wits. The gnomes were so surprised that they let go of Dodder's stick, which whizzed round rapidly, knocking both of them clean off the funnel. They fell on the deck with an awful bump, but luckily were unhurt.

Dodder was very excited. "I felt her move," he shouted. "We're on the right track—that's the secret right enough, boys!"

They climbed down to the sand and tried to push her off, but she would not stir. In starting the engine they had driven her even farther aground, and she had no reversing gear. Baldmoney came down the rope ladder and lent a hand too, using sticks as levers. They pushed and pushed in the moonlight for all they were worth.

"She's moving," gasped Dodder. "One more heave—one, two, three, *now!*" Then . . . very gradually, the *Jeanie Deans* slipped back and the next moment she was floating in deep water just off shore, gently turning round, and showing her full and lovely lines. The excited gnomes clambered back up the rope ladder and the next moment all were aboard. A tiny breeze puffed once across the water and the big ship swung yet farther from the shore.

The gnomes fitted the key into the funnel again and wound the engine up, the ingenious Dodder having found the purpose of the checking lever. Sneezewort and Baldmoney pushed and pulled until they were quite out of breath. At last the key would turn no more—the ship was ready to start.

They made fast the little lifeboats, buttoning on the canvas covers, and when all was ready, Dodder took the wheel. The bows of the *Jeanie Deans* were pointing away from Poplar Island, for the gentle night breeze had taken her out still farther into the lake. Baldmoney went forward to the bridge beside Dodder, and Sneezewort went below to get the supper ready.

The checking lever was pushed down and the next moment the *Jeanie Deans* began to move. Her decks trembled slightly, there was a sweet purring noise from the engine and very gently she gathered speed. What a wonderful moment that was, to feel the ship suddenly become alive, so full of power and movement! Down in the saloon the plates rattled gently on the table, tiny creaks and squeaks sounded on all sides, the pictures of King George VI and his Queen and the two Princesses trembled gently on the walls.

Sneezewort felt very important, as, with sleeves rolled up, he busied himself over the galley stove. I'm afraid he also ate far too many peppermint creams, but it was an opportunity not to be missed.

The ripples chirped merrily under the bows as the ship slipped steadily through the water. The dark mass of Poplar Island dropped astern, and soon they were out on the shining expanse of the moonlit lake. Dodder puffed happily at his pipe, intensely excited at the thrill of the wonderful ship. This was a bit better than sweating at the rough homemade paddles of the *Dragonfly*! A jolly sight better! Over him rose the funnel and the tapering mast and far above he saw the expanse of glittering stars.

Every ten minutes or so it was necessary to wind the engine up again, but even after it had stopped she had considerable "way" on her, so they did not lose much distance.

The gnomes made up a sea chantey to sing whilst they wound the key. It is difficult to translate into English from gnome language, but the gist of it was this:

# CLOCKWORK CHANTY

*Music by* WALTER PITCHFORD

Jean - ie Deans, Our Skip - per's luck - y find, So

heave the key a - round, me boys, And wind, wind, wind.

The stalwart three,
Stout gnomes are we,
See how we pull together;
So heave the key around, me boys
And never mind the weather;
Sing happy ho, the *Jeanie Deans*,
Our skipper's lucky find,
So heave the key around, me boys,
And wind, wind, wind.

It went to a good tune and helped the work along
wonderfully.

Dodder, manning the wheel, was faced with a problem which suddenly presented itself. Should he turn the nose of the *Jeanie Deans* downstream or should he steer north! Now that Poplar Island was left behind it was easier to think more clearly.

With this beautiful boat the whole problem had been altered. It was certainly worth exploring the Folly a little higher. They still had a week or two before winter came. Yes, the fate, not only of the *Jeanie Deans*, but of the gnomes themselves, lay in his hands. It was a tremendous decision to take.

From below came the delicious smell of stewed blackberries; Sneezewort was whistling at his work. Baldmoney, chewing a peppermint cream, was drawing something on his map with a hot skewer, on the top of the cabin skylight. How they trusted him, implicitly! It was rather pathetic, and he suddenly felt very old and wise.

Then, with a silent prayer to Pan, Dodder twiddled the spokes of the wheel. The bows of the *Jeanie Deans* crept round until they pointed northwards. Dodder had made up his mind. They would go ON! They sailed all night, making steady progress, and when Dodder became tired, Baldmoney took a turn at the wheel.

Slowly the moon sank lower, to the east the horizon began to grey, and the starlings left the reed beds where they had been roosting.

On either side the shore began to close in, and very soon they came to the Folly brook again, where it ran into the lake. The same old Folly! It was good to see it, as bright and jolly as ever!

When at last the sun began to climb the sky over the rounded elm trees on the shore, they had left the lake far behind. The engines were still purring sweetly and the gnomes felt exultantly happy.

It was not until they had progressed a long way that Dodder suggested that they should find a quiet place to tie up for the day. The *Jeanie Deans* was a conspicuous object with her shining paintwork, and might attract attention.

At last they rounded a bend in the stream and saw a dense reed bed under some alder bushes. Dodder stopped the propellers by pulling up the checking lever and the *Jeanie Deans* glided as gracefully as a swan among the rusty sedge swords.

Baldmoney and Sneezewort ran forrard and let go the anchor, which went tumbling down with a loud splash into the water, sending terrified minnows darting in all directions. All around were the friendly reeds and rushes; it was good to smell the land again and to know that all chances of starvation were gone. The bushes were thick with berries; as soon as they found some horsehair they could fish again (the Folly was alive with fry—the gnomes had noticed them darting before them upstream). They were back once more in the land of plenty, and all their perils seemed to lie behind them.

After seeing that the ship was securely anchored and safe from prying eyes they went below and turned into their bunks. Worn out with excitement, they slept the sun round, safe in the green sanctuary of the thick reeds.

# CHAPTER 16

# Hallowe'en

HAVE YOU EVER LAIN out of doors by a camp fire, on an
autumn night, far away from anywhere? It is rather a
wonderful experience.

The three gnomes are sitting round their little camp fire
now, watching the wavering sparks going up and up to lose
themselves among the trees. Do you remember the way the
light from the fire illuminated the leaves overhead, making
them so mysterious and lovely, like some sort of theatrical
setting, and the creepy feeling you experienced when you
looked beyond the warm circle of the fire into the blue-
black outer world? The darkness, full of mystery and adventure, crowds around and hems you in.

So it was for the gnomes, and it was Hallowe'en!

Close by ran the Folly, talking to itself in all manner of
different keys; one little waterfall tinkled, another tinkled, it
chuckled and chinkled, playing little hidden tunes all to
itself as if it didn't care whether anybody was listening or

not, any more than the rustling trees and the grass; which always looks so bright a green in the firelight.

Five feet away was the hull of the *Jeanie Deans*; the flicker of the fire's light showed up her name wonderfully clearly, and winked on her portholes. How trim she seemed with her pillar-box-red Plimsoll line, her black hull and creamy white upperworks, her brass-work twinkling in the light of the flames! What a ship indeed to own!

They had anchored there for the very good reason they could go no farther that night. A little way upstream was a mass of sticks and rubbish—flood rubbish—which effectually barred the Folly. The stream had become more and more difficult lately and they had to keep on cutting a passage for the boat. But the gnomes were not sorry; it was a good place to camp, with not a house within miles. They would have some work to do on the morrow to clear the stream, but the ship could be moved.

Dodder was frying eight fat minnows over the embers, and Sneezewort was sitting on an upturned barrel (from the hold of the ship) picking chestnuts out of their hairy casings in readiness for roasting. A most appetizing smell came from the pan as Dodder bent over it, the red light from the flames lighting up his face.

Over a month has passed since we last saw them tucked up in their bed of reeds, and now it is All-Hallows Eve, the greatest night in the gnomes' calendar! In far-off days good

*A view of the* Jeanie Deans *as she plows on her way*

people stayed indoors on this night for fear of spirits and the Little People. They sat round their fires telling ghost stories, until the tiniest scratching mouse made them jump and gibber. They made up silly tales about churchyards giving up their dead, and sheeted figures walking among the graves. Silly nonsense, all of it. But this I must say, that on Hallowe'en you had a better chance of seeing the Little People than at any other time, and for this reason mortals kept indoors.

\* \* \*

The journey up had been strangely uneventful. Only one adventure had happened to them. A boy, hunting for rats up the brook, had passed close to the *Jeanie Deans* and her trembling crew, but so cleverly was the ship hidden under the bank, and so unobservant are most boys, he had not seen them and had passed on, whistling and throwing stones into the water, quite unaware he had missed what would have been the most wonderful experience of his life!

"Here you are, gnomes," said Dodder at last, lifting each piping hot fish on the point of his hunting knife and flicking them on the expectantly proffered plates. "Fine fat minnows, done to a turn. It's your job to be chef tomorrow, Sneezewort, and if you cook 'em as well as these, I shan't grumble. Remember, you burnt the last lot. Come on, Baldmoney, you can finish the map afterwards; the fish will get cold."

Baldmoney, who had been lying full length on his stomach, putting some finishing touches to the map of the journey, obediently put on his waistcoat and climbed on to his barrel. He had found a name for each stopping-place on their journey; this should be called Rampike Dam.

They ate in silence, neatly biting the backs out of the little fish. When they had finished the minnows they had one big crayfish each, fried in the fish fat, and to finish up, stewed crab-apple, sweetened with peppermint cream.

By the time the last mouthful had been eaten each gnome was as tight as a little drum. They helped Dodder wash up the plates, stowing everything neatly away in the cabin cupboard, and then Baldmoney and Dodder lit their pipes. Sneezewort did not smoke because the others considered him too young (he was born long before Julius Caesar landed in Britain, but that is awfully young for a gnome).

"Ah, that's better," grunted Dodder, loosening his belt and settling himself comfortably in front of the dying embers. "There's nothing like a good meal at the end of a long day, and nothing like a good fire to sit by! The only thing lacking is a sip of my Elderberry 1905 to go with the nuts. But that must wait until we get back to the Oak Pool. Hallowe'en doesn't seem the same without my wine."

For some time nobody spoke; it was too perfect a night for talking, and the fire made them drowsy. Sneezewort and Dodder hotched nearer to the embers, they felt the bitter cold of night on their backs. The rushing of the Folly was such a soothing sound that Sneezewort began to nod.

"Listen!" Dodder was sitting bolt upright. His eyes were lifted and his mouth was slightly open as he gazed skywards. The others were wide awake in an instant, their long ears twitching, the firelight glinting on their eyeballs. From far away among the stars and the cold night sky a very faint baying, like a pack of hounds in full cry, came down to them. It grew nearer and nearer, passed right overhead (the gnomes' ears turning with the sound), then dwindled away down the course of the Folly.

"The Heaven Hounds!" exclaimed Dodder. "That means a bad winter. They are steering by the stream; I expect they will pass right over the Oak Pool on their way to the sea." And he remembered the goose feathers he had found on Poplar Island.

"What are the Heaven Hounds?" asked Sneezewort, hooking a hot chestnut out of the embers and tossing it across to Baldmoney.

"Why, the wild geese of course, silly," said Dodder; "they live far away in the land of Northern Lights, the land of the Snow Queen."

"Tell us about them, Dodder—please, *please*, Dodder—before we go to bed; after all, it *is* Hallowe'en!" begged Sneezewort.

"It's time you were in your bunk," said Dodder severely

(they usually sent Sneezewort to bed early because of his age). "But as it's All-Hallows Eve you can stay up a little longer."

\*　　\*　　\*

"Many cuckoo summers ago," began Dodder, "we had a terrible winter on the Folly. You must know the country was very different then, no railways, cars, and no roads to speak of, and only a few fields round the villages. Moss Mill hadn't even been built. Quite a number of gnomes lived up the Folly in those days, and the country was full of them—Elves, Goblins, and Hobgoblins, Pixies, Nixies, Sprites, Brownies, and Jack-o'-Lanterns or the Lantern Men. These Lantern Men were marsh goblins, who always carried a little light with them to see their way over the marshy ground. If any of our people are left, they would be the Lantern Men. The last I heard of were at Fenny Compton, away to the west of us, and they nearly drove a signalman out of his wits.

"Well, we'd had a lean summer, few berries and nuts and no mushrooms. The consequence was, the first frosts caught us unawares with empty larders. In those far-off times there were not many cornfields, and we had to go a long way for our gleanings. How the hobgoblins used to play the poor farmers up too, on Hallowe'en, chasing their horses until they were covered in sweat, milking their cows, and stealing things out of their wattle huts just out of pure mischief. But that's by the way.

"We had the first heavy fall of snow early in November and after it the frost set in. The Folly froze solid, even in the rapids, and you could walk dry shod all the way up to where Moss Mill now stands.

"With the bad season I saw we hadn't nearly enough food to carry us through the winter, so Cloudberry and I volunteered to go upstream and try to catch some fish. They bite well in cold weather, if you can find a deep pool which isn't frozen, and I thought that if we went up to the rapids we might have some luck. We borrowed two extra skin coats from some gnomes who lived at Joppa and made ourselves some snowshoes.

"We had got nearly as far as Lucking's meadows when the snow began to fall, and we half thought of turning back. But as we were so desperate we decided to go on and trust to the snow easing up. But not a bit of it, it came on harder than ever, and we took shelter in a hollow tree. It snowed all day, and the wind got up and blew the stuff into great drifts. All the snow seemed to come down into the valley and the tops of the hills were blown bare, until the grass began to show.

"Just as it got dark we heard the Heaven Hounds. They came out of the north, a long line of them, gaunt grey birds, ravenously hungry. They saw the grass showing on the hill and came bugling over our heads. It was a wonderful sight."

Dodder tossed another stick on the fire, and a sheaf of sparks shot upwards to lose themselves among the trees.

"As soon as they settled they began to feed, plucking at the short grass. As we don't often see these birds in this part of the world, we got out of our tree and climbed the hill towards them. There was a sentry on guard on the brow of the hill and he challenged us. You see he couldn't quite make us out, coming through the snow, he thought we were wood dogs. But when he saw us he was quite friendly. 'Why,' he said, 'if it isn't the Little People!'

"We asked him all sorts of questions, where they came from and where they were going. They had been flying for two days and a night, so he told us, all the way from a place called Spitzbergen, and had lost their way. I told him that we'd never had a snow like this before and he seemed quite amused.

"'Oh,' he said, 'you in Britain don't know what snow is. You should see Spitzbergen!' And then he told us all about the icebergs and glaciers, and how for many months of the year the sun never troubles to get up at all so that all is as dark as it is tonight."

"What an awful place!" remarked Baldmoney, with a shiver, looking beyond the circle of the firelight. "I don't think I should like to go there!"

"Well," said Dodder, "the wild geese don't stay in Spitzbergen in the wintertime; nearly all the birds fly away. They come to Britain, following the sun. But they breed in Spitzbergen, and the wood dogs are worse there than they are in this country, eating their young and stealing their eggs.

"I said I should like to go to their country, and he said, 'Well, why don't you? I will come back in the spring and take you. You can climb on my shoulders and fly back with the skeins. Will you come?' Well, I didn't know what to say . . . I was younger in those days . . . I can tell you I was very tempted, especially when he said he'd bring me back safe and sound in the autumn. Cloudberry got quite excited about it. You remember what a fellow he was for adventure."

"I should have gone if I'd been you," said Sneezewort; "it would have been a wonderful experience."

"Oh! I don't know," said Dodder. "I couldn't bear the thought of leaving the Folly and the other gnomes, and I should have missed the Stream People. Perhaps I was a bit of a coward."

"What happened then, Dodder?" asked Baldmoney.

"Oh, they grazed on the hill until the moon got up, and then they all flew away, and we were left alone on the bare hill. Cloudberry *was* mad with me for turning down the offer, and wouldn't speak to me for days afterwards. If I'd have gone he would have gone too, but he somehow didn't fancy going alone. He said it was the chance of a lifetime and one which would never come again. He always was a restless sort of person; I suppose that's why he came up the stream. I even think that since our meeting with the Heaven Hounds he was more restless than ever, and I don't think he ever quite forgave me for not asking the geese to come back for us in the spring."

\* \* \*

By now the fire had burnt low and the cold was increasing. The sound of the wild geese passing over had aroused strange emotions, a restlessness which was hard to explain. The thought of those great wide-winged birds flying so far over oceans and continents made them feel very earth-bound and small, even discontented with their lot.

"Well," said Dodder, "I don't expect we shall ever get the chance again; it certainly would have been a great adventure." He shivered suddenly. "My! But it's cold tonight. See how the leaves are falling!" As he spoke, a flurry of dead leaves came wavering down in the firelight. Some fell into the red embers, hissing gently.

Old Man Winter was on the prowl; life seemed to shrink into the earth at his approach, as a worm withdraws into the ground. Overhead a remote star showed for an instant and was hidden, and on one side of a blackened log lying in the grey ashes a line of sparks ran swiftly, puffed by a sudden breeze. Up in a thorn-tree a blackbird had rolled up into a ball. Once it withdrew its head to look sleepily at the red glow beneath, but it soon tucked it in again and went on dreaming.

For a long time nobody spoke, each gazed into the red core of the fire, busy with his own thoughts. Far away they heard the howl of a wood dog. Dodder shivered again.

"Gracious! Did you hear that?"

"Yes . . . a wood dog . . . I've heard them before."

It was a strange thing that during the whole of their journey up the Folly they had never once seen a fox. But just as men in lion-infested countries can go for years without as much as catching sight of a lion, so it was with the gnomes.

"You know," remarked Dodder at last, "we can't go much higher. The source must be miles away yet, and there isn't much point in finding it. We haven't come across another trace of Cloudberry. If you ask me, a wood dog had him. This country must be full of them." Again came the long-drawn howl, farther away now, somewhere up the Folly.

And suddenly, whether it was that distant cry in the night, or the wind in the half-bare trees, the three little gnomes felt suddenly dreadfully homesick. If only they could have begged a lift from the wild geese they would have been back at the Oak Pool by now. Instead of that, they were miles away in a country swarming with enemies.

"I believe you are right," said Baldmoney. "We ought to turn before the end of the month."

"We'll go just a little higher," said Dodder, asserting his authority. "Cloudberry may always be just round the next bend, you know."

The others did not reply; they felt perhaps a little rebellious, but Dodder was right.

They gathered up their baggage, and each carrying an empty barrel went back to the boat and were speedily on board, tucked up in their cozy bunks.

*   *   *

The red sparks of the embers burnt like rubies, fanned now and again by a passing gust. One by one they were snuffed out, and when the last had gone, a lithe shadow stole out of the bushes.

It was a wood dog. It gingerly sniffed all round the dead fire and ate up a few fish bones and crumbs that the gnomes had left. Its cunning eyes were like slits, and its brush switched to and fro like an angry cat's!

Suddenly it stopped sniffing, and crouched down on the ground with pricked ears. From the outer darkness by the stream it had heard a most curious sound. It crept slowly forward, its brush still twitching. Then it saw the silent bulk of the *Jeanie Deans* anchored serenely to the bank. The hairs on its back bristled and it backed away into the shadows.

And inside the cozy cabin, Dodder lay on his back, the moleskin bag drawn up over his head, snoring so loudly that the little wooden bunk vibrated, not caring if all the wood dogs in the world were prowling about outside!

CHAPTER 17

# A Smell in the Air

THEY GOT AWAY NEXT morning bright and early, with a frosty sun showing its cheery red face through the tangled branches of the streamside thorns. It was quite a business cutting a way for the ship through the flood jam, but at last it was done and the ship safely through.

Dodder, as usual, was steering, Baldmoney was polishing the brass fittings on deck until they winked and flashed, and Sneezewort was busy washing up the breakfast things in the galley (poor Sneezewort always seemed to get the more menial jobs). It would have done any sailor's heart good to see the way they kept that ship.

"Baldmoney" (it was Dodder who called).

Baldmoney stopped polishing and looked up to see Dodder sniffing the air.

"Yes, Skipper—did you call?"

"Come up here a moment."

"Aye, aye, sir" (they had become very nautical lately). He

266

climbed the little ladder to the bridge.

"Do you smell anything?"

Baldmoney sniffed and sniffed.

"Ye—e—es, I think I do."

"What is it?"

"Wood dog!"

"Right, just as I thought," said Dodder triumphantly.

Baldmoney looked fearfully at the banks, passing in slow procession on either side: dense blackthorn, clothed in unbelievably lovely colors, rose-red brambles, and old withered rush; a continuous jungle of exquisite beauty on either hand. At other times the gnomes would have journeyed slowly, noting every painted leaf and examining with the keenest delight, this wonderful pageantry of autumn, but time was passing swiftly and there was so much work to be done. In vain did they strive to see through the tangle of leaves.

"I don't like it," muttered Dodder, taking out his pipe and filling it slowly as Baldmoney took over the wheel. "I've smelt it a lot lately; I believe we're being trailed."

Baldmoney shuddered. "But surely we should have seen THEM?"

"Not necessarily—they're cunning brutes. They trail you for days, waiting their chance. Then one night, when you are sitting round the fire perhaps, talking as we were last night, spinning yarns, they're on you before you can say knife!" Dodder, his pipe drawing well, resumed steering.

"Horrible!" Baldmoney blew his nose loudly. "Worse than stoats! We'd better keep a good fire burning tonight and go to bed early."

"It might be wiser," said Dodder reflectively, his eyes still searching the banks. "It won't do to run any risks. I know what these wood dogs are. They are bold and hunt by day in this wild country."

\* \* \*

For the rest of the morning they kept a sharp look out but saw no trace; now and then, however, an eddy of wind would bring them just a hint of something that shouldn't be there. Mixed with the delicious spicy smell of the autumn foliage and the hint of frost was this faint rank odor of fox. It was most unsettling.

After midday the sun turned a dull rose-red and gradually the distant hedgerows and trees began to vanish silently in mist; it would be dark early.

The beat of the *Jeanie Deans'* screw seemed quite loud, for the Folly was sluggish and silent, flowing tortuously by spinneys and woods, past high hedges and motionless reed beds, where the bulrush heads were a dark vandyke brown.

Moorhens scattered when they saw the ship, diving in great alarm. At last they came to a little copse composed mostly of birch with an underwood of hazel. Dodder's attention was immediately arrested by quantities of ripe nuts hanging in clusters among the round yellowing leaves. Never before had he seen nuts in such abundance or of such size. It was a late crop too, due no doubt to the sheltered valley. They had run out of nuts long ago and had not tasted really ripe ones since they had been Squirrel's guests in Tree Top House. There were enough here to fill the hold. It was an opportunity not to be missed. Already the blackberries had been finished and the fruit barrels were empty.

The anchor went down and the ship swung round under the overhanging branches. They could pick quite a number without even stirring from the deck, but the finest were a little way up the bank.

"There's enough here to carry us right through the winter," said the delighted Baldmoney, reaching up and picking a beautiful bunch hanging just over his head. "Why not fill the hold? We shan't get a chance like this again, and we shall travel better with more ballast."

"Good idea," said Dodder, "but keep a sharp look out! I'll stay on board and look after the ship. Don't go out of call. There are some beauties just up the bank."

Baldmoney and Sneezewort, glad of the opportunity of stretching their legs, were soon ashore. Dodder could see them moving about among the bundles of hazel rods.

The hazel has a curious growth. Round the root it sends up straight rod-like suckers, and as the gnomes had to climb the trees to get the fruit it took them quite a time to force their way through. Dodder saw the branches shaking, and now and then a yellow leaf dropped to the ground.

What a lovely afternoon it was to be sure, golden and pearly, with no sound but the "caw, caw" of the rooks feasting on the acorns in the oaks, and the robins singing all around. One was sitting on a yellow hazel bough just across the stream, watching them, and now and again piping its mournful but sweet little song, which sounded like falling water. It was rather shy and would not talk, and seemed quite as selfish and self-centered as the robin of Poplar Island. From a great distance came the sleepy hum of a threshing machine at some lonely farm steading. Industrious men, like the bees, were busy over their harvest from the fields, the golden fruits of the summer sunlight.

The hazel bushes shook and rustled as nut after nut was thrown down from above until the grass was littered with fruit. Dodder smoked his pipe contentedly. He was thinking very deeply as he puffed away, watching tiny blue smoke rings go up and up into the tranquil air. There was nothing he enjoyed more than a quiet pipe of nettle tobacco.

It was time they gave up looking for Cloudberry, and as for the chance of finding the Folly Source, it was as far away as ever. There was certainly no time to reach it now with winter so close, and this frost was exceptional for nearly November. Not only that, the stream was becoming difficult to navigate. At Rampike Dam it had been an awful business cutting a way for the ship, and the higher they got the worse it would be. It only needed a big "fall" of timber entirely to block their passage.

His word was law: if he decided they must go no farther, well, that was that.

Dodder suddenly noticed that the robin was not singing. It was sitting on its branch and flirting its tail and saying "tic, tic, tic!" in an urgent voice and cocking its bright black eye.

Baldmoney and Sneezewort were so busy packing the fruits into the little bags and barrels (they had carried them ashore) that they never even heard the alarm note of the robin.

Dodder's long pointed ears moved like a donkey's and he had put his pipe back in his pocket. The robin began to be quite hysterical. It had certainly seen something among the bushes and soon a blackbird flew across and began crying "zinc, zinc, zinc!" in a very loud voice.

Baldmoney and Sneezewort stopped work; their wood-craft told them something was amiss.

Dodder called to them, "Better come back, there's something in the bushes!"

They came staggering down the bank, each carrying a load; so well had they worked that all the barrels and sacks were full, neatly stacked in the grass. The gangway was down and they carried up their precious cargo, dumping it in a neat row on the deck, working as deftly as mice.

"What a racket!" exclaimed Dodder. "There must be something there."

The blackbird was a handsome rogue with the bright gold bill of an old bird, which matched the hazel leaves, and he sat among the autumn foliage, flirting his tail. Zinc! Zinc! Zinc!

"Hurry up!" said Dodder. "It might be the wood dog. It isn't worth taking chances." (He could only just see Sneezewort's head among the leaves.)

"There are only two more loads," called Baldmoney, scurrying back down the bank.

Sneezewort grabbed a barrel and Baldmoney a sack as they began to run towards the gangway.

Then things happened very quickly. The blackbird flew up into the air with a shriek, and the robin flicked into the bushes as the red lithe form of a wood dog sprang out like a panther.

Dodder had a snapshot glimpse of Baldmoney, still clutching the sack, making a leap for the gangway, of a barrel rolling down the bank into the stream, spilling the nuts broadcast, of a scuffle of leaves and grass, a despairing shriek from Sneezewort, a further rustling and then—all was still!

"Where is he?" shouted Dodder." Where's Sneezewort?"

Baldmoney lay sobbing and trembling on the deck with nuts scattered all around.

"The wood dog got him," he gasped. "It all happened so quickly. Oh! Oh! Oh!"

Dodder, with surprising agility, was on the bank in an instant, peering into the thick bushes.

Parting the slender hazel rods he saw, a few yards away, the form of a fox. It was standing looking back over its shoulder, and there, sticking out of its mouth were two kicking legs. Sneezewort! The fox had not killed him; he was going to play with him as a cat plays with a mouse. With superb courage Dodder advanced on the wood dog waving his stick.

"You great brute, put him down—put him down, I tell you! If you kill him I'll tell Pan; we are the last gnomes in England—you shall not kill him!"

The fox could not reply because he had to keep a tight hold on the wriggling Sneezewort. He was going to have some fun and games with the juicy little morsel, so he just grinned and laid back his ears.

Then he lay down, pretending to take no notice of Dodder, and opened his mouth. With a shrill shriek his victim made to dart away, but out shot a velvet paw and pinned the unhappy Sneezewort to the leaves, where he lay squealing like a pig.

"Come nearer, little gnome," wheedled the fox to Dodder. "Come nearer and I'll let him go."

Dodder was playing for time; also he was frantically

praying to Pan under his breath.

"O good god Pan, help Sneezewort to get away; never mind me—I don't mind dying, but let Sneezewort live!"

Dodder advanced on the fox, quietly and unafraid. Just then, with an extra wriggle, Sneezewort broke away but he was deftly caught by the back of his skin breeches. Sneezewort, half crazed with fear, drew his knife. The fox tossed him up and caught him by the middle and shook him like a terrier shakes a rat. The bright blade flew sideways into the hazel; Sneezewort lay horribly still.

"No, you don't, my fine fellow," growled the fox. "I'm only going to let you go when your brother comes a little closer. I want to talk to him."

"I talk with *you* first, Red Robber," said Dodder, "and you will listen. Many cuckoo summers ago, long before even your forebears were thought of, I was a-hunting up the Folly. A wood dog trailed and caught me. I got away, how makes no matter, but ever since I have gone through life maimed and halting. Pan heard of it, and he put a curse upon you and all your kind. From thenceforth you have been hunted by the Devil Hounds, and so you shall be hunted to the end."

Dodder came still nearer, his little eyes ablaze, fixed on the grinning, mocking mask of the fox. It was looking down at Sneezewort, lying motionless between its front paws; the eyes almost vanished in a wide smile, its long pink tongue hung out.

"Ah, ha, see how still he lies! I've killed him, and in a minute I shall kill you too, one-legged gnome who cannot run away. But first I will eat Sneezewort; I've been tracking you gnomes for days. I have watched you round your fires at night, but I feared the bright sparks that burn."

"Listen, red wood dog—do you hear what I hear?"

The fox lowered its head and snarled. "I hear nothing but the Folly water and a frightened blackbird among the bushes. I hear nothing but wild sounds, and I smell nothing but warm blood, Dodder," and a little rope of saliva drooled from his jaws.

"Then an old lame gnome must have better ears than the young red wood dog," observed Dodder. "Listen again—listen well, Red Stinker to Heaven."

The fox's ears switched abruptly.

Far away came the sound of a horn and the faint "tow row" of hounds.

He snarled once, looked down at the motionless figure of Sneezewort, then at Dodder, stood irresolute, swung round and vanished like a shadow!

\*   \*   \*

Dodder ran to the little figure which lay face downwards among the leaves.

"Dear old Sneezewort, are you hurt?" asked Dodder tenderly, bending over him.

The wee mouseskin jacket was ripped and the toothless

mouth agape. Sneezewort did not reply.

Despite his game leg Dodder picked him up as if he were a baby and with Baldmoney's help laid him on the deck, and took off his coat. There was an ugly gash across the breastbone, but it was only a surface wound.

"He'll be all right," said Dodder. "Let's get him down into his bunk; he's only knocked out." They brewed some nettle tea and covered him up with skins. After a while Sneezewort opened his eyes wonderingly.

"You'll be all right, little man," said Dodder, "just lie still. The wood dog's gone now and won't come back—ever!"

*   *   *

He went up on deck again. In the distance was the thundering of hooves, loud cracklings and crashings in the bushes. The tip of a hound's stern waved among the hazels and the terrified blackbird, silent now, flew swiftly down the stream. Other hounds were coming up the Folly on either bank.

As Dodder stood watching, well screened under the hanging branches and hazel trunks, he saw the huge barrel of a horse's body, a grey horse with a scarlet rider on his back, shoot like a bolt from one side of the stream to the other, landing with a soft double-thud. The man had a hand across his face to shield it from the whip of the branches. The next instant rider and horse had vanished.

In the distance were excited shouts, and the tremendous, blood-stirring sounds of a pack of hounds in full cry.

Fainter and fainter they became until at last all was still. Dodder felt a movement behind him; Baldmoney, still very white about the gills, was at his elbow.

"How is he?" asked Dodder, tossing his head towards the cabin.

"Oh, he's all right, only a bit shaken; he'll be as right as rain in the morning."

"Good. . . . Baldmoney."

"Yes, Dodder?"

"We're turning back tomorrow."

"Aye, aye, Skipper, I'm mighty glad."

Silence fell. The robin began to sing again and a broken nut branch, with leaves still green, came floating down the stream. It had been knocked off by the jumping horseman.

Dodder held up his hand. "Hark!"

Baldmoney listened, his teeth faintly chattering.

From quite a distance they heard the horn again, a burst of short clear notes. It was sounding the "kill."

Dodder slowly removed his cap.

"Amen," said Baldmoney in a low voice, "so perish all the enemies of the Little People."

\*   \*   \*

Robin Clobber, attired in tweed jacket, breeches, gaiters, a velvet hunting cap, and mounted on a globular Shetland pony Sweep, was hacking home with Daddy, feeling quite grown up.

"Well, Robin," his father said, "you've had your first run with hounds; how did you like it?"

"Ripping," gasped Robin, almost speechless with happiness.

They jogged on until they came to the Folly bank and they stopped the horses to look at the brown rushing water with its hurrying leaves. Something caught Robin's eye, a minute pale object which bobbed swiftly down the current. It was a tiny barrel! Why, it must have come from the *Jeanie Deans*—however did it get there? Robin remembered the bitter moment when he saw his lovely ship sailing away. Still . . . he had Sweep now; Daddy had bought him the pony to make up for his disappointment, and a pony was *ever* so much better than a boat! Funny about the barrel, though; perhaps those little men he saw by the bridge had a hand in it. Perhaps they'd even got hold of the *Jeanie Deans*. Well, if they had he was glad; she would be in good custody, and they would find more use for her.

They rode on towards the house.

# CHAPTER 18

# Down Stream

"MY WORD!" EXCLAIMED Dodder, swinging his arms to and fro like a cabman to warm himself, "there's ice on the water. If we get up full steam we may push our way through; it is not thick enough to worry about."

Though the weather was so cold it was divine on deck, as beautiful in its way as a most perfect summer morning. Dodder's breath came in puffs like a kettle on the boil; the grass was crisp, white, flashing diamonds, and the air smelt of sliced apple. From the rimy hedges, spangled starlings whistled merrily, the sun winking on their burnished bodies. All along the edges of the Folly old Jack Frost had been busy during the night making a double fringe of sharp daggers and dragons' teeth of ice. There was ice round the screw of the *Jeanie Deans*, her stern and decks were covered with ice crystals. Dodder breathed deeply and clapped his arms once more, his senses alert to the beauty of the scene. Not far away was a graceful group of birches growing in a little clearing in the hazel bushes. Quite a lot of leaves still remained upon them, round-shaped leaves like minute shields, of a beautiful clear amber yellow. They made a rare contrast to the slender black and silver stems.

Dodder felt "good." He blew out his cheeks, puffed on his nails, and shouted, "Hullo, below there! Show a leg! Show a leg! A lovely day for the journey down! Show a leg!"

Sneezewort and Baldmoney (the former now fully recovered and quite his old self despite his terrible ordeal) nipped up the funnel and began to wind the key vigorously. With long practice they had quite got the knack of starting her up.

"One more turn," shouted Dodder to the straining gnomes. Sneezewort put one foot against the funnel and pulled until his naturally red face turned a deep purple. There was a loud click and a sudden horrid screech from the bowels of the ship. Dodder pushed the starting lever and nothing happened!

"That's done it," said Dodder in a bitter voice. "The engine's broken now."

Sneezewort began to cry. "Oh dear, we are in a mess; we shall never get home, and now the wood dogs *will* get us. What are we to do?"

"Shut up, you sniveling baby," growled Dodder; "don't you see we shan't need the engine any more if we keep in the current? It will take us right down to the Oak Pool. If you ask me, it is a very good thing this *has* happened; if we'd been tempted to go any higher we should have been frozen in."

They broke the thin film of ice round the ship with oars and after much hauling and pushing they got the nose of the *Jeanie Deans* round. A moment later the current took her and, free of ice, she began to drift as silently as a fallen leaf downstream. Dodder could not resist one last look at the hazel thickets which had been the scene of such exciting happenings the day before. I think Sneezewort had forgotten all about his narrow escape, for gnomes take everything as it comes.

Baldmoney went down into the cabin with the map and wrote upon it (in gnome language) "Farthest North. Our last camp, Wood Dog Wood, Sneezewort nearly eaten here." He could not suppress a sigh that the real object of all their efforts had not been attained. . . . Cloudberry had not been found.

\* \* \*

The gnomes went back down the Folly with a great company. Each tree as they passed it flung some dead leaves down to them, the stream was full; hawthorn, maple, chestnut, elm, oak, lime, willow, ash, and alder, poplar and wild apple, all were drifting with the current, smoothly and silently, in a colored carpet.

There was nothing to do all day but stand about the

deck, smoke and gossip, admire the scenery, and lean over the side to watch the endless procession of colored leaves sliding past, to watch the darting fish in the clear water, and wave to astonished water-voles.

It is a strange thing that before the floods in late autumn, rivers, streams, and ponds become crystal clear.

It was possible for the gnomes to see every pebble and leaf on the stream bed, and the waving cresses, some like green hair, and neat pillows of tight, green weeds, seemed to belong to a fantastic submarine fairyland.

*   *   *

A friendly wind helped them across the lake and they could not suppress a shudder when they saw hated Poplar Island, barren and wild, on the starboard side, half hidden by mist. Were it not for the *Jeanie Deans*, perhaps their bones would be bleaching on its grim shore. And so they went on, past places hardly recognizable now that the trees were stripped almost bare.

They dropped anchor in Crow Wood and paid Squirrel a visit. They felt they could not go past without looking him up. He was overjoyed to see them back again, and many a yarn they exchanged with him up in Tree Top House.

There, in Crow Wood, were the marks of their old fires, recalling the night of the animal banquet, when Owl told them ghost stories, and, as for the gibbet, it had been torn down by the animals and the poor bones given a decent burial by the moles and sexton beetles. No other giant had been seen in Crow Wood since the gnomes had left, and everybody lived in peace and harmony.

As Squirrel was a lonely soul they persuaded him to go back to the Oak Pool with them. I think he was a little regretful at saying good-bye to Tree Top House, but the picture the gnomes painted of the Oak Pool proved irresistible. And when he saw the *Jeanie Deans* anchored to a pine branch he was too excited to speak.

Soon after leaving Crow Wood it began to snow, so that the conifers seemed like trees on a Christmas card and the gnomes like little snowmen. Hundreds of fieldfares and red-wings feasting on the scarlet berries in a hedgerow stopped their banquet to watch the *Jeanie Deans* drift by. The sky was a heavy ocher-grey, promising snow for days and days, but nobody minded.

They managed the Folly Falls with ease because more water was coming down than in summer, and though the steamer was buffeted out of her usual stately dignity by the swift rush, she was soon serenely gliding on towards the Oak Pool.

What a happy party it was on board, to be sure! It was good to see the familiar landmarks, and it wasn't long before they fell in with many old acquaintances. Some, like the hedge-pigs, dormice, and fern-bears, missed the fun, for they were tucked up for the winter and would not appear again until the spring. But kingfishers, moorhens, Bub'ms, water-voles, moles, Spink, and Bluebutton, all recognized them and gave them a warm welcome as they went past. As you can well imagine, they were speechless at the sight of the *Jeanie Deans*. Truly this homecoming was going to give the Stream People much to talk about for many a long winter's night. Dodder, Sneezewort, Baldmoney, and Squirrel all waving frantically from the bridge of the big ship, the snow falling thickly, all the animals running along the bank, trying to keep up with her, why, it was as good as a play!

Sneezewort had found a little Union Jack in one of the cabin lockers, and this was run up to the forepeak. They didn't care who saw them, even the miller's brats, or the peppery old Colonel from Joppa!

\*   \*   \*

Snow was still falling in big feathery flakes when they passed Moss Mill, and ice daggers a yard long were hanging from the now motionless buckets of the giant wheel. The mill pool was partly frozen over too, but in midstream the water was clear, which was a lucky thing for the *Jeanie Deans*. And just as dusk was falling they passed Lucking's meadows. A cozy light was burning in the farmhouse window, where Farmer Lucking was just sitting down to discuss an enormous ham of his own curing, and presently they came to the rapids above the Oak Pool.

How strange it seemed, this silent white landscape. Last time they were here all was dressed in summer finery. Now the trees were black and bare and hardly a rush blade was to be seen along the banks.

"If only we had found Cloudberry," said Dodder sadly to Squirrel, his eyes greedily taking in each dear familiar landmark, "it would have made this trip just perfect. But we've at least found one thing, this lovely ship. Baldmoney will soon mend the engine—he's as clever as anything at making and mending things. Perhaps one day we'll go up the Folly again—who knows?"

The *Jeanie Deans* glided on, ice tinkling along her sides. In another moment they had rounded the bend, and there was the oak and the Oak Pool. What a moment! What a picture! The snow-covered branches hanging over the inky stream, each twig encrusted with frost, the dear old oak tree sturdily awaiting them, and the excited cries of the crowds on either shore!

All at once Dodder uttered an exclamation, his hands gripped the wheel of the *Jeanie Deans* convulsively. "Sneezewort! Baldmoney! Squirrel! *Someone's lit a fire in our house!*"

"Who can it be, in our house?" exclaimed Baldmoney.

"Perhaps the Stream People heard we were coming and lit a fire to welcome us home," suggested Sneezewort nervously.

"Nobody's any business in our house," shouted Dodder, getting very excited. "Not even the Stream People."

Slowly they drew nearer, the Folly bearing them ever onward until they were close to the oak root.

"Let go the anchor," called Dodder, and it went tumbling down into the icy water. The *Jeanie Deans* swung her nose round and Sneezewort lowered the gangway. The next instant they had the greatest thrill of the whole adventure.

The door opened and there, waving frantically, was Cloudberry, dear old Cloudberry, beaming all over his face. He looked just the same (though perhaps a trifle thinner) as when he left the Oak Pool two years before!

\*     \*     \*

The door of Oak Pool House is shut fast and a merry fire is blazing within; never has the old oak re-echoed to such uproarious merriment. Outside, the snowflakes whirl, and the Folly is still hurrying on between jagged ice-floes.

The *Jeanie Deans*, safely anchored, lifts slightly to the ripples talking under her keel, small fragments of floating ice dwell lovingly along her sides and are then swept onwards on their cold and lonely journey. The snow lies thick on her decks, darkness is cloaking the wild winter fields.

But within the oak root all is high revelry and fun. Most of the Stream People who can squeeze in are there—nobody has been left out in the cold. Truly the finest animal banquet ever! And with them round the blaze, full of supper and toasting their toes, sit Dodder, Sneezewort, Cloudberry, Baldmoney, and Squirrel. Cloudberry, with his mouth full of peppermint cream, is telling them of his adventures.

"After scratching my name on the bridge," he is saying, "I went on up the side of the big lake, and whom do you think I met? Why, the Heaven Hounds! They were resting there before their long journey back to Spitzbergen. They asked me to go with them—how could I refuse such an offer? Ever since Dodder and I met them up the Folly years before I had always longed to go. So I went, and came back on Hallowe'en!"

"We heard the Heaven Hounds passing over," exclaimed Dodder, "when we were right up the Folly—then you must have been with them!"

"Yes, I was with them; and now I come to think of it, I saw a little bright spark far below us which looked like a fire. I thought it was some lonely old tramp cooking his supper" (here Dodder grunted indignantly) "or a Lantern Man. It was very cold up there, I can tell you, tucked up on the old leader's back, with my arms round his neck. They put me down in Lucking's water meadow. It gave me quite a turn when I found this house empty—I couldn't think what had happened to you."

"So you never went up to the Folly Source after all!" exclaimed Baldmoney.

"Of course not. I knew I would never get such a chance again so I took it. But I've done with wandering now. I've seen Spitzbergen and the Land of Northern Lights, and it will take me the rest of the winter to tell you of all my adventures and the strange things I've seen."

"And to think we've been all those miles up the Folly for nothing," grunted Dodder in an aggrieved tone, half laughing in spite of himself. "It's just the same old Cloudberry, he hasn't changed a bit—has he, gnomes?"

There was a slight movement above them and a piece of bark fell down. It was only Ben, staring down at them, his eyes like carriage-lamps in the firelight, listening with all his ears.

\* \* \*

So here we will leave the Little Grey Men, for they have much to talk about. Baldmoney has spread out his waist-coat map and is tracing, with a grubby finger, the course of their adventurous journey. Dodder, with great ceremony, has produced a shell of his precious Elderberry 1905, with the result that already Squirrel and Cloudberry are a little too unreserved, having no "head" for elderberry wine, and (though I hardly like to mention it) Sneezewort can be observed making ineffectual efforts to stifle a hiccup, as tipsy as a bumble bee in a foxglove finger.

Our last glimpse of them is in the cozy flamelight, with their crooked shadows thrown on the interior of the old hollow oak. And the last sound we hear is of the Folly brook, chuckling on past the Oak Tree Pool as it has done for a thousand, thousand cuckoo years, on its long journey to the distant sea.

*Words and music of the Folly Brook Song can be found on pp. 290–291.*

# THE FOLLY BROOK SONG

*This is the song sung by the Folly brook as it passes the Oak Tree House*

From woodland and fallow,
With music, with laughter,
Through deep and through
    shallow,
Bright bubbles stream after,
Through lilies and cresses
With trailing green tresses,

I journey unceasing
By steep dell and dingle,
My brown ripples creasing
O'er shillet and shingle,
Past flowery hedges
And quivering sedges.

White lambs, running races,
Are puzzled to see
Their black chubby faces
Reflected in me,
And the first swallow dips
As he thankfully sips.

I leap at the mill
(You should hear the wheel's
    thunder!),
In the pool I am still,
Silver fishes swim under,
And dragonflies play
Where arrowheads sway.

The spotted trout rise
By the old mossy piles,

They are ancient and wise
To the angler's wiles,
And red cattle dream
At the bend of the stream.

And when summer's glory
Is over and done,
It is still the same story,
I rush, and I run;
Though leaden the sky
I go hurrying by.

When trees begin weeping
Their yellow leaves fall,
And safe in my keeping
I gather them all,
Away to the sea
They travel with me.

When snowflakes are twirling
And reeds are a-shiver,
With flood rubbish whirling
I haste to the river,
I plunge, and I roar,
I bubble, and bore.

No sleeping, no slowing,
The sky in my face.
Eternally flowing,
I ripple, I race
Impatient to rest
On the Grey Mother's breast.

# THE FOLLY BROOK SONG

*Music by* WALTER PITCHFORD

# About the Author

**BB** is the pseudonym for Denys Watkins-Pitchford (1905–1990), a prolific author who published many children's books from 1938 to 1975, including *Down the Bright Stream*, the sequel to *The Little Grey Men*. BB was also the author of many nonfiction titles for adults about the natural world and the illustrator of many beautiful books about England and its wildlife.

**The BB Society** was formed in 1999 with the full support of BB's Trustees. The goal of the BB Society is to encourage a wide interest in the works of Denys Watkins-Pitchford, particularly among the young.

The society produces a yearly publication, *Sky Gypsy*, and regular newsletters, and arranges annual events, meetings, exhibitions, and lectures. The centenary of BB's birth is 2005, and several events and publications will commemorate this year.

Details of membership can be obtained from Yvonne Seward, Membership Secretary, Lantern Cottage, Little Comberton, Pershore, Worcestershire, WR10 3EH, United Kingdom, or by e-mailing membership@bb-society.com.

Did you like this book? Julie Andrews would love to read your review of THE LITTLE GREY MEN, or any of the books in the Julie Andrews Collection. Write to her at:

JULIE ANDREWS
THE JULIE ANDREWS COLLECTION
HARPERCOLLINS CHILDREN'S BOOKS
1350 AVENUE OF THE AMERICAS
NEW YORK, NY 10019

or

INFO@JULIEANDREWSCOLLECTION.COM

From time to time we will post reader reviews on the Julie Andrews Collection website. Please include permission to quote you, including your name and location, when you submit your review.

Other books you might enjoy in the Julie Andrews Collection:

BLUE WOLF by Catherine Creedon

DRAGON: *Hound of Honor*
by Julie Andrews Edwards and Emma Walton Hamilton

DUMPY AND THE FIREFIGHTERS
by Julie Andrews Edwards and Emma Walton Hamilton,
illustrated by Tony Walton

DUMPY TO THE RESCUE!
by Julie Andrews Edwards and Emma Walton Hamilton,
illustrated by Tony Walton

DUMPY'S APPLE SHOP
by Julie Andrews Edwards and Emma Walton Hamilton,
illustrated by Tony Walton

GRATEFUL: *A Song of Giving Thanks*
by John Bucchino, illustrated by Anna-Liisa Hakkarainen

THE LAST OF THE REALLY GREAT WHANGDOODLES
by Julie Andrews Edwards

THE LEGEND OF HOLLY CLAUS by Brittney Ryan

MANDY by Julie Andrews Edwards

SIMEON'S GIFT
by Julie Andrews Edwards and Emma Walton Hamilton,
illustrated by Gennady Spirin